They Had

Your favourite authors love *They Had It Coming*

'The very best kind of thriller – taut, well researched
and superbly written. I've read all of Nikki Smith's books
and this is my favourite so far'
Fiona Cummins

'Nikki's skilful characterization and sharp prose, together
with whiplash-inducing twists and turns, left me turning
the pages late into the night'
Sarah Pearse

'This clever and twist-packed thriller will make you wish you
were in Bali – just maybe not with these two warring couples!'
Ellery Lloyd

'An expertly crafted page-turner that confirms the author's flair
for destinations both sun-drenched and dangerous. *They Had
It Coming* is my favourite Nikki Smith to date!'
Louise Candlish

'Absolutely gripping. No matter how far you travel, you
can never escape yourself or your secrets'
Jo Callaghan

'Kept me up until 2 a.m. Twisty, tense, toxic, tropical and timely.
They Had It Coming is TERRIFIC'
Nikki May

'Nikki Smith has written the ultimate dream
destination / nightmare scenario glam thriller. Gives
Liane Moriarty a run for her money!'
Helen Fields

'Another excellent destination thriller from Nikki Smith. The
twists and turns left me breathless. Highly recommended!'
B. A. Paris

'Nikki Smith has done it again with this clever, complex, twisty, page-turning thriller that will have you guessing right up until the last page. Brilliant!'
Charlotte Levin

'Sharp, addictive and impossible to put down, this is a must-read'
Lesley Kara

'An edge-of-your-seat, twist-after-twist thriller with some truly unforgettable characters. A wild ride from start to finish'
B. P. Walter

'Evocative, with palpable tension simmering in the shadows of paradise, Nikki's latest thriller is creepily tense. You won't know who to trust'
Karen Hamilton

'Nikki Smith is the go-to for scorchingly twisted summer thrillers'
L. V. Matthews

'An addictive, twist-packed tale of revenge, secrets and lies, all set against the breathtaking backdrop of Bali. It's utterly unputdownable – I devoured every page!'
Emily Freud

'The undisputed queen of the destination thriller. This peels back the glossy sheen that coats the lives of digital nomads in Bali and reveals the torment and trouble lurking below. Exquisitely plotted'
Emma Christie

'A deliciously dark thriller set on the paradise island of Bali, with a cast of intriguingly complex characters, carrying long-held secrets and telling dangerous lies'
Frances Quinn

'The perfect airport novel. Fiendishly plotted and packed with dodgy characters, with twists and turns galore in a beautiful setting; what more could you want?'
Trevor Wood

'The seemingly perfect world of digital nomads isn't quite what it seems – a stunning location and characters with secrets. Nikki Smith at her best'
Catherine Cooper

They Had It Coming

NIKKI SMITH

PENGUIN BOOKS

PENGUIN BOOKS

UK | USA | Canada | Ireland | Australia
India | New Zealand | South Africa

Penguin Books is part of the Penguin Random House group of companies
whose addresses can be found at global.penguinrandomhouse.com.

Penguin Random House UK,
One Embassy Gardens, 8 Viaduct Gardens, London SW11 7BW

penguin.co.uk

Penguin
Random House
UK

First published 2025

001

Set in 12.5/14.75 pt Garamond MT Std
Typeset by Jouve (UK), Milton Keynes

Printed and bound in Great Britain by Clays Ltd, Elcograf S.p.A.

The authorized representative in the EEA is Penguin Random House Ireland,
Morrison Chambers, 32 Nassau Street, Dublin D02 YH68

A CIP catalogue record for this book is available from the British Library

ISBN: 978–1–405–97471–4

To Martin – who has stuck around despite the fact that I spend most of my time plotting to kill someone.
Not him.
Usually.

'It is in the character of very few men to honour without envy a friend who has prospered.'

— *Aeschylus*

Prologue

She can't see her friends. There is only a hot, sticky mass of people, their faces distorted under the strobe lights. Searing flashes of white that cut through the club's darkness, illuminating the dance floor for fractions of a second.

They were here only a minute ago. She's sure they were; she remembers the four of them dancing together, hands intertwined. Shortly before that they were downing shots of flaming sambuca. The hot barman – a Robert Pattinson lookalike – had grinned as he'd filled up their glasses. Or was that earlier on? Time has stopped being measurable. She could have been here for a few seconds or a few hours; she has no idea. She can only focus on the music that pulses through her body, synchronizing with the hundreds of people on the dance floor, all moving as one to the same beat.

Flash.

The bodies around her are too close. Drops of perspiration slide down her forehead; her own, someone else's, she can't tell. She needs to get out. Find somewhere she can breathe.

Flash.

Someone puts their hands on her shoulders and leans in towards her, their pupils blown, their eyes staring into hers, unseeing. She pulls away, bumping into people, weaving her way across the floor.

Flash.

If she can just get to the loos, she'll be able to gather the thoughts that are rapidly spiralling out of her control.

Why did you drink so much?

How could you be so stupid as to lose your phone?

You shouldn't have let them leave you.

She sounds like her mother. Irritated; an attempt to hide the panic that rises up, sweet and sickly, in the back of her throat. Her friends wouldn't have gone without her. It's their golden rule. Never leave anyone behind. They would have made sure she was with them. Wouldn't they?

Flash.

Another face appears in front of her, their mouth wide in a rictus grin, and she recoils, the noise of protest that comes out of her swallowed up instantly by the music. He tries to grab her hand, his sweaty palm slipping up and down against hers in the dark, and she pulls away, wraps her arms across her chest.

Flash.

She can see the sign for the loos, and a tear slides down her cheek. She wants to splash her face with cold water and lock herself in a cubicle, just for a few minutes, just until the floor stops feeling like it's sliding away beneath her feet. She'll ask to use someone's phone, explain that she's lost hers, along with her wallet. Call her friends, and if they don't answer, grab a taxi. Tell them she'll pay when she gets home.

It will be fine.

She repeats the words like a mantra as she staggers towards the sign that seems to get further away from her with each step, the floor stretching like bubblegum beneath her feet.

Flash.

Are the lights getting brighter? She can't see properly and holds her arms out in front of her to stop anyone getting too close.

'There you are.'

A familiar voice cuts through the music and relief floods her body, like someone has poured a glass of cool water down her parched throat.

'Where did you go?' he asks. 'I turned around and you'd gone.'

It takes her a few seconds to be able to speak. Her tongue feels as if it's swollen in her mouth, squashing the words she's trying to say. An unintelligible mumble comes out instead, and he frowns.

'Your friends?' he says.

She nods, his breath hot against her ear.

'They went home a while ago,' he says. 'You wanted to stay with me, remember?'

She stares at him blankly, jumbled memories running through her head: him buying her a drink and making her laugh. She doesn't understand how the evening has become so muddled in her brain.

'Are you OK?'

She shakes her head, watches his face blur into a swirl of fleshy pink as the room spins. She stumbles and holds on to his arm to stop herself falling over.

'Do you want to me to get you a cab?' he asks.

She holds up her thumb, incapable of speech, and leans on him as they make for the exit, glad that she'll be home soon and that her mother's voice, still buzzing in her head, will finally fall silent. The noise of the dance floor becomes muffled as they leave it further behind, heading down the corridor towards the exit.

He runs his finger across her cheek as her legs give way beneath her.

'You don't need to worry,' he says. 'I've got you.'

Any second now and she'll be outside. Will feel the breeze on her face. Breathe clean air. Hear the familiar sound of traffic passing along the main road.

But that moment never comes.

1. Sophie

When Sophie walks up the path to the communal front door of their block of flats, there is no indication that anything is wrong, no hint that her world is about to shift in a way she couldn't possibly have foreseen.

Edge Court – the 1970s-style block that includes their one-bedroom rental – is technically located in Raynes Park rather than Wimbledon, but she tends to ignore this detail if anyone asks where she lives. *Up near the Village. Just along from the station.* Generalizations that slip out more easily than the whole truth. Being only two roads away from the postcode she really wants to be in, as far as she is concerned, is close enough to claim residency.

It's quicker to walk from Raynes Park station, but she likes to get off at Wimbledon, head up the hill, pop into Gail's and grab a cortado – a hundred and thirty-five calories less than a latte and still tastes practically the same. Sometimes she stops in to see Jess, her sister, or peruses the latest range of leggings in Sweaty Betty – she's got plenty of pairs already, but it never hurts to have additional motivation for a HIIT class and Jude doesn't need to know if she saves a bit less than they agreed towards their 'it's never enough' house deposit this month. It makes her feel like a local, as if she still belongs here.

Today, like always, she'd passed Headquarters' glass window and smiled at her stylist, Ruth, who does a full head of blonde highlights for her every six weeks. She always tells her she wants the style and colour to match Holly Willoughby's – Jude stares at the TV for longer than he normally does whenever that woman comes on – but Ruth never manages to get it quite right. Maybe if Sophie was taller, if she had the extra two inches of height that Holly does, it would look more like she expected. But her appointments do give her the chance to catch up on the latest gossip. She gets to bitch about her shitty salary and lack of promotion, to hear Ruth sympathize when she tells her (again) that the role which had been sold to her as a PR account manager for a fashion brand had turned out to be more of an executive assistant. And Ruth will no doubt divulge which client's husband has got some fucking fantastic new job and is buying a house, or who is moving out of London to start a family. Information she is desperate to know, but which also stings sharply when she hears it, like squeezing lemon into a cut.

As she'd walked along Southside Common, she'd passed the road that led to her old school, had anticipated the burn of acid indigestion and swallowed down the memories before they had a chance to bubble up. A few dozen steps further on, she'd played the game she usually plays with herself and pretended she wasn't going to look at the place she'd called home until she was thirteen but had done it anyway.

A large Victorian property in one of the cul-de-sacs, altered almost beyond recognition after twenty-two years. The red-brick, ivy-covered porch had been demolished by the new owners after the fire, the exterior repainted in an off-white and an extension added to one side. The kind of house that will always be out of her and Jude's reach, even if he had got that bloody promotion he'd been so desperate for. Not that she'd ever set foot inside it again, no matter how much money she had.

She'd turned off the main road by the travel agent's on the corner, had felt a tugging sensation in her stomach when she'd caught a glimpse of the TV screens in the window displaying images of gorgeous beaches and turquoise water. She and Jude could do with a holiday – they haven't spent much time together recently. She misses the long, lazy lie-ins they have when they're away – entire mornings in bed, the smell of his skin next to hers, sticky with the heat. Layla and Nate keep asking them to go out to Bali, stay in their flash villa, but she's not sure Jude should take the time off work. She smiles as she remembers the four of them in Puerto Banús a couple of years ago – Layla climbing up on to a podium in one of the nightclubs, a bottle of Grey Goose in one hand, pulling Sophie up after her; the two of them dancing, their skin slick with sweat. The feeling of being in a bubble of happiness, completely absorbed in the moment, while Nate and Jude wolf-whistled from the floor below.

She turns her key in their front door, the same way she's done a hundred times before, hears the latch click and kicks off her trainers on to the mat. What happens after she hangs up her coat and walks inside is just a blur as she finds herself in their small living room, staring at her treasured objects lying scattered across the wooden floorboards.

Why aren't they on the shelf, where they usually are?

She bends down, tries to gather them up, put them

7

back where they belong. Her brain doesn't fully comprehend what has happened and spins to catch up, but deep in her gut she already knows. A primal instinct, something dark and full of fear that she doesn't want to acknowledge.

She feels a sharp stab of pain, and winces. Drops of blood fall on to her Marc Jacobs leather tote bag, a TK Maxx bargain, as the glass from a broken champagne flute slices into her skin. *Stupid.* She should have just left it where it was, along with everything else. Drawers open, their contents rifled through. The matching candle holders she'd spent ages choosing now in jagged pieces on the marble hearth. A silver photo frame of her and Jude on their wedding day, the glass smashed, distorting their smiling faces into something out of a nightmare.

She trembles as her uninjured hand digs around in her bag for her phone, the vibrations of destruction continuing to echo around the room. She finally finds it, together with a tissue that she wraps around her finger to stem the bleeding. *Shit.* It's out of juice. She'll have to see if Mrs Taylor is in next door. She's eighty-six and almost completely deaf, so Sophie doubts she heard anything, but she won't know unless she asks. And she can borrow her landline to call the police.

As she backs out of the living room into the hallway, she glances at their bedroom, doesn't want to face the horror in there. She needs to speak to Jude; can imagine the way his face will crumple when she tells him. She takes a deep breath, refuses to give in to the temptation to fall apart, reassures herself that this is all fixable, that they are only possessions, that they are insured.

It's only when she walks past the kitchen that she freezes, blood pounding in her ears, and wishes, too late, that she'd paid more attention to the sensation she'd been conscious of when she'd left the station. *A premonition.* The same feeling she'd had all those years ago, the one she'd ignored when it had told her to go back. And look what had happened then.

The noise that cuts through the silence is the unmistakable sound of the bathroom fan. Jude had insisted the landlord instal it a few weeks ago after spots of black mould appeared on the ceiling. Brand new, it only comes on when it's activated by movement.

2. Jude

The burglary is the final straw. They need to get out of London.

It had taken the police fifty minutes to arrive, despite being told there was an intruder still at the scene. By then, of course, the flat was empty, but Sophie, usually unflappable, had insisted on staying with Mrs Taylor next door until he'd got home. He doesn't blame her. He still feels guilty for not being the first one home, even though he knows there isn't anything he could have done. The scumbag had trashed the place and then, according to the police, had probably jumped out of the window and run off through the communal gardens. No wonder his wife doesn't feel fucking safe. Even he'd been shocked after seeing the damage – he'd taken dozens of photos of the mess on his iPhone before clearing it up and had spent his lunch break googling *ring doorbells* and *tamperproof window locks* – Christ, he'll put bars on the windows if it makes Sophie feel more secure.

He joins the escalators going down into Canary Wharf underground station, feels as if he's being dragged along with the other commuters into some kind of modern-day version of hell. The jostling, the smell of stale sweat, being forced to listen to one-sided conversations by people on their phones at full volume. He's not sure if he can face coming back tomorrow to listen to Patrick make yet another speech about touching base, drilling down and staying ahead of the curve. He hates his boss almost as much as his job at Bearman Brothers, and Patrick has recently made it very clear the feeling is mutual.

His unofficial uniform of Tod's athleisure sneakers, Euro-style grey trousers, pale blue shirt and padded Patagonia gilet act as a good camouflage, but he has never belonged in this environment. He's felt like an outsider for years – not part of the in-crowd, the ones that matter. He hasn't got the cut-throat mentality necessary to do this job – he thought he did when he first started, but his ambition has drained away after years of watching others overtake him, and now he can't wait to be out of the whole toxic charade. He rubs his neatly trimmed box beard as the tube pulls in and the glass doors slide open. Jude squeezes himself on and pulls down the bottom of his gilet as he adjusts his grip on the rail above. He's lost weight recently thanks to all the stress at work, but despite Sophie saying this one looked better, it still feels a bit on the small side.

He thinks of Nate and Layla, imagines them lying on a beach in the Bali sunshine sipping cocktails. He hopes his best friend won't take too long to reply to his WhatsApp, that the offer he's made several times before still stands. After he'd finally cleared up the mess last night he'd shown Sophie the photos Nate had sent over of their new Balinese villa-in-progress, had seen her blue eyes widen at the sheer size of the place.

Until yesterday, Sophie had always refused to entertain the idea of moving anywhere else in London, despite him dropping the suggestion into their conversations on a relatively frequent basis. She'd insisted she couldn't leave Wimbledon, that it was where she'd grown up, that it wasn't the right time. A plethora of excuses which have gradually worn thinner over the seven years they've been together and have now reached the point where they both just pretend to believe she's telling the truth.

But the break-in has changed all that – last night she said she didn't want to renew the lease on their flat and instead suggested they get away for a while; spend some proper time together. He'd floated the idea of him taking a sabbatical and had been surprised when she didn't object. Usually he gets the impression that she's reluctant for him to do anything that might negatively affect his career.

If Nate and Layla agree they can come and stay, he'll buy the plane tickets for their first-year wedding anniversary in a few weeks. That would fit with the paper theme. Sod the expense. Sophie deserves the best. He knows he's lucky to have her. The kind of woman that everyone, him included, had always considered out of his league. She'd reminded him of Kate Bosworth with dimples when he first met her: petite, blonde hair, a perfect round face with flawless peaches-and-cream skin. A smile that exuded warmth and made him feel as if he was standing under a spotlight; the only person in the room who mattered to her. She thinks he's joking when he tells people he'd known from their first date that he'd marry her, but bumping into her like that in Pret and realizing who she was – it really had felt like fate.

His Tom Ford glasses mist up with the lack of air-conditioning and he takes them off, wipes them on his shirt, tries to ignore the tinny music coming from the iPhone of the woman in front of him, which is giving him a headache. Only Southwark to go and then he'll be at Waterloo. He catches a glimpse of his reflection in the tube window, sees the dark circles under his eyes, the grey flecks in his deep brown comb-over more obvious than he remembers.

This time last year, Nate was doing this commute with him. Sometimes they'd stop off at Clapham Junction, grab a beer and discuss office politics before Nate headed back to his flat in Streatham and Jude went home to Wimbledon. He misses those outings more than he thought he would. The chance to reminisce about university; the place where, looking back, he remembers being happiest. Getting hammered with Nate in one of the student union bars and laughing so hard his stomach hurt; he'd never felt like an outsider back then, never had to make an effort to fit in – something he hadn't appreciated enough at the time.

Jude had been tempted to phone him today, tell him what had happened at work. Nate would have understood – he always had – but then Patrick had called him into another bloody meeting and he hadn't had a chance.

He thinks about not having to face his boss every morning, of not having to squash himself into the tube like this every night, breathing in everyone else's germs. Of the possibility of being thousands of miles away when the shit he's got himself into really hits the fan. Assuming Sophie hasn't changed her mind about the sabbatical since last night, he'll make sure they have such an amazing time in Bali that she won't want to come home.

This could be his chance to get out of the rat race. To start over and decide what he *really* wants to do with his life. Not end up like his parents. Spend more time with his wife. Nurture his passions. Make a baby. There are so many possibilities dangling in front of him, he's spoilt for choice.

3. Layla

Layla finishes her early-morning yoga practice in an Upavistha Konasana pose, stretches her hamstrings, takes a deep breath and lets her worries float away into the cosmos. The monsoon downpours have finally stopped, vanishing along with the worst of the mosquitoes, thank God, but as a result, the garden is suffering – patches of brown have begun to appear on the grass beside her yoga mat and she hates feeling responsible for anything dying, even if it is just a plant. She needs to remember to ask Nate to switch the sprinklers on more regularly.

Her morning wellness smoothie is waiting for her in a blender in the fridge. Fresh ginger, half a lemon, honey, carrot and orange juice. The drink has separated out into layers and she swirls around the thick, vivid colour that has settled at the bottom to mix them together. She pours it into a glass, adds a bamboo straw and snaps a photo of it on her phone, manipulating the filters to blur the background and increase the brightness before uploading it to Insta, adding the caption 'Seek to be whole, not perfect.'

She's neglected her grid recently, needs to create some more content, persuade Nate this isn't just another one of her temporary passion projects. Canggu is already full of influencers trying to *live their best lives* – beautiful, young, tanned women who curate every one of their social media posts to goad envy and maximize the number of comments. She can't compete with them, and doesn't want to. Since coming out here, her aim has been to cultivate more meaningful relationships with others through her work as a life coach. Channel her own experiences to help others tap into the spiritual side of themselves. It's the first job she's ever done that she feels passionate about. Her current list of clients is made up of people who work long hours in stressful jobs around the world, all seeking a better way of life, all curious to know whether it's possible to live as a digital nomad.

She carries her smoothie back out into the garden, kisses the tip of her forefinger and presses it on to the photo frame on the shelf in the living room; the picture inside one of her with her parents, taken a couple of years ago.

She dives into the pool and swims a length before turning over and floating on her back. The sun draws patterns on her closed eyelids and she relishes its heat in contrast to the coolness of the water.

A shadow falls across her face, bringing her back to reality with a jolt. She looks up to see Nate standing on the side.

'Earth to Layla. Did you hear me?' he asks.

'What?' She squints up at him.

'I said Jude had his sabbatical approved. He and Sophie are going to come and stay.'

He clenches his fist and punches the air. 'How cool is that?' His grin lights up his entire face, and for a moment all Layla can see are his teeth; large and very white. She feels a sharp pain behind her eyes as if someone has pricked her with a needle.

'I thought you said he wasn't going to get it?'

She massages her forehead, sees his smile fade slightly, clearly confused by her reticence.

'I said I didn't *think* Jude was going to get it. He must have had to do some serious arse-licking to get Patrick to agree to it. What a fucking result!'

Layla ignores his exuberance as she pulls herself through the water, reaches for the chrome handles of the steps and gets out. She gives her long hair a quick towel-dry, ruffling the dark strands that she hasn't had cut since they arrived in Bali. If the Blackwells are coming, she needs to make an appointment to get it done.

'You're going to have to do most of the entertaining,' she says. 'I'm going to be busy with all my life-coaching stuff.'

'I said I would, didn't I?'

Nate wouldn't care if she said he had to cook and clean as well – not that he needs to, as their housekeeper takes care of most of it – anything so long as he can spend time with Jude.

'And anyway,' he continues, 'it's not like you have to work all the time. That's why we came out here in the first place. For a more relaxed pace of life. You haven't seen Sophie since the wedding, and it'll be nice for you to spend some time together.'

'Will it?'

He doesn't meet her eyes, and she can tell they're both thinking the same thing.

'You apologized,' he says. 'And Jude said it's all water under the bridge. You still message each other, don't you?'

She nods. She and Sophie do exchange the occasional

WhatsApp and comment on each other's Insta posts, but their words are meaningless phrases that disguise what they both really feel. *OMG that sunset is to die for. Yay, go you!! Gorgeous dress, darling x. Soo excited for you to come and visit.*

'Jude wouldn't have asked to stay with us if there was still an issue,' Nate continues. 'And Sophie wouldn't have agreed to come. Think of all the time you two spent together.'

'That was before the wedding,' Layla says.

Nate shakes his head. 'Fucking up on one day doesn't wipe out all that history. And having them both here for a few months will give you and Sophie time to reconnect. Sort things out properly.'

'*A few months?*' Layla's voice comes out as a shriek and she forces herself to take a breath. 'When we agreed they could come a couple of weeks ago, you told me it would be one month – max. Now you're saying it's – what – three?'

Nate stares at her.

'They're not going to be staying with us all the time. They want to go travelling. Anyway, does it matter? We've got a spare room, and it's going to be great to have someone here who can give me a hand with decorating the villa. The sooner it's finished, the sooner we can move in, and that's what we both want, right?'

Layla closes her eyes briefly, tries to centre herself, find the happy place that she'd drifted into in the pool.

'Three months is a long time, Nate.'

'I just said they won't be with us all the time. Jeez, Layla. I thought we'd agreed all this. Why are you being so weird? I thought you were happy about it.'

She swallows the lump that seems to have appeared in her throat.

'I am happy.'

'Well, you don't look it. It's like I've just announced my mother is coming to stay or something.'

He flashes one of his goofy grins and nudges her arm, but she doesn't smile back.

'I know you really want to see Jude,' she says, 'but I like it being just us here. Having other people around changes things.'

Nate wraps his arms around her in a tight hug.

'I won't let that happen. And Jude and Sophie aren't just "other people". He's my best mate. Our best friends. It'll be so good to see them. Just like old times.'

She studies his face – the strong jawline and dark brown eyes that she'd fallen in love with, the slightly crooked nose that he'd broken playing rugby when he was a teenager. He reminds her of a giant Labrador puppy; overeager with excitement. He kisses her on her forehead and she can feel the damp patch he leaves behind.

'You need to go and get changed,' he says. 'You're shivering.'

She nods and presses her teeth together to stop them chattering as she heads across the lawn, stopping briefly in front of the sliding glass doors before turning back towards him.

'When are they getting here?' she asks.

'They fly out in two weeks. They've already handed in their notice on their flat.'

Layla walks down the corridor into their bedroom, shuts the door behind her, pulls off her wet bikini and drops it on the bathroom floor as she turns on the shower.

Sophie's coming. Here.

The thought grows in her mind until it feels like it's taking over her brain, squeezing out everything else. She tells herself it will be fine but can't bring herself to shut her eyes in the stream of warm water, convinced she'll open them only to see Sophie standing in front of her.

Her reflection gazes back at her – blurry in the steamed-up mirror. She repeats the words to herself, then writes them on the glass with the tip of her finger – IT WILL BE FINE – gradually revealing her face, cut up like a jigsaw puzzle.

She thinks back to the wedding, to the part she can actually remember; of Sophie walking down the aisle in her white Caroline Castigliano silk dress, of the look of hostility her friend had given her as their eyes met, briefly, before Sophie moved on, past the next pew.

She can hear Nate in the garden, singing along to one of the playlists he and Jude used to listen to in London. He couldn't be happier.

It will be fine.

But the sick feeling in her stomach tells her she's not convincing anyone, least of all herself.

'Nate?' she shouts.

No answer.

'I'm just going out.' She pulls a white maxi dress out of the pile of clean laundry and sticks it over her head. 'I won't be long.'

She picks up the keys to her moped from the bowl on

the dark wooden sideboard in the hallway and slides her feet into her flip-flops.

The traffic on the ten-minute ride into the centre of Canggu is as bad as ever. The original coastal fishing village is now a town; a cluster of roads with giant banana palms and red frangipani crammed in between the dozens of luxury villas, restaurants and shops that stretch inland from the ten-kilometre sandy beach. A haven for surfers and digital nomads, packed with Westerners and Australians seeking a more meaningful life.

She parks her scooter outside the Warung Canteen café, catches the occasional waft of incense from the various offerings laid out on the pavement. It's one of her favourite spots, and Nate rarely comes here. She heads inside, twisting her still-damp wavy hair up into a messy bun. Old surfboards are fixed high up on the dark walls; below them hang dozens of framed surfing pictures and vintage memorabilia.

She sees who she's looking for immediately; he's sitting alone at a table near the back. Part of her had hoped that he wouldn't show up; that he'd have changed his mind. Then she could go back home to Nate, carry on as normal.

As she sits down opposite him, she adjusts the gold chains around her neck, twisting the talisman evil-eye pendant so the turquoise-blue charm faces outwards. She wonders if he can see her pulse beating through her skin, which feels as if it is transparent, revealing everything inside her. He grins, displaying one missing tooth.

'I knew you'd come,' he says.

4. Nate

Nate hears Layla's scooter start up outside as he rolls over in bed and looks at his Apple Watch. An hour before he has to leave for the airport, and his health stats show he only had thirty-two minutes of deep sleep last night. Layla had woken him up when she'd got out of bed at 3 a.m., and she hadn't come back for an hour. She's been doing the same thing for a while now; says she can't sleep, and it's got worse since he told her Jude and Sophie were coming.

He doesn't remember her saying she had a client meeting this morning, but she must have done – either that or she's gone to another yoga class. She's starting to become obsessive about them, and when he thinks about this, together with her nightly wanderings, something in his stomach twinges, as if he's suddenly remembered something unpleasant he needs to do.

He stretches as he sits up, his tanned skin browner than ever against the white sheets. He relishes these lazy mornings. It almost feels like being back at university – long lie-ins, often only waking up to catch an episode of *Home and Away* – except now he's in luxury accommodation without the shit food. None of Jude's dodgy fry-ups of cheap bacon that had constantly set off the fire alarm. Enough time to catch a few waves, then drop in for a massage before settling down in the co-working space at

ConnectZen or HiveHub, ready for when the Vauxhall office comes online. The small consultancy firm that employs him remotely as a freelance project manager only pays a quarter of the salary he used to get in London, but he can do the job with his eyes shut. Living here is almost like being on a permanent holiday – he gets to chill out in the sunshine, eat at amazing restaurants, watch the sunset from beanbags on the beach and then come home to have hot, sweaty sex with Layla. He wouldn't swap it for anything.

He jumps in the shower, then scrapes his brown hair back off his face, ties it up into a bun. He'd grown it out after leaving London, had a barber here punctuate the length with a sharp undercut, and now he blends in perfectly with the rest of the digital nomad crowd. His co-workers are a mix of the unconventional, encompassing every profession from spirituality to cryptocurrency. All plugged into their Macs, working across various time zones – not just for a better work–life balance, but a better life, full stop.

The low cost of living in Canggu means they have the equivalent of a six-figure-salary lifestyle back in London. And everyone here knows it. Bragging is evident in every social media post, disguised behind hashtags such as *#blessed #betterlife #laptoplifestyle*. It's one of the main discussion topics in Tide beach club, which is filled with like-minded settlers from all over the world; Australians and British, mostly, but recently even Russians and Ukrainians, ironically living side by side in harmony, despite the fighting raging back at home.

He makes a mental note to check in with Nyoman

Suardika before he leaves to collect Jude and Sophie. His site manager owes him an update on their new villa; he pushes away the feeling of irritation that arises with this thought as he sticks on a pair of shorts and glances at his messages. He reads the first one, feels goosebumps rise up on his arms, then deletes it before the temptation to reply becomes too much. He wishes he could, but it's too risky at the moment and, if Layla finds out, she'll kill him.

He sends her a text.

Missed you this morning, sexy 😘

Her reply comes back a few seconds later.

Will make it up to you tonight 😏

He glances out of the window at the cerulean sky and blazing sunshine and has a flashback to being squashed into a packed tube train with Jude after walking to the station in the dark, damp drizzle running down the back of his neck, his mind running over all the emails marked *urgent* that he'd need to reply to later that night. The constant backstabbing of office politics meant he'd had to keep a bottle of Gaviscon permanently in his desk drawer. He can't believe he did it for so long.

If it wasn't for Layla, he'd still be there. Her parents had paid for all this. A sixty-mile-an-hour head-on collision with a lorry driving on the wrong side of the road had resulted in an untimely legacy and a chance for them to break free of the nine-to-five. Sometimes it takes a tragedy to make you re-evaluate your life – something he is already only too well aware of.

Layla hadn't cried, not even at the funeral. Instead, she'd gone out every night, drunk until she threw up, and paced around their flat sticking dozens of Post-it notes with different quotes on to the walls. *Everything happens for a reason; it's figuring out the reason that's the hard part. Often it's the deepest pain which empowers you to grow into your highest self.*

He'd found it hard enough losing two people he'd come to regard as his second family, but it had been worse watching Layla teeter on an invisible tightrope, terrified as to which way she was going to fall. It hadn't been until he'd switched on a crappy Netflix film set in Bali that he'd seen a spark of interest in her eyes that hadn't been there for weeks. She'd told him she wanted to move. Get away from all the memories. Start again somewhere new. And he'd agreed, relieved she'd found something to focus on, even though he'd had to bring the flights forward after the complete shitshow of Jude and Sophie's wedding.

His oldest friend is the only thing he misses about London. He has plenty of mates out here – he knows all the right people and has established a reputation in Canggu as being the life and soul of the party – but it would still be nice to spend time with someone who has known him for longer than a few months. Someone with whom he shares a history that is buried deep into his skin, who knows him better than anyone else, the bad stuff as well as the good.

He checks his Apple Watch again – needs to get a move on or he'll be late to the airport. He goes to put on his Cole Buxton white T-shirt but can't find it in the pile of clean laundry. He's sure he remembers putting it in the wash. What has the bloody housekeeper done with it? He contemplates texting Layla to ask her but knows she won't want to be disturbed when she's with a client.

Shit.

He really wants to wear it today. Jude had always said never to underestimate the importance of a first impression, and even though Nate knows this isn't that, for some reason it feels like it is. He wants everything to be perfect for their arrival, wants his best mate to see that his poky flat in Streatham where they could barely all fit around the table for dinner is long gone; that he and Layla are living their best lives out here. Which they are. A villa five times the size of his old flat, their own private pool, no more cheap self-assembly furniture. He couldn't be happier, apart from having to deal with his site manager – he should have listened when everyone told him building projects are bloody stressful.

He searches through his wardrobe, moves the metal hangers from one side to another, flinches at the scraping sound, but his T-shirt definitely isn't in there. He hesitates, then opens the other door, to Layla's side. Maybe she's taken it by mistake. He rifles through her dresses, but there's still no sign of it. *Fuck.* He really needs to go. The black one it is.

He catches sight of them as he goes to shut the door. Marks on the dark wood at the back of her wardrobe. He pushes her clothes to one side to get a better look and runs his fingers over the dozens of scratches, his stomach contracting as he realizes they aren't just marks. They're letters. Whole words have been carved into the teak with something sharp. He shines his phone torch over them, trying to keep his hand from shaking.

I wish it had never happened.

He moves the light further down.

I'm sorry.

The same phrase, etched deep into the wood over and over again.

Then another.

It was all my fault.

He can't face reading the others and swallows as he moves her hangers back into place, covering up the horror as he shuts the door.

Fucking hell, Layla.

He'd thought she was better. Why hadn't she told him she was struggling? She'd been over and over the accident with her therapist. How it wasn't her fault that her parents crashed on their way to visit her, how no one could have foreseen that happening.

Maybe these markings are from when they first got out here, before she started the counselling sessions, which she'd then stopped after her therapist said she didn't need them any more. Or at least that's what Layla had told him. He's not going to know unless he asks her, but he can't have that conversation now and start an argument just before Jude and Sophie arrive.

She'd said she was fine.

She's clearly not.

He sniffs the black T-shirt lying at the bottom of his bed, then pulls it over his head, sprays another blast of deodorant under his arms just to be on the safe side. He checks his hair in the mirror and scrutinizes his reflection, pleased that his weight training seems to be paying off. Three pounds of muscle gain in a month, according to his trainer.

He orders a taxi on the Grab app, then scrolls across to

his photo albums, clicks on the one labelled *Exeter* and looks at the pictures of him and Jude at university, ones that he's never shown Layla. Most of them are blurry, unfocused shots of the two of them on nights out at Cheesy Tuesday or Dirty Sexy People in Arena nightclub. He remembers the smell of Lynx, of trying to avoid the VKs spilt on the already sticky carpet as they'd staggered back to the student house they shared, stuffing slices of Domino's into their mouths en route in an attempt to stave off a hangover.

He hesitates when he gets to a group of pictures that were all taken on the same night and scrolls through these ones more slowly. Appearance-wise, Jude hasn't changed much over the past seventeen years. He wears glasses now, rather than contact lenses, the geek-chic style favoured by celebrities, and his hair has a few salt-and-pepper streaks through its once glossy dark brown that he wears in a comb-over style to fit in with everyone else at Bearmans'.

But Nate barely recognizes the photos of himself. He's at least seventy pounds heavier – one of the many reasons he never shows them to anyone. His pudgy face is framed by a bleached-blond tousled mop of curly hair that had ended up being far lighter than the box of dye had promised; the result of a dare he'd lost to Jude over who could drink the most shots in thirty seconds. Jude hadn't been a big drinker back then; when they'd gone out clubbing he was the one they relied on to sweet-talk the bouncers and make sure they got home safely. But that night, he'd downed six more shots than Nate; the result hadn't even been close. Despite insisting that he didn't give a shit, Jude was actually a lot more competitive than Nate had realized.

Looking at these photos, he's surprised Jude had wanted to hang out with him at all. Many of the students on his corridor in Halls hadn't. He'd heard the comments whispered behind his back. But Jude hadn't cared. Had taken him under his wing. And for that, Nate will always feel like he owes him, despite what happened later.

He texts Layla as his taxi heads down the main road, accompanied by dozens of scooters, past the local warungs, past the telephone cables hanging like thick black spiders' webs from the poles at the side of the road.

Am going to collect J&S now. Meet you back at the villa.

She messages back straight away.

Great, then we can go out and grab some lunch at Groove Lounge? Will book us a table. XX

He types a thumbs-up emoji, but remembers the words carved into her wardrobe and sends it without a kiss. His mind flicks back to the text message he'd deleted earlier, and he wonders if the offer still stands. Perhaps he should consider it after all.

5. 2007

There's only seven of them this time — a family of three and two couples. I'm well acquainted with the hotel they've asked to be collected from. The Amari Yara. A five-star resort with a kidney-shaped infinity pool built at the top of a valley, overlooking the canopy of the Ubud jungle, which spreads out for miles beneath. Four-posters in all the rooms, with origami-folded towels in the shape of swans at the foot of each bed; guests names spelt out in flowers; rose petals sprinkled on top of the bathwater.

I used to work here as a gardener. Twelve-hour days with only thirty minutes for lunch in a small staff canteen with no air-conditioning, one day off in every ten. A uniform made of stiff shiny cotton that we were supposed to keep clean and tidy, despite our instructions to stop the jungle from encroaching into the hotel gardens or the infinity pool — a Sisyphean task that kept twenty of us occupied day after day in the boiling heat. I managed eight years before they decided to cut back on staff costs. Told me that my services, along with a few of my colleagues', were no longer required. The vegetable garden we'd conscientiously tended vanished completely within a matter of weeks, abandoned to the advances of the wilderness. I went back once to see it, but it was already buried beneath a thick layer of impenetrable undergrowth.

That was two years ago. Before I left, as a parting gift, I sprinkled running bamboo seeds over the flowerbeds around the side of the hotel. The hotel management are still trying to get rid of it. That stuff grows into every nook and cranny, penetrates through skirting boards and wallpaper. Now and then, I see the specialist removal van outside reception when I go to pick up guests; the men in their logoed jumpsuits with spraying equipment and sharp digging tools carrying around bags full of vegetation.

My experience at the Amari taught me four things:

1. Loyalty gets you nowhere.
2. Wealth does not buy manners or empathy.
3. You can't control nature.
4. Pierre Choderlos de Laclos was right. Revenge is a dish best served cold.

All these lessons have proved invaluable. Especially in the job I do now. White-water rafting on the River Ayung. Picking up tourists and trekking down four hundred steps into the steep canyon. Helping to lower the boats into the water, riding the rapids, stopping under the waterfalls and then taking the guests back to their hotel. The tips make it just about worthwhile. But only just.

Luckily, over the past couple of years I've learned that there are other ways to make money.

This group had booked in last week. At the time, we hadn't expected the rains for another fortnight, but they'd arrived without warning, staining the bright blue sky a dark grey. The long lines of tourists who'd climbed down to reach the canyon earlier in the season – a red river with their helmets and life jackets – have thinned out to a small dribble over the past few days. If it weren't for the added extras, there wouldn't be enough of them to justify putting on the trips at all.

I'm surprised this lot still want to go. I left a message with the hotel yesterday to double-check, but they all confirmed and paid a deposit up front, so who am I to argue? I would have thought, with such unpredictable weather, guests staying at the Amari Yara would be happier lying in the spa, working up a sweat in the sauna or just sitting in one of the many restaurants, sampling a tasting menu and specially selected paired wines. I know I would.

I half expect them to have bailed out when I arrive at reception, but they are all there, waiting for me. An American couple from Louisiana – Dan, the husband, is the first to shake hands, with an overenthusiastic pumping action; two girls from Australia on a backpacking tour; and a family from London – middle-aged parents on holiday with their eighteen-year-old son, who looks as if he doesn't want to be here at all.

I check their footwear and send the two girls to change into trainers. Ashley glances at her friend nervously, but it's the Americans I'm most worried about. Dan looks much older than fifty-two, the age he's put on the form, and a heart attack would be terrible for business.

'Ready?' I ask. They nod. 'Let's head out to the minibus, then.'

They follow me like sheep. Dan tells me how many lengths he did earlier in the pool, his loud Southern drawl already beginning to grate as we climb into the bus. I watch him carefully, note how tightly he has to hold on to the handrail – never a good sign – but I can see a large bulge in the back pocket of his shorts. A much better sign: he's brought his wallet, and I can see Ashley has hers with her too.

Often, clients decide to leave their valuables behind at the hotel, so I can never be sure how things will work out at the start of a trip, but so far, everything looks even more promising than I'd hoped.

6. Sophie

Ngurah airport isn't what Sophie expected. For some reason she'd thought it would be smaller; that there would be more bamboo and wicker, but the glass-and-metal air-bridge they'd walked through to get into the terminal hadn't felt that different from disembarking at Heathrow, and the immigration process had, if anything, been quicker and more efficient. She'd stood with Jude in a short queue, making bets on how long it would take. They'd walked away with a temporary visa within a matter of minutes, Jude insisting that she owed him, as his guess was closer.

She fiddles with the solitaire diamond on the thin gold chain around her neck, a recent birthday present from her husband, wishes there was somewhere she could freshen up while they wait for their bags to appear. She wants to reapply her make-up, or at least put on some perfume, before she sees Layla. Her lululemon hoodie currently smells of stale crisps and plane seats, but she's not sure whether to risk the toilets after some of the horror stories she's heard about travelling in developing countries.

'You'd think the airlines would have designed something to stop your head constantly falling forward,' she says, stifling a yawn. 'I only managed to sleep for a couple of hours on the flight to Kuala Lumpur.'

'They have,' Jude says. 'It's called first class.'

'Always the comedian.' She rolls her eyes as he reaches for her hand and squeezes it. 'Did you finish your book?'

He nods. His reading habits couldn't be more different to hers. He's been working his way slowly through one called *12 Rules for Life*, apparently something to do with psychology, taking his time to study every word. He only ever buys non-fiction. She prefers something more pacy and gripping – she'd grabbed a copy of *The Guests* from the shelves of Heathrow's WHSmith and is now wondering whether they could stop off in the Maldives on the way back to London.

She twists her head from side to side, stretching her neck. Jude walks behind her and kneads her shoulders, but his efforts do nothing to ease the large knots that seem to have hardened permanently into her muscles since the day of the burglary.

'Is that better, Mrs Blackwell?'

She nods, doesn't want to hurt his feelings.

'Doesn't mean you get out of carrying your rucksack,' Jude grins. 'Although I'm sure Nate will be more than happy to take yours; he said he's been working out more since they got here, and you know how he loves to show off.'

She hears the note of envy that has crept into her husband's tone. Unlike Nate, he doesn't belong to a gym and isn't really into team sports – his way of de-stressing is to go for a long run on his own around Wimbledon Common at the weekend. He puts his arms around her and she slides her hands into the back pockets of his jeans as she leans against him; something she'd done on their first date and which has now become a shared habit.

A grey rucksack appears through the plastic flaps and travels along the conveyor belt, the bright pink ribbons she'd carefully tied around the handle still clearly visible, although she'd also put an Air Tag inside to track it, just in case. Jude always laughs at how she likes to be prepared for all possible emergencies.

'Grab it, that's yours,' she says, prodding him.

Hers appears a few moments later and she hoists it over her shoulder, trying not to grimace under the weight. They buy a couple of SIM cards for their phones after passing through security, and head out into the main terminal, past WHSmith and Starbucks. She finds it discombobulating to see the same brands here as the ones that were in Heathrow, seven and a half thousand miles away.

Jude walks ahead, holding his iPhone up in the air, taking photos. Being six foot three, it helps that he can see over the heads and shoulders of most of the other tourists heading towards the arrivals hall. She knows he'll record their entire trip from start to finish. Sometimes she thinks he should have been a photographer; he has a passion for it that he doesn't have for finance, and he's talented – has a way of capturing images which have an intensity she never manages to achieve, even if she plays around with the filters. He knows exactly where to point the camera to uncover something unusual. But there's more money in banking than photography, and if they're ever going to buy their own place, or try for the baby he says he wants, they need every penny Bearmans' pays him.

Unlike Layla, she isn't going to be the recipient of some huge inheritance. Her mother, contrary to all expectations, continues to cling stubbornly to life. Sophie suspects by the time she finally passes away, the insanely expensive care home that always smells of overcooked vegetables will have swallowed not only every penny her father left – that ran out last year – but also a large proportion of Jude's income. Her salary doesn't stretch much further than their rent and bills in London, which is why she'd been looking for another job even before they decided to come out here. A step up, something with more money. Jude had suggested there wasn't any point working in PR for a fashion company that didn't appreciate her and that it would be better to spend their time in Bali thinking about her options. She'd handed in her notice the day after the burglary.

The ceiling in this part of the airport has been painted white, and is curved, like a series of giant, undulating waves. Soulful Indonesian music echoes through speakers attached to the walls of a giant tropical garden, where potted palms fronds vibrate in the air-conditioning. Everything is so much cleaner than she thought it would be – she probably should have risked the toilets.

She spots Nate before Jude does, dressed in surf shorts, flip-flops and a black T-shirt. He's grown his hair out since he left London – his neat banker's cut now a slicked-back man-bun. His face breaks into a broad grin when he sees them.

'Mate! It's so good to see you!'

He hugs Jude first, slaps him on the back, and then embraces her. He smells divine – something spicy and floral – and for a moment she doesn't want to let go of him. His physique has changed from when she last saw him a year ago. His muscles are more defined and he's lost the beer paunch common to so many men of his age working in the City.

'I can't believe how bloody tanned you are!' Jude says, staring at him. Sophie could swear her husband is standing up straighter, maximizing his couple of inches of height advantage.

'Well, you get a lot of time to sunbathe out here,' Nate says. 'I can't wait to show you around. It's a different world compared to London. You're going to love it.' He turns towards her.

'Layla can't wait to see you, Soph.'

'She's not here?'

'She had to meet a client but sends her love. She'll meet us back at the villa.'

'That's a shame,' Sophie says.

'Yeah. She was gutted.' Nate rubs his hands together. 'But there'll be plenty of time to catch up while you're here. You'll be delighted to hear that we've got in a few bottles of Aperol in your honour.'

'Oh God.' Sophie covers her face in mock horror. 'That whole Circle Line pub crawl is still such a blur. I wish I'd drunk halves like the rest of you. I swear Jude cheated and was drinking ginger beers in those last few.'

Nate laughs. 'We told you that you were being optimistic. Twenty-six pubs in one day! That's quite a feat; even for us. Anyway, we're not planning anything that hardcore for today – Layla is going to book us somewhere chilled out and local for lunch.'

He picks up her rucksack and casually lifts it over one shoulder. Jude flashes her a look that says *I told you so*.

'I've got a taxi waiting in the parking lot.' Nate sets off across the terminal, Jude walking beside him.

Sophie slows her pace and drops behind, distracted by the sound of a young woman shrieking with delight as she spots her family waiting for her. They embrace; a mother, father and someone who Sophie presumes is the woman's sister clinging to one another in a tight circle, oblivious to everyone else around them.

She thinks of Jess and feels something tug at her insides, knows this is a situation that she will never get to experience. Once upon a time, it would perhaps have been possible, but not since the fire. Sophie's life as she'd known it had come to a sharp halt after that. They'd moved house and she'd had to change school, leave behind everything familiar. Her mother hasn't been the same since, and for the last few years she hasn't even been able to stand up without help, let alone hug anyone. Although she'd never done much of that. Not to Sophie, anyway.

Jude and Nate are too busy talking to notice she's fallen behind and she hurries to catch up. Knowing Jess is so far away makes her miss her sister more than ever, and her eyes well up. She can hear her now, telling her to pull herself together and go and have a great time, which is, after all, why she's here.

It's just not the only reason.

She thinks about Layla, of when they'd first met three years ago. An evening event she'd organized for the fashion brand she worked for. Layla had been hired to serve drinks – another temping job she'd quit after only a couple of months. The two of them had started chatting and, later, once everyone had left, they'd ended up in a bar, where Layla had her in hysterics, relating various anecdotes about her work as a film extra and waitressing on a cruise ship. They'd finally got into a cab at 2 a.m. and Sophie had been so hung-over the next day she hadn't been able to go into work.

She'd introduced Layla to Nate a few days later – had known they would hit it off. Nate had been captivated by the fact Layla wasn't constrained by the unspoken rules their friends tended to adhere to – she hadn't been to university and wasn't in the least bit bothered about having a career. She was basically living the life that Nate had always wanted for himself but had been too scared to pursue.

Sophie isn't surprised Layla hasn't come to meet her, but her once closest friend isn't going to be able to avoid her much longer.

When they get to the villa, Sophie will have access to every aspect of Layla's life. And then she's going to make her pay for what she's done.

7. Jude

Jude goes to get in the passenger seat of the taxi, but Sophie nudges him out of the way.

'You go in the back with Nate.'

'Are you sure?'

'Yes. It'll give you both a chance to catch up and, anyway, I won't feel sick if I sit in the front.'

He leans forward to give her a kiss, but she's already halfway inside and he catches the side of her head instead, gets a mouthful of hair and the bitter taste of shampoo. He shuffles along the back seat, leaving a space for Nate, who is helping the driver put their rucksacks in the boot.

He can't believe how different his oldest friend looks after a year away from London. Positively fucking glowing. It makes him feel paler and even more washed out than usual. He needs this break so badly – both he and Sophie do.

The taxi heads out of the airport, then north on the bypass, ignoring the exits for the tourist towns of Kuta and Seminyak. The air-conditioning kicks in after a few minutes, but the heat is glorious – it's like sitting in a bath, and it spreads through his entire body in a way it never does in the UK, even at the height of summer.

'Kuta is basically the Balinese equivalent of Magaluf,' Nate says. 'A load of drunk tourists have turned the place into a party resort and now it's a bit of a shithole – reminds

me of that trip we did to Malia at uni. Seminyak is nicer –
huge beach, more upmarket resorts and good shopping,
but it still feels pretty overcrowded compared to where we
are. Canggu is the dog's bollocks. Amazing beaches, great
surfing. Just an all-round incredible vibe.'

The road is wider than the motorways at home, the
three lanes on either side crammed full of traffic, and
with more scooters than Jude has ever seen in his life.
It's noisier and more built up than he thought it would
be. Outlet stores, garages, banks and fast-food restaurants line the pavement, interspersed every now and again
with palm trees and patches of dark green vegetation.
The edge of the carriageway is marked by kerbstones
painted with black-and-white stripes which blur into one
another as they go past, making him dizzy. Could he see
himself living here? He's never been to South-east Asia
before, and at the moment it feels alien, but he's also
buzzing with an excitement that he hasn't felt in damp,
grey London for a long time.

'How far is it to Canggu?' he asks.

'Depends on the traffic,' Nate says. 'About an hour? In
rush hour it can be double that, but you've timed it well.
And unlike in London, this journey will cost us under
twenty quid.'

Jude lets out a low whistle.

'I know, right?' Nate grins. 'I said you'd love it out here.
Three whole months, mate! You won't want to go home.'
He leans across and claps Jude on the shoulder. 'I still
can't believe you managed to persuade Patrick to give you
a sabbatical.'

'Yeah. Me neither,' Jude says, trying to brush something

brown off his T-shirt which he realizes is actually a stain. He catches the occasional sour whiff of his own stale perspiration and wonders if Nate can smell it too. He's desperate to jump in a shower and get changed.

'How is Bearmans'?' Nate asks.

'Oh, same old, same old. You know.'

Jude focuses on looking out of the window as another scooter flies past, sounding its horn. A young child clings to his father's back, his small hands tight around his waist. Jude doesn't want to talk about work. His relationship with Nate had changed after they started there – a gap opening up between them as Nate deliberately pulled away. Jude understood why – it had been a difficult time for them both – but it still brings a lump to his throat when he thinks about it.

He glances at Sophie, who is busy chatting to the driver, and lowers his voice.

'I'll talk to you about it later. Tell me how the build is going – I can't wait to see it. The photos you sent look bloody amazing. I can't believe you've got an infinity pool.'

He tries hard to stop the resentment that threatens to creep into his voice.

'It's brilliant,' Nate says. 'And the place we're renting while it gets finished is great too – you'll see – so there's no massive rush to move out.' He shuffles forward on his seat, adjusts the black leather plaited bracelet around his wrist as he taps Sophie on the arm.

'I was really sorry to hear about the burglary,' he says gently. 'What a nightmare, coming home to find that.'

Jude tenses, wishes Nate hadn't brought it up. Sophie hasn't been the same since it happened. She's more distant. Angrier. Has been going to bed early and sleeping with her back to him. The whole incident has been completely traumatic and she doesn't need reminding of it.

She twists round in her seat to look at Nate, threads the fine chain around her neck through her fingers.

'Yeah. It wasn't one of my favourite moments. But I guess everything happens for a reason – it means we get to come and see you guys.' She takes a sip out of the bottle of water the driver has given her.

'And at least you're rid of that couple upstairs who played opera at a zillion decibels at six in the morning,' Nate adds.

'There is that,' Sophie says, managing a small smile. 'Anyway, how's Layla? Jude said her life-coaching business has really started to take off.'

'Yeah, she's good.' Nate hesitates. 'She's got several clients now.'

'How long has she been doing it?' Jude asks.

'A few months. On and off.'

'Do you think she's going to stick at it?' Sophie asks.

Nate doesn't answer.

'Come on, Nate,' Sophie says. 'Layla would be the first to admit she struggles with routine. She's had more jobs than anyone else we know. What makes you think this will be any different?'

'Because she really loves it,' he replies. 'Says she's helping people on their journey of self-discovery.' He hesitates, then flashes her a grin. 'Her words, not mine. I'm just happy she's happy. She's not under any pressure to make it a success – her inheritance is enough to keep everything ticking over.'

Jude sees Sophie's pinched expression as she turns back around in her seat, and as Nate starts talking about Instagram posts, time differences and co-working spaces, he feels his eyes getting heavier. The rhythm of the car drowns out their voices as he's sucked into the oblivion that had evaded him on the plane. He wakes with a jerk what feels like a couple of minutes later when Nate shakes his shoulder.

'Wake up, sleepyhead. We're almost there.'

Jude yawns.

'Sorry. Didn't get any shut-eye on the flight over.'

Nate grins. 'I'm expecting you to stay awake for our afternoon drinking session. Imagine some of our best nights out at Rocket or Vagabond in Canary Wharf but in twenty-nine-degree heat with views of the ocean and much cheaper drinks. Fucking incredible.'

Jude smiles, but he already feels as if he's downed a couple of pints, thanks to a thumping headache. He'll have to take a couple of paracetamol when they get to the villa.

He can see the road has narrowed to a single lane on each carriageway, the patches of dark green vegetation now denser and more frequent. The traffic has thinned out; there are only a few scooters ahead of them as the taxi pulls up outside a pair of large carved wooden gates inset into a long wall.

'Hopefully Layla's back by now,' Nate says. 'She's dying to see you both.'

Jude takes their rucksacks out of the boot and flinches as Sophie slams the passenger door so hard that it rocks the taxi. Nate exchanges pleasantries with the driver before handing him a few twenty-thousand rupiah notes.

'Thank you, Mr Osborne. Very kind. Much appreciated.'

Nate smiles. 'My pleasure.' He holds up his hand as the taxi pulls away, then presses his key fob against the panel by the side of the gates.

'He's a big fan of yours, isn't he?' Jude rests the rucksacks on the ground.

'It's good to keep on the right side of taxi drivers out here,' Nate says. 'They know everyone, and word gets around quickly if you're an arse.'

'What about you?' Jude asks. 'Do you know everyone?' He remembers all the client dinners in London that Nate had been invited to, all the times he'd been left standing at the side of the room at some work event, trying to gather up the courage to break into one of the cliques before Nate had marched in and got everyone laughing in the space of a couple of minutes. He still wonders how Nate had managed to develop such effortless charm when he'd spent the first term at university sitting mostly in his room by himself, eating chips and playing *Call of Duty* on his PlayStation.

'Not everyone,' Nate says. 'But I do know the people who matter.' The gates open and he reaches out and picks up both the rucksacks, swings them over his shoulders. 'That's something I learned from you, mate.'

Was he someone who knew the right people? Maybe he had been once, but that was years ago. And Jude knows he's definitely not any more.

'Let me know how much the taxi was and I'll pay you back,' he says.

'No way,' Nate says. 'My treat.'

The villa reveals itself as the gates open slowly, like stage curtains being drawn back.

Jude hears Sophie's intake of breath.

'Fucking hell,' she says. 'This is amazing.'

The gates shut silently behind them and he pulls out his phone to take a photograph of their teak surface, ornately carved with stems and flowers. He reaches out to touch them, runs his fingers over the leaves, feels the curves and knots in the wood, suddenly conscious of how isolated they are here. Just the four of them locked inside Nate and Layla's little piece of paradise.

He walks up the path towards the two statues of cross-legged Buddhas that sit either side of the front door. Just then, Layla opens it, holding a bottle of champagne, and throws her arms around him, her numerous gold bracelets pressing uncomfortably into his neck. He's not sure whether it's the jetlag, but it feels as if she's trembling.

'It's *so* good to see you!' she says. 'I hope the journey wasn't too much of a nightmare.'

'I can't believe it's been a year,' he says, pulling away. 'We've missed you guys!' He rubs his forehead, and Layla frowns.

'You OK?'

He nods. 'Yeah. Just a bit dehydrated. Can feel a headache coming on.'

Layla grimaces. 'Long-haul really messes with your biorhythms. I've got some arnica and gelsemium for that.'

The look on his face must show he has no idea what she's talking about.

'Homeopathic remedies,' she says. 'Much better than

46

paracetamol or ibuprofen. I'll find them for you in a sec. Come in!'

She steps back into the hallway and Jude looks around for his wife.

Sophie is staring at a large terracotta pot on the driveway which holds a large orchid, the white petals of each flower bleeding dark pink towards the centre. She reaches down and plucks off a few, crushing them in her palm before discarding them like confetti into the bottom of the pot.

'Soph,' he says loudly. 'Are you coming inside?'

She turns at the sound of his voice and wipes her palms on the front of her wide-leg linen trousers as she walks towards him, her trainers crunching on the gravel.

'I am indeed,' she replies. 'Let's get this party started.'

8. Layla

'I can't believe you're finally here!' Layla holds up the bottle of champagne as she leads the way into the kitchen. 'Let's do a toast, then I'll show you around the villa. You can dump your bags in your room and have a quick shower before we go for lunch. If that's OK with you, I mean?'

She doesn't give Sophie or Jude a chance to reply before adding, 'Or maybe you just want to chill out by the pool for a bit? Sorry, you're probably knackered. It's just Nate – we! – have been excited for *weeks* about you coming.'

She pauses briefly and holds her breath as she untwists the muselet from the top of the bottle, wiggles the cork until it pops out with a loud bang, followed by a steady stream of frothy liquid that splashes on to the marble counter.

'Shit! Nate, can you grab a tea-towel and mop that up before the ants descend on us.'

Calm the fuck down. You sound like you're on speed. She takes a deep breath and lets it out slowly as she fills the four coupe glasses up to the brim, her bracelets jangling against the side of the bottle. She hands one to Sophie and gives another to Jude.

'So,' Nate says, taking a glass and raising it, 'here's to you guys coming out to visit. It's been too long, but better late than never. Cheers.'

'Cheers,' Jude repeats. Layla is overwhelmed by a

48

feeling of déjà vu, convinced that if she so much as blinks, she'll open her eyes to find them all back in the tiny kitchen of their flat in Streatham, talking excitedly over one another, empty bottles of prosecco discarded on the counter while Imagine Dragons or Hozier play on repeat in the background.

They clink glasses and she stifles a sneeze as the bubbles go up her nose. Sophie hasn't changed at all. She's still as stunning as ever – doesn't even look tired, despite the fact she's just got off a seventeen-hour flight. There's a Tiffany gold chain with a solitaire diamond around her neck which matches the one around her wrist. Layla doesn't remember her wearing that in London. Another present from Jude, no doubt. He's always buying her stuff. She reminds Layla of a cat – all smooth movements with elegant curves. Beside her, Layla suddenly feels like she's all awkward angles and frizzy hair.

'Have you thought about what you'd like to do while you're out here?' she asks.

'We've got lots of ideas, but you guys are the experts,' Sophie says. 'It's the trip of a lifetime for us – Jude isn't going to be able to take another sabbatical at Bearmans' – so it's all about making memories. Things we can tell our kids about.'

Layla swallows what's left in her glass as she notices Jude's eyebrows rise a fraction. Nate pours Layla another drink, then leans towards her and plants a brief kiss on her lips.

'We can talk about it over lunch,' she says. 'We thought we'd take you to Groove Lounge.'

Nate searches Google on his phone and holds it up to

show Jude. 'This place,' he says. 'It was set up by this pro-surfer guy who started off serving margaritas out of a combi van on a patch of grass by the sea, and now it's this incredible beach club. It's got a huge pool, the food is great, and it has these giant sofas we can chill out on.'

'Sounds amazing,' Sophie says.

'Let me show you where you guys are sleeping and you can unpack,' Layla says. Jude goes to follow her, but Sophie puts her hand on his arm.

'You stay and talk to Nate. Layla and I can take the bags.'

Sophie smiles, but Layla feels something in her stomach tighten at the thought of the two of them being alone for the first time since the wedding. She heads out of the living room, Sophie following, and points at the pool through the huge glass doors.

'The villa is all on one floor and made up of three rectangles, so it's shaped like a U,' she says. 'All the rooms have sliding patio doors that look out on to the garden. Because the bedrooms face one another across the pool, it does mean you'll have to remember to put the blinds down if you want some privacy, and we'll do the same on our side.'

Her hands slip on the door handle as she turns it to reveal a large room, painted white, with dark wooden furniture and a king-size bed, above which are hung four black-and-white photos. She's bought brand-new matching candles and other accessories in beige and earthy tones to make it look as good as possible and just hopes Sophie appreciates it. Layla's done her best with this rented villa but can't wait to be able to start from scratch with their own.

She puts down Jude's rucksack and walks over to the opposite side of the room.

'The bathroom is behind here,' she says, sliding the door to one side so Sophie can see the large rain shower, open to the elements and surrounded by tall bamboo that acts as a natural wall. 'I've left out various toiletries – help yourself to anything you need,' she says. 'What's ours is yours!'

She winces at the desperation she can hear in her voice. There's only so much she can do to make this visit a success – she can't make Sophie forgive her.

Sophie smiles. 'That's very generous.'

Layla watches her examine the black-and-white prints above the bed. Her and Nate together: the two of them on the beach; standing in front of a waterfall; in a swimming pool with their arms around each other; two naked silhouettes embracing in front of a sunset. She feels her face flush.

'There's none of you in London,' Sophie says.

Layla hesitates. 'I guess I wanted a fresh start.'

She has a sudden recollection of kneeling over the toilet in some dodgy bar, her head spinning, her tights wet from the puddle of God-knows-what liquid on the floor, Sophie holding her hair back and passing hand towels to wipe her mouth after she'd finally finished throwing up.

Sophie lifts her rucksack on to the bed and unclips the straps.

'We bought you something,' she says, holding out a rectangular shape wrapped in pink tissue paper. 'It's for when you move into your new place, really, but you can use it here.'

'That's so kind of you.' Layla's hands shake slightly as she tears off the paper and looks at the wooden chopping board. 'You didn't have to.'

She'd left Nate to choose Sophie and Jude's wedding present, can't even remember what it was he'd bought. She and Sophie are going to have to talk about what happened at some point, but she doesn't want to bring it up when Sophie has only just arrived. She needs to give her a chance to settle in, for them to re-establish some kind of neutral ground, to not say anything that will permanently shatter their friendship, which currently feels as fragile as an eggshell.

Layla crumples the discarded tissue paper up into a ball and throws it in the bin.

'Jude insisted.' Sophie fishes out her make-up bag, runs a brush through her already sleek blonde hair, applies some pink Charlotte Tilbury lipstick and a mascara and sprays an atomizer on her neck and wrists. Layla recognizes it as the perfume she always wore in London. Jo Malone's Pear and Freesia. 'We got your names engraved on it, and today's date. I'm sure you won't forget us descending on you, but it's just a little something to remember our visit.'

Sophie leans in for a hug and Layla embraces her awkwardly, inhaling the cloying scent of her perfume. She hopes Sophie can't feel the dampness under her arms. The chopping board feels as if it's weighing her down and she forces herself to tighten her grip so she doesn't drop it as she sits clumsily on the edge of the bed.

'Are you OK?'

Sophie's voice sounds blurry, as if she's speaking

underwater. Is she OK? She's not sure. She's too hot. Needs some air.

'Put your head between your knees.'

She feels Sophie's hand on the back of her neck and recoils from the intimate skin-on-skin contact.

'I'm fine,' she says hurriedly. 'I think I drank that champagne too fast.' She sits up slowly and fans herself with one hand. Sophie disappears into the bathroom and comes back with a cold flannel, which she presses against Layla's forehead.

'Thanks.' Layla lets out a strained laugh as Sophie's flawless features swim back into focus. 'I can't believe you're the one with jetlag and I'm the one who almost passed out. I'm exhausted at the moment. I might have to have a nap at the beach club after lunch.'

'Did you not get much sleep last night?' Sophie asks.

Layla takes the flannel and moves it to the back of her neck. She shouldn't have said anything. Nate already thinks she's going crazy. He'd checked several times, in every room – had even opened all the cupboards and assured her there was nothing there.

She swallows. 'It's the heat combined with too much champagne. Bit of a lethal combination.'

She laughs again, but can tell from the creases on Sophie's forehead that she doesn't believe her. She stiffens as Sophie puts her hand on Layla's arm.

'I know we didn't leave things on the best of terms,' Sophie says. 'But as I'm going to be here for a while, I want us to get on. Start over. But we can only do that if we're honest with each other, right?'

Sophie tightens her grip, and Layla flinches. She thinks

of the number of times she'd cried on this woman's shoulder after her parents' accident, of how Sophie had come over and cooked meals for her, tried to get her to force down a few mouthfuls of food. How Sophie had been happy to sit with her in silence, unlike Nate, who had constantly pushed Layla to talk when she hadn't been capable of putting her feelings into words. Something heavy pulls in her chest as she gets up off the bed.

'I keep waking up in the middle of the night,' she says quietly. 'I think I can hear noises.'

Sophie frowns. 'What kind of noises?'

Layla looks at her.

'You'll think I'm mad,' she says, 'but I'm convinced I can hear someone walking around the villa.'

9. Nate

Jude has changed into a navy polo shirt, and Nate wonders if he should offer to lend him something so he doesn't look quite so much like a tourist. His best mate needs to kick back, chill out a bit. Not be so bloody stiff. His bare legs stick out from underneath his shorts, reminding Nate of a couple of pale twigs. Has he lost weight, or is Nate imagining it? The stress of City life seems to turn people into cartoon versions of themselves – either bloated from too many business lunches, or thinner and depleted, their shoulders permanently hunched over as if they are fixed to a laptop. Jude has clearly fallen into the latter category. Nate is so fucking glad he and Layla decided to come out here and get away from it all.

'Is it far from here to your new place?' Jude looks out through the glass doors to where the turquoise pool is sparkling in the sunshine. 'Can we drop in and see it on the way to the club?'

Nate puts his hand up to shade his eyes from the sun and realizes Jude isn't looking at the pool at all. He's staring into the bedroom across the other side of the garden, where Sophie is having what looks like a serious conversation with Layla.

'I'll check what time Layla's booked the table for,' he says. 'But it might be tricky to squeeze in a visit before lunch.' He nudges Jude's arm. 'So, Bearmans'. You started telling me about it in the taxi. How have things been?'

Jude wrinkles his nose. 'Pretty shitty. The usual toxic stuff that always happens around promotion time. Lots of cliques and meetings held behind closed doors. That grim feeling when you walk into a room and everyone suddenly stops talking and you're supposed to pretend that you haven't noticed.'

Nate laughs drily. 'No change there, then. You shouldn't let it wind you up.'

'Easy for you to say when you don't have to do it.' Jude's voice sounds tight. 'We're trying to save for a house deposit, and Sophie's mum's care-home fees are a fucking fortune. I've no idea how long we're going to have to pay them, and I don't think Sophie realizes how much we're forking out every month. It's not like the two of them are even that close. Sophie only visited her a handful of times last year.'

Nate sees a muscle twitch in Jude's cheek.

'I don't expect you to understand,' Jude continues. 'When you were at Bearmans', you were one of the people behind the doors, weren't you?'

Nate feels his throat tighten. Jude is right. He was one of those people. And he'd made the deliberate decision to distance himself from Jude when they'd started work – he'd needed some space after their last term at university. He has a sudden flashback to being in their student house, of walking along the corridor towards the bathroom with Jude following, mumbling something Nate couldn't hear above the sound of blood rushing in his ears. Of turning the door handle and thinking he was going to be sick. He's tried so hard to forget what happened, has buried it in the depths of his brain.

'It's crap whatever rung of the ladder you're on,' Nate says quickly. 'That's just Bearmans' for you.' His Apple Watch pings and he glances at the notification, grateful for the interruption. 'Taxi's here. We should get going.'

'Layla's just been telling me about your new villa,' Sophie says as she walks across the garden. 'I bet you can't wait to move out of here, with all the weird—'

'Sophie and Jude bought us a present.' Layla nudges Nate's arm and holds out the chopping board so he can see the engraved lettering. 'How nice is that? Perfect for slicing limes for our tequila shots later!'

'Ah, thanks, mate, that's epic!' Nate looks at Jude and grins as he locks the patio doors, then he turns and puts his hand firmly on Jude's shoulder. 'Shall we make a move?'

The taxi is waiting outside, pulled up in front of the gates.

'Shame we haven't got time to stop in and see the new place,' Jude says as he climbs into the back.

''Course there's time,' Layla says, frowning. 'Groove Lounge know us. They'll hold our reservation.' She leans forward and says something to the driver.

Nate swivels around in the front seat, unease swilling around in his stomach. 'Why don't we see it after we've eaten?'

'If our past outings are anything to go by,' Jude says, 'we might not be in a fit state after we've eaten. Do you remember when we went out for lunch for my birthday and you guys ended up sleeping on our sofa because we didn't get back until 4 a.m.? I could barely stand up, let alone see anything.'

'We're passing it on the way,' Layla says. 'We'll only be five minutes. The taxi will wait, won't you?' The driver nods. 'See? He doesn't mind. And I'd like to see it too. It's been a while since I last went in. I bet it looks really different now all the windows and doors have been fitted.'

Nate tries to think of something to dissuade Layla, but his mind is completely blank. He turns back around and stares out through the windscreen.

'What made you decide to buy around here?' Jude asks, breaking the silence.

'It's further away from the tourists,' Nate replies, 'but still only takes around ten minutes to get into the centre of town; quicker if you do it on a scooter.'

Jude points out of the window at a patch of brown earth covered in planks and scaffolding.

'Looks like they're building everywhere.'

Nate nods. 'After the bombings in 2002, tourist numbers here fell through the floor. The Iraq War and SARS didn't help the situation – carpetbaggers from Noosa realized they could pick up property for next to nothing. And that was before the pandemic. But now people have cottoned on to the fact that you get a shitload more for your money out here than you do at home, whether that's London, Sydney, Paris, wherever. And Covid has forced businesses to wake up to the fact most people can do their job from anywhere.'

'Canggu has more of a hipster vibe than other places,' Layla says. 'And it's heaven for digital nomads. There's so many of us now; it's a proper community. We just wanted to feel part of something, didn't we, Nate? You don't really get that in London.'

She puts her hand on Nate's shoulder, and he squeezes it, then points at an ultra-modern building with a flat roof set back from the road. A wooden bridge arches over a small lake, leading up to four giant stone pillars at the entrance.

'That hotel only opened recently,' he says. 'It's got this incredible restaurant called Kayana – run by a celebrity chef. Everyone says it's amazing. We should go there for lunch. One of the investors hangs out in the same co-working place as I do – Alex – he's such a great guy, isn't he, Layla? He keeps asking us to visit and said he'll give us a discount.'

Layla doesn't reply as the taxi pulls up outside the building site. A line of perspiration runs down Nate's back as he leads the others through an alleyway and along the side of a corrugated-metal fence. The place sounds suspiciously silent and when he pushes open a makeshift gate in the fence to reveal their villa, it looks exactly the same as when he'd last been here. He wishes he could have confronted Nyoman without the others being there.

Layla crosses her arms. 'What happened to the doors and windows? I thought they were supposed to be going in two weeks ago?'

Nate studies the holes in the walls. 'That's what Nyoman said.'

'Where are they then?' she asks.

He grits his teeth as his heart starts to race. 'I don't know, Layla. I'm chasing him all the bloody time. You're welcome to see if you can do a better job, but you said you wanted me to handle it.'

Sophie steps carefully around the edge of the empty swimming pool that has only been half tiled across the bottom and tilts her head to one side.

'Well, it doesn't look quite like what I was expecting from the photos, but I'm sure it's going to be amazing when it's finished.'

'What photos?' Layla frowns.

'The ones Nate sent over,' Jude says. 'The pool was full of water, for a start.'

Layla looks at Nate. 'You didn't tell me you'd sent photos?'

He flushes, then thinks of the words carved into the back of her wardrobe.

'We don't always tell each other everything.'

He can't hide the snappiness in his voice and Layla turns away without answering. She's right, he should have told Jude the photos were AI-generated images – how the villa will look once it's completed, not what it looks like at the moment. He'd had a perverse need to impress him, to show that he could manage a project as successfully as he did at Bearmans', but now he just feels stupid.

There's an awkward silence where he can feel Layla's annoyance hanging in the air like a shimmering heatwave.

'It's going to be huge,' Sophie says, running her fingers along one of the walls. 'We'd never be able to afford anything even a quarter of this size in London.'

'It only looks like that because it's empty,' Layla says quickly. 'Wait until it's finished and we've got all the furniture in.'

'Nyoman?' Nate calls out.

No answer.

'Nyoman!' Nate barks his site manager's name.

A man holding a spirit level appears through a door-shaped gap in the wall.

'Nate.' Nyoman smiles and nods his head as he speaks. 'Layla.'

'These are our friends who've come to stay with us,' Nate says. 'Jude and Sophie.'

Nyoman nods again. 'Nice to meet you. You like the villa?'

'It's going to be incredible,' Sophie says. 'There's so much space.'

'Where are all the site crew?' Nate asks.

'They are on a break,' Nyoman says. 'They will be back soon.'

Nate steps through the gap, walks down a corridor and comes back out again. 'Maybe this is just me, but it doesn't look like anything has changed since I was last here,' he says, trying to keep his tone steady. 'Why are we still waiting for the bifold doors? I thought we were aiming to get those in a couple of weeks ago?'

Nyoman smiles but doesn't reply as he holds the spirit level over a section of the wall and makes a note of something on the pad he keeps in his pocket.

Nate knew coming here was a mistake. It stresses him out every time he visits. He wishes he hadn't hired this man. The friend who'd recommended him said he was one of the best site managers in Canggu. Nate had been impressed by his experience and Nyoman had seemed keen to get the contract – had even gone to the effort of showing him around another site he was working on. But now he gets the distinct feeling that despite his constant smiles, his site manager doesn't like him and is trying to drag this job out for as long as possible. Squeeze him for every last fucking rupiah. But if Nate confronts him, he's worried Nyoman will simply disappear off the site, taking with him the large amount of cash Nate paid up front to secure a discount.

'We were aiming for that, but there have just been a few delays,' Nyoman says, staring at him pointedly. 'Hopefully not too much longer.'

'I really hope so.' Nate glances at Layla, then swats a mosquito as it lands on his arm, wishes it was Nyoman's face underneath his palm. 'Because if things don't start moving soon, I might have to look at getting someone else in to help.'

Nyoman lets one end of his spirit level drop on to the ground with a thud.

'Canggu is a small place, Nate. It may not be that easy to find someone else.' He pulls the metal post along the ground, the scraping sound like nails along a blackboard, and Nate winces.

'How about you focus on your job,' Nyoman says, his smile still fixed in place, 'and let me get on with my mine.'

10. Sophie

Sophie can see immediately why Nate and Layla like Groove Lounge so much. If a place was created to match a couple, it would have been built specifically for them. Laid-back with a cool bohemian vibe and a DJ playing the latest tracks, staffed by slick local waitresses who must be under instructions to encourage clientele to bring their friends, as the place is full of people who seem to know each other.

Everyone has the same 'look', despite the variety of languages being spoken: tanned, dressed casually in linen shirts, trousers and maxi dresses, as if they haven't made an effort, when she's fully aware they wouldn't look like that unless they had. Most of them are adorned with a few fine-line or discreet script tattoos, with beaded leather bracelets around their wrists. They want to give the impression they aren't all about the money – but she's beginning to realize that places like this only exist out here *because* of the money. A constant influx of digital nomads who can afford to come here for months at a time and spend their pounds or roubles or dollars.

A long rectangular infinity pool lies in front of dozens of low wooden sofas with taupe cushions and cream canvas parasols, all overlooking the beach and the sea beyond. It even smells luxurious – a mix of designer perfumes and colognes, rather than the aroma of incense that seems to permeate much of the air here.

For lunch, they'd eaten lobster nachos and plates of ceviche followed by vegetarian poke bowls; the acidic tang of lime was still sharp in Sophie's mouth as she sipped on watermelon mint margaritas while the sun slipped below the horizon, filling the sky with an orange glow. The heat has infused into her limbs, relaxing the knots that Jude had tried unsuccessfully to get rid of in the airport. Layla is so lucky that she gets to do this whenever she wants.

Sophie thinks about what she would be doing if she was in her flat in Wimbledon – probably sticking a couple of ready meals in the microwave while she waited for Jude to get back from work – and swallows the spiky ball of envy that rises up in her throat. She'd happily put up with a few strange noises at night if she got to do this every day.

Nate orders another round of Long Dawn Daiquiris from the waitress as she collects their empty glasses. He and Layla seem to have made up after their earlier dis-agreement and are now unable to keep their hands off each other.

'We should talk about plans for while you're here,' Nate says.

Sophie can feel the beat of the music in the ground below her feet as the music kicks up a notch. More people have arrived since it got dark; the bar area is crowded, the place filled with an excited buzz. She's at the point of being perfectly drunk; a fizziness inside her that makes her want to dance.

'We've got a few ideas,' she says, looking at the people

standing in front of the DJ with their arms in the air. 'What do you think we should do first?'

'He's going to offer to teach you to surf,' Layla laughs, sliding her hand around Nate's shoulder. Their constant touching and stroking makes Sophie uncomfortable. She's never been into public displays of affection, and it forces her to acknowledge the gap that has opened up between her and Jude recently.

She shakes her head.

'Not my thing. But I bet Jude is on for it, aren't you?'

Jude flashes a grin at the waitress as she reappears with their drinks, a flower tucked behind her ear.

'It's been a while, but I'm happy to give it a go.' He looks at Nate. 'I thought you weren't keen on going in the sea?'

Nate shrugs. 'I decided I needed to get used to it after we got out here.'

'Well, if you can manage it,' Jude says. 'I'm sure it can't be that hard. I tried it on holidays in Cornwall back in my teens. On a good day I could do a three-sixty.'

Nate leans across and fist-bumps him.

'Definitely got to see that, mate. I'll take you to the beach this week.'

Layla rolls her eyes. 'Well, for those of us who aren't going surfing, there's obviously yoga, art galleries, more temples than you can shake a stick at, the Monkey Forest, or we could head out to the Nusa Islands if you fancy sunning yourself on a stunning beach.'

'What about white-water rafting?' Sophie takes a few large sips of her drink, relishing the hit of cinnamon that follows the heat of the rum. 'Have you guys done that yet?'

Nate shakes his head. 'You can't do it in Canggu.'

'There are places not too far away where you can, though, aren't there?' Layla says.

'I think so. Maybe in Ubud?' Nate stands up. 'I've got to take a leak. Then we hit the dance floor.' He leans down and plants a kiss on Layla's lips before walking past the bar, stopping to high-five several people who look delighted to see him.

'Popular, isn't he?' Sophie swallows another mouthful of her cocktail as Jude gets up to take some photos.

Layla rolls her eyes. 'Yup. Nate knows anyone worth knowing out here. One of the perks of spending every day in a co-working space.'

Sophie points at a man with a short fade haircut and stubble beard holding a drink in one hand, standing among a group of people, clearly the centre of attention. There's something so charismatic about him that she doesn't want to look away, a tight feeling in the pit of her stomach.

'Who's he?' she asks.

Layla hesitates. 'That's Alex. A crypto trader. Absolutely loaded. He's the one who invested in that new flash hotel with the fancy restaurant. One of Nate's new best friends.'

Sophie grins. 'He's fit. Reminds me a bit of Theo James. Look at those cheekbones.'

Layla doesn't reply as she twists the turquoise charm around on her pendant.

'You don't like him?' Sophie asks.

Layla shrugs.

'I don't really know him.' She hesitates. 'He's got a reputation as a bit of a player.'

Sophie raises her eyebrows. 'Well, I can see he wouldn't be short of admirers. But if he's that awful, why is Nate hanging around with him?'

'You know what Nate's like,' Layla replies. 'He loves being the life and soul, and Alex and his crowd are definitely all that.'

Sophie detects a bitterness in Layla's voice as her straw sucks up the last of her daiquiri. That's not like Layla. Live and let live has always been more her motto.

Jude comes and sits back down, plants a kiss on Sophie's cheek and puts his hand on her thigh, but she moves away, pretends to adjust her skirt. He's drunk. Her own head starts to spin and she feels her balloon of happiness begin to deflate, wishes she'd drunk more water and fewer cocktails.

'You OK?' Jude's forehead creases in concern.

'I'm fine.' She hopes Nate will come back from the gents so they can get up and dance. She wants to lose herself in the music. Jude puts his arm around her shoulders, but it feels like a heavy weight that presses into her skin and makes her head spin even faster.

A woman brushes against their table, her hair the same shade of red as her sister's. For a moment Sophie thinks she's Jess, then realizes of course it isn't her, and a lump rises up in her throat. She wishes it was. Jess would love it here, and it would mean she'd have someone to confide in at moments like this when things don't feel quite right.

'Are we dancing then, or what?' Nate has reappeared and is holding his hand out to Layla.

Sophie nods and follows them on to the dance floor. Her mind has slid from a pleasant blurriness to being unable to focus and she can't make her body stay in time with the beat of the music. She holds on to Jude's shoulder to keep herself upright as she looks across at Layla and Nate, their arms wrapped around one another, thinks of their new villa, their infinity pool, their kitchen that will be at least triple the size of the one she and Jude had in Wimbledon. Thinks how Nate doesn't care whether Layla's life-coaching business is successful, how she's managed to sail through the last three years, barely having to work at all. How happy she looks. She feels a hot, sticky jealousy slide over her skin.

After they've finally staggered back to the villa a few hours later, she lies next to her husband in the king-size bed and breathes in the smell of the unfamiliar washing powder on the pillowcase. Something floral and exotic.

She remembers Layla dancing, wearing her vulnerability like a scent, her long, floaty dress spreading out around her, the reflections from the mirror balls set around the DJ booth catching on the gold chains around her neck. Sophie kicks off the sheet, wishes she could sleep, but still feels wired despite refusing the tequila shots the others had done when they got home.

Jude starts to snore and she gets up, goes into the bathroom, pulls on a towelling robe, turns on the tap, cups her hands underneath and then hesitates. Is the water safe to drink? Hadn't Nate said they were supposed to stick to bottled stuff?

She opens the bedroom door and heads down the corridor towards the living room, trying not to make any noise, the wooden boards cool under her bare feet. She opens the fridge, takes out a bottle of water and gulps it down thirstily. There's a soft glow from the cabinet lighting in the kitchen that comes on automatically at night, and through the floor-to-ceiling glass doors she can see the swimming pool, lit up in the darkness by the solar lights set into the surrounding grass.

The movement of Nate's silhouette catches her eye as he appears behind his bedroom window. It takes her a couple of seconds to realize he's naked, but still, she doesn't turn away as he walks towards Layla lying on the bed, and continues to watch as he kisses her, working his way down her body until their two silhouettes merge into one.

She feels a pulling sensation in the bottom of her stomach, a heat that prickles over her skin as she watches them move in a way that is both familiar and so very different, until they finally finish. She thinks of Jude in their room and what has become of their ever shorter, perfunctory efforts, which finally petered out after the burglary, and her heart shrinks.

Outside in the garden, the surface of the pool is completely still, as if inviting her to walk across it. She knows it's impossible, but desire has brought on a recklessness that makes her half tempted to slide open the patio doors and try it anyway.

Something solid settles below her ribs, like a large stone that she can feel every time she swallows. She wanders around the room, trying to clear the heaviness, inspects the objects on the tall shelving unit: several framed photos of Layla and Nate when they were younger, and then Layla with her parents, a set of painted bowls, various ornaments, books and Buddha sculptures.

Why is she still living in a shitty rented flat when they get to have all of this? She hopes Layla is lying awake in the dark now, straining to decipher the sounds of Sophie moving around the kitchen: the thud of an empty bottle hitting the bin, the click of a fridge door. Sounds that she hopes will crawl through Layla's brain and eat up her rational thoughts.

She hesitates as she feels the darkness seep through her skin and expand inside her. She walks back to the shelves, picks up one of the small painted wooden geckos and slips it into her dressing-gown pocket before heading back along the corridor to where Jude is still snoring.

She opens the drawer of her bedside table and slides the gecko inside, the swirls of bright blue and green paint disappearing beneath her passport, before slipping off her towelling robe and lying down next to her husband, her skin still on fire.

She presses her hands together over her heart; a prayer for forgiveness — a ritual that she hasn't performed since she was thirteen, in those weeks after the fire — and waits for sleep to come.

11. Jude

When Jude wakes up the following morning, his wife isn't in bed beside him. He goes to sit up, but it feels as if there's an elastic band stretched around his head, and he collapses back on to the pillow. What the fuck is that taste? Ash? Was he smoking last night? He hasn't touched a cigarette for years. Christ, he must have been pissed.

He waits for the room to stop spinning, staggers into the bathroom and stares at his bloodshot eyes in the mirror. His beard could do with a trim, but his hands are shaking too much right now to use a razor. He turns on the shower, hopes the water can perform some kind of miracle, as if bringing a shrivelled plant back to life.

'Afternoon!' Nate looks at him over the top of his sunglasses as Jude steps out through the glass patio doors. 'We were wondering when you were going to make an appearance. Coffee? I sense you might need one.'

Jude nods. 'Please. And a new head if you've got one, but failing that, some painkillers.'

Nate laughs. 'Sure thing, mate.'

Sophie is lying on her stomach on a lounger, her head poking over the edge as she peers at her phone on the grass in front of her. He leans down and plants a kiss on the back of her neck. Her skin smells of suncream and something floral that he doesn't recognize, and if he didn't feel so crap, he'd kneel down beside her and run his hands over her back; give her a long massage.

'You were snoring like a pig last night,' she says.

'Was I? Sorry.'

She raises her calves to make a space for him and he lowers himself down gingerly on to the end of her lounger, rubbing his temples.

'Nate has broken me,' he mumbles. 'I feel like shit. No sleep on the flight over followed by cocktails and God knows how many tequila shots does not go down well. Was I smoking? When I woke up, I swear I could taste—'

'You both were,' Layla says from her lounger, sipping from a water bottle. 'Nate accosted some poor backpacker and persuaded him to give you his packet of Lucky Strikes.'

Jude feels his stomach roll over.

'I feel like I'm dying and I've not even been here twenty-four hours.'

'Here you go, mate.' Nate reappears from the kitchen carrying a mug, a couple of wraps of sugar and a blister packet of tablets. 'You still have it black with two, yes?'

Jude nods, unsure whether the liquid will stay down if he takes a sip.

'I've got some belladonna if you'd rather take that?' Layla says. 'Paracetamol makes me break out in a rash.'

Jude ignores her as he pops a couple of tablets and shoves them into his mouth, winces as the coffee burns his lips.

'I think I feel worse than I did after your twenty-first,' he groans. 'Your mate Alex just kept buying me drinks.'

'I told you he was generous,' Nate says. 'You can sleep

it off by the pool. We thought we'd just hang around here today, give you a chance to recover. I've got to log on later this afternoon and do a bit of work. You can come with me to ConnectZen if you're feeling up to it – it's one of the co-working places we use – they've got a pool and a bar you can chill out in. And I'm going to have to visit the site again at some point this morning. Find out if Nyoman has made any fucking progress since yesterday.'

He screws up one of Jude's discarded sugar wrappers and flicks the tiny paper ball across the grass.

Jude can't remember the last time he saw Nate really pissed off. Even when things had been shit at work he'd always managed to keep a smile on his face. People are drawn to his affability, the fact he seems so easy-going. Always up for a laugh and a joke. They don't get to see the person underneath – the one Jude knows can be ruthless if it comes to it.

'God help Nyoman,' he says.

Nate smiles. 'Layla's going to stay here. So—'

'No, I'm not,' she interrupts. 'I've got a client meeting.' Nate frowns, and she raises her eyebrows. 'What?'

Sophie sits up on her lounger. 'We don't expect you to look after us all the time. We're not children. If you guys need to work, that's totally fine. We'll just hang around here, or I might go and find one of those nail bars you were telling me about last night.'

Nate scrapes his hair back off his face and ties it up in a band. 'We want to spend time with you. That's why we asked you out here, right, Lay?'

Jude sees Layla hesitate for a fraction of a second before she answers.

''Course,' she says. 'And when I get back, we can plan what we're doing for the rest of the week. Maybe go and visit some waterfalls or do some snorkelling.'

Jude can feel himself starting to perspire. The heat or his hangover? Either way, his skin feels unpleasantly slick and clammy. He watches Nate give Layla a kiss as she sets the table. Perhaps now isn't the best time to ask why his best friend digitally manipulated those villa photos.

'I made some nasi goreng earlier,' Layla says, looking at him. 'It'll help soak up the alcohol from last night. Fancy some?'

They eat outside under the shade of a large umbrella, the cream linen providing welcome respite from the sun. Jude can't remember the last time he and Sophie ate outdoors. The previous summer? Their flat doesn't even have a garden, so it was probably a rare lunch outing to a pub on the Common.

'Do you remember those donor kebabs we used to have after a night out at Fabric?' Nate says, laughing. 'From that dodgy van? The sauce that used to leak straight through the paper bag on the bus home.'

The memories flash into Jude's head. The crowd with their hands in the air. Dark corridors, filthy toilets and damp tarmac; the loud, thumping beat. He usually spent the next morning recovering while Nate made breakfast in their kitchen.

Layla giggles. 'The good old N87. Never turned up on time and had seats that smelled of vomit. I don't know how you two managed to avoid getting food poisoning from eating that shit. God knows what they put in those things.'

'You still used to have the salad and the sauce,' Nate says with a grin.

'Yes, but not the meat!' Layla says. 'Or whatever it is they slice off that rotating pole.'

Jude looks at her. 'I read somewhere that they take—'

'Don't tell me.' She covers her ears. 'I don't want to know.'

Jude laughs. 'Well, this meal tasted infinitely better. Thanks so much, Layla.'

Sophie puts her fork down and pushes her bowl to one side. 'Yes, thanks, Layla, that was great. You could really taste the garlic and chilli.'

Jude notices she's left most of hers. Since the burglary, her appetite has shrivelled to almost nothing. He doesn't know how she isn't permanently starving. He watches as she gets up and goes to lie down on one of the inflatables by the side of the pool while he carries their bowls into the kitchen.

Layla is standing in front of the shelves in the living room, frowning as she studies the various framed photos.

'Everything OK?' he asks. Her body seems to stiffen at the sound of his voice. 'I hope we're not making things inconvenient for you by being here.'

'No, you're really not. It's lovely to see you both.' She points to the dishwasher. 'Can you stick those in there?'

He scrapes the leftovers into the bin, then bends down and stacks the plates in neat rows, adjusting all the crockery that's already in the top section so it fits in properly. One of his pet hates. He can't bear things to be all out of order.

'I'm sorry we didn't get to see you after the wedding,' he says, squirting soap on to his hands and running them under the kitchen tap.

She doesn't look at him. 'We moved our flights forward. Nate did text you.'

'I know,' he says. 'He just didn't say why. You weren't supposed to leave for another week. We got back from honeymoon and you'd already gone.'

'I think you know why,' she says.

Jude follows her gaze outside, to where Nate is rubbing suncream on to Sophie's back, and feels something tighten in his stomach. He sticks a tablet into the dishwasher drawer, clicks the door shut and presses the button to turn it on.

'Everything's OK between you and Sophie now though, right?' he asks.

She nods. A movement so quick he wonders whether he's imagined it.

'Can I ask,' she says, 'have you seen one of these anywhere?'

She holds a small wooden ornament on her outstretched palm.

Jude folds the tea-towel he's holding in half, hangs it over the rail on the oven and walks over to her. The carved creature in her hand is painted in different shades of blue and green with lime-green spirals and dots covering its body.

'A lizard?' he asks.

'It's a gecko,' she says. 'There were three of them on this shelf, but now there's only two. I just wondered if you'd seen one anywhere.'

He shakes his head. 'Sorry,' he says. 'Are you sure? That there were three, I mean?'

'Yes. I'm quite sure.' He notices the edge to her tone as Nate pokes his head through the patio doors.

'Your phone's bleeping, mate.'

Jude is conscious of the heat of the sun on his forehead as he walks past the pool, and remembers he hasn't put any cream on. He thought he'd turned his mobile off. He picks it up off the grass and sees he's had three missed calls, all from the same number.

Fuck.

He tries to look casual as he dials his voicemail while Nate glances at him, tries to ignore the rush of adrenaline he can feel shoot through him.

He's surprised it's taken them this long. A message from Kathy in HR at Bearmans' asking him to get in touch. Is she having a laugh? There's no way he's going to do that. As far as he's concerned, any interaction between them ceased the moment they fired him. He presses the phone into his ear so there's no chance of anyone else, especially Sophie, hearing what she's saying.

When Kathy's finished speaking, he deletes her voicemail and blocks her number. He has no intention of speaking to someone who is currently several thousand miles away and in no position to ask him to do anything.

She can make all the demands she wants, but there's no fucking way he's going back there.

12. 2007

'You can't expect us to go down there. That's insane.'

Dan's Southern American drawl bristles with indignation.

'Yeah, that is insane.' His wife – who we have all discovered on the twenty-minute minibus drive makes a mean crawfish étouffée, likes line dancing and is actually called Jen, despite Dan only referring to her as 'babe' – echoes her husband's comment.

'Mr Landry—'

'Dan.'

'Dan, I did warn you about the steps,' I say.

'I didn't realize there would be that many,' he says.

I want to ask him what he thought four hundred steps would look like but restrain myself. My five other guests are waiting at the entrance to the pathway that leads through the jungle and down to the bottom of the canyon. I don't like to leave clients standing around for too long. It gives them time to think.

'Maybe you should wait in the minibus if you don't think you can manage it?'

James, a banker from London, looks at his wife and son before announcing this loudly, as if he's just expressing what the rest of the group are all thinking.

'I mean, it does look pretty bloody steep,' he adds, 'and we've all got equipment to carry.'

Jen's eyes widen and she pats her stiffly permed hair, as if already feeling the restrictions of the safety helmet.

'I can carry your oars for you,' I say. 'But you have to be sure that you can manage the steps.'

Dan walks over to the edge of the path and looks down into the jungle below. The steps are cut into the steep rockface and there's a metal handrail, installed several years ago, across the narrower sections to avoid repetition of one particularly nasty accident. The grey boulders are covered in greenery — different species of ferns, palms, banana trees, papaya and snake-fruit trees. I know them all, including which ones are poisonous.

Dan turns to his wife. 'I think we can do it, babe.'

She looks unconvinced but takes the red helmet I hand her and gingerly lowers it on to her head while I give the rest of the group theirs, together with lifejackets and paddles. The aluminium poles with their nylon blades vary in length and I check each of the guests to make sure they come between shoulder and eye height when they hold it upright.

Mia, one of the backpackers, looks so fragile that I doubt she's going to be able to paddle for long. With eight of us in the boat, let's hope the others do most of the work.

'I'll take a dry bag,' I say, 'but if there's anything you'd rather leave in the minibus — wallets, jewellery, phones — shout now before I lock up.'

I've perfected the art of sounding casual at this point in the proceedings, but what happens now will determine just how lucrative this trip is going to become.

Luckily, Dan, Ashley and James get out their wallets. Kristin, James's wife, also hands over her purse — Mulberry, I think, a favourite of clients who come from London — and Mia gives me her watch. That isn't going be any use, but I take it anyway, put it in the glove compartment together with the wallets and check that James is watching before I lock the doors of the van.

In peak season, dozens of vehicles are crammed into this area, but today the place is almost empty.

'If you all stand together, I'll get a photo of you,' I say.

The group hold up their paddles and I take a couple of pictures with my phone. They're set to upload to Flickr and I'll email everyone a copy later — clients love an added personal touch.

The sky is now covered in a layer of dark grey cloud and tiny flies have begun to hover in black clusters. Kristin swats them away from her face as we start down the steps and I offer up a prayer that it won't rain. Once we've left the van, we can't come back. At least not for an hour.

Below us, I can only see three inflatable boats tied up along the concrete ledge at the side of the riverbank. Usually, there'd be a queue of tourists heading towards them, but today there's no sign of anyone else and a feeling of unease begins to circle in my gut.

Dan is already struggling even before we reach the bottom — wheezing as he grips the handrail. James's son is carrying Mia's paddle for her. Jen is attempting to have a conversation with Kristin, but it's not easy when you're in single file with a helmet covering your ears.

None of them are looking at me, and so none of them see the look of horror on my face when I see the river — at least a foot higher than the last time I was here and flowing twice as fast, its roar fiercer than a caged wild animal.

13. Layla

Layla heads inland on her scooter, away from the beach. She wants to make the most of the time before her meeting, just needs a few minutes to meditate and clear her head.

Sophie and Jude have only been here a day.

The thought circles around continuously in her brain, making her dizzy.

Last night had gone better than she'd expected – they'd got drunk, danced, laughed until her stomach hurt, in that way you can only do with really good friends – and when they'd finally collapsed into bed, Nate had said it had been just like old times. And he's right, it had. But whenever she thinks about spending time with Sophie on her own, she experiences a sensation similar to vertigo, as if she's standing on a high bridge, staring over the edge at the drop below.

Since moving to Bali, she has tried not to think about the person she was when they left London. Arriving in Canggu had been like drawing a line in the sand, a point from which she has focused solely on looking forward. And becoming more Zen. But having Sophie and Jude here has stirred up the past and she's worried that things she thought she'd left behind, confident they had sunk without a trace, are going to float back up to the surface, where everyone can see them.

She drives a few kilometres away from the shops and

restaurants to where there are no builders or machinery or flash new hotels. This is the place she sees on post-cards, where she can hear herself think. The old Bali – whose spiritual heartbeat is much louder here than it is in Canggu. She loves being part of the digital nomad community, but when she is out in the countryside she feels she can breathe. Nate's new friends would never come here. There's none of the glamour, the gadgets, the places-to-be-seen-in, the opportunity for not-so-subtle one-upmanship. Nothing that would appeal to people like Alex.

His face slips into her head and she forces it out again as she stops the scooter and looks out over the lush green fields – rice paddies that stretch away into the distance, the outline of Mount Batur rising up in a triangle behind them. A woman in a red straw hat is bending down, up to her knees in water, tending to the young shoots that, close up, Layla can see are actually hundreds of individual plants, not the sea of green you see in photos.

So much in life comes down to perspective.

She shuts her eyes and inhales the smell of damp earth before getting out her phone and taking several shots for her Instagram grid, filtering them to get the best light. A quick glance at the time tells her she's got ten minutes before she needs to be at HiveHub.

As she heads back into the centre of Pererenan, she passes a couple of warungs, their customers spilling out on to the metal tables and chairs set up on the pavement. All locals – the tourists will still be in bed after a late night of partying. She sees an elderly couple holding hands and for a fraction of a second she thinks of her parents and her heart leaps, before she remembers it isn't them and that she will never see them again. Almost a year and a half since the accident and it still doesn't feel real.

It had almost killed her. Literally. The shock had detached something in her brain so, to begin with, she couldn't feel anything. She had started cutting herself just to prove she was still alive, to show that, physically, her body was still functioning beneath the numbness; that her skin still slid apart when she drew a razor blade across it and blood still oozed out of her veins. And then she'd gone out and drunk bottle after bottle of pretty much anything she could get her hands on, trying to blot out the pain which had arrived a few weeks later. A grief that had taken her breath away with its intensity, twisting her insides into knots so tight that she'd had to crawl into bed and lie under the duvet in the dark until it receded. For more days and nights than she could count, she'd teetered on the edge of a swirling blackness that had threatened to swallow her whole.

Sometimes she pretends that it never happened, imagines her parents are both still pottering around their house at home; her dad fixing something on the kitchen table, his toolbox balanced on a chair; her mum cooking a Sunday roast, the smell of rosemary and garlic coming from the oven. They'd always wanted to visit Bali, and she'd made sure the lorry driver hadn't taken that away from them too: she'd brought them with her – they're currently sitting in an urn on top of the unit in her living room. After the nightmare of losing them, she couldn't bear the thought of them lying in the ground somewhere cold and dark and never seeing the sun again.

Nate still thinks they were the reason she wanted to leave London. And she hasn't corrected him because he's right, they were. Just not the only one.

She parks her scooter on the pavement outside Hive-Hub and pulls off her helmet. The huge L-shaped building has an industrial-style black iron framework with cream panels filling in the gaps between the struts. It's buzzing, as usual – a hostel as well as a co-working space, with rooms kitted out better than most of the local homestays. The open-plan ground floor is covered with dozens of different-sized tables and large potted palms. Other digital nomads slouch on brightly coloured beanbags in front of the huge pool, behind which is a couple of acres of scrubby grassland.

He should be here already, but she can't see him. She orders a passion-fruit iced tea at the bar, then sits down at the table they normally meet at and gets out her phone. She logs on to Instagram, posts one of the photos she took earlier and adds the caption 'I chased success because I thought it would make me happy' underneath it, together with *#LiveYourBestLife #LoveBali #PowerToChange*. She scrolls through all her messages, replies with positive affirmations and heart emojis to a few DMs and books in a call with another prospective client.

She's almost finished her iced tea, and there's still no sign of him. He asked to meet; the least he can do is turn up on time. A ticking sound makes her look up as a tokay gecko slithers down the metal strut next to her table. She reaches for her phone to take a photo, thinks of the one that has gone missing off her shelf in the living room. She feels stupid for asking Jude about it earlier – what on earth would he want with a wooden ornament? But she'd needed to state its absence out loud. To prove she's not imagining it. She thinks other things in the house have disappeared recently, but Nate doesn't believe her, says their housekeeper has probably just moved them. And she's not a hundred per cent sure – she wonders if her mind is playing tricks on her, like it had done when she was drinking.

Even though she's no longer waking up with blanks in her memory, she's not certain whether it's anxiety that's making her imagine the noises that Nate says aren't there. She thought she heard something again last night – the sound of the lock catching on the patio doors in the living room, the way it always does if you don't push it up far enough before you open them, but she had forced herself to lie still and not get up. Nate would have asked what she was doing, and she couldn't bear the thought of him going to investigate and not finding anything, again.

She looks up as a shadow falls across the table. The man she's here to see slides into the seat opposite her and she snaps her laptop shut.

'You're looking well,' he says.

She leans forward, closing the gap between them. 'You can't just message me and expect me to drop everything, meet you at a moment's notice and then make me wait twenty minutes for you. We have guests staying with us. What do you want?'

He grins, displaying his missing tooth.

'The same as before.'

'I told you: I need more time.'

'So you said. But things have changed.'

He pushes a piece of paper across the table.

'Instructions are on there. Three days.'

As Layla opens her mouth to argue, she catches sight of two familiar figures walking over to the bar.

Shit.

'You need to leave,' she hisses. 'Right now.'

The man looks at her but doesn't make any attempt to get up. She slides the piece of paper off the table, folds it up into a small square and sticks it in her pocket. 'I will deal with this,' she says. 'Just go. Please.'

He walks away as Nate heads across the tiled floor towards her.

'Finished your meeting?' he asks.

She nods, her heart thumping beneath her ribs.

'Want anything else to drink?'

'Can you get me another iced tea?' she says. 'I thought you said you were going to ConnectZen?'

Sophie pulls out the now empty seat opposite Layla.

'We were,' she says, 'but then we decided HiveHub was nearer. Jude has flaked out by the pool for the afternoon, so I asked Nate if I could come and see what all the fuss is about with these co-working spaces. Maybe meet some of your friends.' She turns towards him. 'Can I get an iced tea too?'

Nate puts his thumbs up and walks over towards the bar.

'And speaking of friends,' Sophie says, 'who were you just with?' She smiles, showing her dimples. Layla experiences a lurch of guilt, remembering the horror of the wedding all over again.

She turns away and swallows as she watches the thin figure slip out through the entrance.

'He's not a friend,' she says. 'Just someone interested in life coaching. I had to tell him I only work remotely with clients in other countries.'

Sophie frowns.

'Visa restrictions,' Layla adds.

Sophie nods, but Layla can tell she doesn't believe her. The corner of the folded paper in her pocket digs into her stomach as she leans forward, each sharp stab a painful reminder of what she has to do.

14. Nate

'Ready for Echo Beach?'

Jude's reply is lost in the whirr of the smoothie blender as Nate takes four glasses from the cupboard, fills each to the top and hands one to Jude.

'Here you go. All your vitamins and minerals for the day.'

'When did you get so health conscious?' Jude asks.

'Since getting out here,' Nate says. 'I realized you've got to look after yourself. Only got one body, and all that. And yes, before you say anything, I remember what I was like at uni, but that was seventeen years ago.' He pats his sixpack. 'I hope I've lost a few pounds and my nutrition knowledge has expanded slightly since then.' He picks up the other two glasses and puts them in the fridge. 'The girls can have theirs when they get up. Layla had a bit of a rough night, so I don't want to wake her, and it's best to get out early if we want to avoid the crowds.'

Jude swallows a mouthful of green liquid and nods his appreciation. He's swapped his glasses for contact lenses and, without the dark frames, Nate thinks his face looks paler than ever.

'How's Layla doing?' Jude asks. 'I guess losing both your parents at once isn't something you ever really recover from.'

Nate hesitates. 'She's good. You saw her before we

left London – things had got really tricky. Your wedding was, well, you know . . .' He trails off, unsure what to say.

Jude reaches out and puts his hand on Nate's shoulder.

'It's in the past, bro. Forget about it. I'm just pleased she's feeling better.'

Nate takes a gulp of his smoothie, his brain conjuring up unwanted images of the words carved into the back of Layla's wardrobe.

I'm sorry.
I wish it had never happened.
It was all my fault.

Layla clearly isn't doing as well as he's making out. He fiddles with his leather bracelet, debating whether to say anything. 'She's been a bit restless at night recently,' he blurts out. 'Says she can hear noises. I've checked all around the villa; thought it might be the air-con switching on and off, or that we had rats or something, but there's nothing there.'

Jude raises his eyebrows. 'Maybe it's tinnitus? Has she been to see a doctor?'

'Not yet. I was kind of hoping it would just sort itself out without having to go down that route.'

'I'm sure it will,' Jude says. He gazes out through the glass doors. 'She couldn't be anywhere more relaxing. You're so lucky – you've got such an amazing life here.'

Nate grins. 'I know, right? Who would have thought this was where I'd end up. How things change, eh, mate?'

Jude stares at him. 'Yes,' he says. 'They really do.'

Nate drains the dregs of his smoothie. 'You ready to surf, then?'

Jude puts his still half-full glass on the counter.

'Absolutely,' he says. 'Let's go.'

They park the scooters on a strip of wasteland behind Echo Beach alongside dozens of others and walk down a narrow path to a crude hand-painted sign propped up in the sand advertising surf lessons. Behind it stands a large bamboo shack covered in wooden planks with a corrugated-iron roof. Nate beckons Jude inside and greets the man behind the counter with a fist-bump.

'This is Bryce,' he says. 'He came over from Noosa on a gap year and hasn't left yet. Which has been great for me, as there's nothing he doesn't know about surfing. Bryce, this is Jude. Can we get him kitted out with a board? I'll grab my usual one, if it's not out.'

'Sure.' Bryce glances at Jude. 'You might want to stick on a rash vest too, mate.' He laughs. 'Looks like you haven't seen the sun for a while.'

He pulls a blue one from under the counter and hands it to Jude, who turns to peruse the surfing photos and postcard ads that are stuck all over the wall of the shack.

'Going to the river-mouth surf spot?' Bryce searches through a rack of boards before taking out a couple.

Nate nods. 'Yup. It's been a while since Jude's done this, so we're starting off slow.'

Bryce nods. 'It's pretty calm out there today and the crowds haven't descended yet, so you should be fine.' Jude doesn't take the board Bryce goes to give him and points at a different one instead.

'Can I take that?'

Bryce frowns.

'You sure? It's a shortboard.'

Jude nods. 'I know, I've surfed before. I'll be fine with it.'

Bryce exchanges a glance with Nate, then shrugs. 'Your choice.' He passes it to Jude, then fist-bumps Nate again. 'Maybe catch up with you properly in the next few days? Alex told me you might—'

Nate shakes his head a fraction and glances at Jude, who is now trying on a pair of OluKai flip-flops.

'Yes, let's do that,' Nate says. 'I'll call you. Stick all that on my tab, can you? I'll settle up next time I'm in. Jude, come on, mate, let's go and do this.'

They stand outside on the sand while Jude struggles to pull on his rash vest, the poly-elastane material getting stuck over his head. Nate has to help him, conscious Bryce is grinning at them from inside the surf shack. Jude reminds Nate of a grasshopper – his skinny arms and legs too long for his body.

'If only Patrick could see you now,' Nate says.

Jude stiffens. 'Yeah, but he's a million miles away and, while I'm here, I don't really want to think about him, or Bearmans'.' He looks at the other surfers sitting on their boards in the take-off zone. 'Are you sure I need this vest?' he asks. 'No one else seems to be wearing one and I'm already covered in bloody suncream.'

Nate shrugs. 'Up to you, but better safe than sorry. I've been burned to shit out here before. It's hotter than you think and the UVB rays are pretty lethal.'

They walk up the beach along the dark brown sand, past rows of loungers shaded by red umbrellas, to where the swell is calmer.

'Stay in the white water to start with,' Nate says. 'I'll

come back in a bit and see how you're getting on. Don't go further without me, OK? It's more full on out there than you realize.'

Jude nods as they lie down on their boards and paddle out towards the breaking waves. Nate squeezes his knees and feet together to create a straight line from his sternum to his toes and digs his entire forearm into the water with each stroke to pull himself along. As he gets further out, small waves begin to hit him and he looks back to see Jude struggling to stay on his board.

'Do a plank, mate!' he shouts. 'Push yourself up so the waves go between you and your board.'

'I'm going to stop here!' Jude yells.

Nate holds up his thumb, then keeps paddling, looking back every now and again to check on him. He watches Jude pop up on his board as he catches a small wave before wiping out close to the beach.

Nate continues on until he's past the breakers, where the water is calmer, then sits on his board and moves into the line-up with the other surfers, watches the waves coming towards him, working out the best one to catch.

He waits until he sees the peak he is looking for, then starts paddling, hears the roar of the water, pops up on his board and heads down the line. When he'd first started surfing in Bali, the sea had terrified him. He'd hated the feeling of being out of his depth, of not knowing which way was up when he went underwater, of fighting to get a breath. After a few lessons, Bryce had seen he was struggling and taken him to visit a hypnotist, someone recommended by one of Layla's woo-woo friends, and now he relishes the visceral power of the water, the sensation of speed combined with the rush of adrenaline. It's one of the most addictive feelings in the world – second only to sex – and it makes him want to do it over and over.

He heads out again and again past the breakers, eventually stopping close to the beach. The salt stings his skin and he wipes his face with his hand. He can't see Jude anywhere. Has he got out? A quick glance along the beach and the row of empty loungers tells him that's not the case. There are a few surfers hanging around in the white water, but none of them is Jude.

When did he last see him? Five minutes ago? Ten? He's not completely sure. He paddles out further, rests on his board, looks around. Still no sign of him. Maybe he did get out. Nate takes his board in, walks along the shore, checks all the loungers and asks Bryce if he's seen him, but Jude seems to have vanished.

Fuck, Jude. Where are you?

Nate's heart begins to speed up. He heads out again, double-checking all the surfers he can see, but none of them is wearing a rash vest. He sits on his board, forces himself to stay calm as he looks around in the water. Still no sign of him.

Don't panic. He knows it's the worst thing he could do at this moment, but he can't stop the pressure that is expanding in his chest, making it difficult to breathe.

The waves rise and fall beneath him. He's going to have to check the beach again. He turns his board around and has started to paddle when there's a flash of blue on his left side. Something punches into him and there's a tangled mess of boards and colours and a metallic taste in his mouth before he realizes he's upside down in the water, being rolled around, trying to work out which way is up among the streams of bubbles.

He gasps for air as he surfaces, reaches down for his leash and brings his board back towards him, but struggles to get on it, turning his head to check whether he's got enough time before the next wave hits.

What the fuck just happened?

He looks up to see Jude floating in the water beside him, holding on to his board.

'I'm so sorry, mate.' Jude raises his hand in an apology. 'I couldn't turn in time. Are you OK?'

Nate swallows the expletives he was about to hurl at some kook and tries to move his arm. It's throbbing but doesn't seem to be broken.

'What the hell are you doing out this far?'

Jude shrugs. 'Sorry. I thought I could handle it.'

'I said to stay in the shallows,' Nate says. 'A shortboard is fucking dangerous when you can't control it. You're lucky you didn't break my arm.' He glares at Jude, anger burning in his chest.

He lies down and paddles through the water towards the beach, not waiting for Jude to follow, his body shaking with frustration. Why didn't Jude just stay where he'd told him to? He never bloody listens. Just goes off and does his own thing. He'd been the same at university, and when they'd started work together at Bearmans'. Always taking unnecessary risks and then expecting him to deal with the consequences.

Jude needs to learn he can't behave like that out here. Things are different now. Nate can't afford to be around anyone he doesn't trust a hundred per cent.

15. Sophie

Sophie opens her bedside drawer and moves her passport to one side. The painted wooden gecko stares back at her accusingly. She turns it over so she can't see its eyes and looks at the small china elephant beside it, something else she'd taken off the shelving unit in the living room last night, her excuse of needing a bottle of water at the ready in case anyone found her wandering around. She wonders how long it will take Layla to notice, whether she'll say anything if she does.

She'd relished the feeling of being alone in the dark; of no one knowing she was there. She'd opened drawers and cupboards, looking through their contents, making the most of her temporary invisibility until she'd found herself peering out through the patio doors, her face pressed up against the glass.

The pool had glowed a fluorescent turquoise blue, but across the grass, Nate and Layla's bedroom had merged into the pitch-blackness of the night. She'd stood for a minute, feeling her pulse quicken as she'd imagined their shapes in the darkness, before finally pulling away and heading back to her room, a sense of disappointment heavy in her chest.

She runs her fingers over the china elephant's trunk before she shuts the drawer. The fragility of the small ornament reminds her of Layla – something that's easily broken. She had felt sorry for her after the accident; she knows only too well how grief eats away at a person until it has consumed all their softness, leaving only a hard shell behind.

But after the wedding, her sympathy had shrivelled up, and now it has become twisted into something spiteful that wants to hurt Layla as much as Layla has hurt her. She'd taken the gecko on impulse, but the flush of satisfaction had ebbed away too quickly and been replaced by an urge to take something else. She wonders if this is going to become a habit. Something that will push Layla back towards the edge she was close to before leaving London.

Physically, Layla looks so much better than she did before she flew out here. The hollows and dark circles under her eyes have filled out and her face has lost its swollen, puffy look, but if Sophie scratched beneath the surface, she isn't sure what she'd find. Appearances can be so deceptive.

Layla reminds her of a butterfly – attracted to colourful things but unable to stay still for long, flitting from one job to another, claiming she doesn't want to be tied down, that life shouldn't be taken too seriously. Sophie is convinced that life coaching is just another one of Layla's fads, something she'll give up once she's bored with it, and what she actually wants is something else entirely.

When Layla and Nate got together, Sophie hadn't questioned his decision to let her move into the flat his parents had paid for so he could support her. She'd thought Layla was just another one of his pet projects – Jude had said Nate had a tendency to take on causes and then quickly lose interest – and she'd assumed their relationship wouldn't last. But they are still together, three years later, and judging from the way they're still all over each other, Nate is as infatuated as ever. Something that makes Sophie's insides twist uncomfortably when she thinks about it.

Nate and Jude reappear in the afternoon while she and Layla are sunbathing by the pool. A jug of sparkling water with giant ice cubes and slices of lime rests on the side table next to them, together with a small woven basket containing a dozen laklak cakes. Sophie sits up on her lounger, takes her AirPods out of her ears.

'How was surfing?' she asks.

Jude flops down beside her and peels off his damp T-shirt.

'Good. Harder than I remembered.'

Nate walks past Layla without saying a word and slides into the pool, swimming a length underwater before re-emerging, his forehead creased in a frown.

'I hope you haven't traumatized Jude,' Layla says. 'He looks knackered.'

'I think Jude can look after himself,' Nate says stiffly. 'We called in at the site on the way back. Nyoman wasn't there and the doors and windows still aren't in. I'm going to have to phone him later.'

Layla rolls her eyes. 'I really don't know what the fuck he's playing at.'

'Have you guys eaten?' Nate asks.

Layla shakes her head. Nate puts his hands on the edge of the pool and pulls himself out, smooths his hair back off his face.

'Let's go to Kayana,' he says. 'I'm starving.'

'Isn't it a bit pricey?' Layla says. 'And tricky to get a reservation last minute.'

Nate shrugs. 'I'll get Alex to pull a few strings.'

Layla rolls her eyes. 'Your new BFF is happy to do that for you, is he?'

Nate ignores her. 'It would be nice to treat ourselves, wouldn't it? Jude, you all right with that?'

Jude mutters something unintelligible, his foot tapping in the air to an invisible beat.

'Great,' Nate says. 'I'll sort it. You guys get ready.'

Sophie looks at her husband lying on the grass with his eyes shut. He's failed to put suncream along his hairline and the top of his forehead has turned a bright red colour. He'd better not offer to pay for lunch today – the drinks might have been cheap last night, but they'd had far more than she'd realized, and even with Alex picking up the tab for some of them, the bill had still been eyewatering.

Kayana is only a ten-minute walk away, but it feels longer in the midday heat. Nate points out the dozens of luxurious villas set back from the main road that are rented by other digital nomads. A mix of traditional Balinese-style architecture with hip roofs covered in clay tiles and vast modern buildings that look like something out of *Grand Designs*. Sophie gets the occasional glimpse of one of them when the high wall that surrounds the property gives way to metal gates at the entrance. All of them are set in manicured gardens with swimming pools and she can hear music and people shrieking as they jump into the water.

Jude keeps stopping to take photos, pushing his phone between the metal bars to get a better shot. Sophie wonders if something happened when he and Nate were surfing – he's barely said anything since they got back and she knows her husband well enough to tell something isn't right. She hopes he snaps out of it before they eat, or lunch is going to be an uncomfortable experience.

Her arms are starting to burn by the time they get to Kayana – her skin feels hot when she touches it – but when they walk across the wooden decking over the lake and into the restaurant, she's glad they made the effort, despite the fact Jude still hasn't said much.

'It's stunning,' she says as they sit down and order a round of drinks.

'Very handy for us,' Nate says. 'And it does incredible food – Middle Eastern and Mediterranean. Loads of vegetarian stuff, which is brilliant for Layla.'

Jude peruses the menu. 'Looks great,' he says. 'And this is our treat, by the way.'

Sophie's heart sinks. They'll burn through their savings if they carry on spending at this rate.

Nate shakes his head. 'You don't have to do that, mate.'

'My way of apologizing for what happened earlier.'

Sophie frowns, her suspicions confirmed. 'What happened earlier?'

'It was an accident,' Jude says. 'I went out a bit too far on my board, tried catching one of the bigger waves, couldn't turn and hit Nate by mistake.'

Nate rubs his arm. 'Don't worry – it's just about stopped throbbing.' He laughs, but Sophie hears a hardness behind his words.

Jude looks at Layla. 'In my defence, your other half did decide to abandon me so he could go and show off.'

The smile slides off Nate's face.

'Not sure it was me showing off, mate. I wasn't the one who insisted on hiring a shortboard when a foamie would have done the job just as well.'

Jude frowns at him. 'I said I was sorry. You don't have to go on about it. You're hardly one to talk about showing off when you sent us fake photos of your villa.'

'Whoa, guys!' Sophie holds up her hands. 'Let's calm it down a bit. Chill out. We're all just here to have a good time.'

She lifts up the frozen margarita the waiter puts down in front of her.

'A toast. To Nate and Layla for having us, and to the surprise I've planned for tomorrow. While you two were off splashing around, I booked us a trip. It involves a bit of an early start, but I thought it wouldn't matter as it's the weekend. The taxi is collecting us at 1 a.m. and we're going to hike up Mount Batur.'

She notices Layla hesitate before she raises her glass and clinks it against her own.

'I've wanted to do that since we got here,' Layla says eventually. 'We just never got around to it. The photos I've seen of the views are incredible.'

'We start in the dark so that we can get to the top for sunrise,' Sophie says, 'but we've got a guide and they provide headtorches.'

Nate raises his glass to Jude's.

'Sorry, mate,' he says. 'I'm hung-over and starving. Hiking sounds great. I can't wait.'

Jude grins and raises his glass. 'Me neither.'

Sophie smiles but, under the table, she can feel Jude's leg jiggling beside hers, his foot tapping silently on the floor.

They stay in the hotel until late in the evening, moving from the restaurant to the outside terrace bar as the sky turns orange and the sun sinks below the horizon. The crowd from Groove Lounge arrives, and Sophie watches Nate gravitate towards Alex. She can see why. It's not just that he's good-looking, he has a charisma that draws people in, pays attention to each person individually but leaves them wanting more. He reminds her of some of the highly successful people she's met in PR – he has the ability to make others feel noticed and special.

Alex flashes her a grin and her stomach flips as she smiles back. She's about to go over when Layla introduces her to someone called Harmony who works in graphic design and also does Tarot readings. She gives Sophie a list of places to get her hair done, as well as the names of a couple of tattoo parlours where she can get a discount if she mentions her name, and when Sophie next looks at the bar, Alex has disappeared.

It's eleven o'clock by the time she slides into bed beside Jude for the second time, two hours until the taxi comes to pick them up to take them to Mount Batur. Sophie knows she shouldn't have risked it; they only got back to the villa an hour ago. Layla could have come into the living room at any moment. But she hadn't. And as Sophie lowers the set of keys she'd taken off the hall shelf into her bedside-table drawer, she feels the adrenaline flood her body and her pulse speed up in response.

She wants to make Layla pay for what she's done, but part of her wonders if it's this sensation she craves more. Something she hasn't felt in a long, long time. The thrill of doing something terrible and thinking you've got away with it.

16. Jude

As the taxi winds its way along the road in the darkness, Jude unzips the front pocket of the rucksack he's borrowed off Nate and double-checks he's got his phone. It's still there, along with a couple of bottles of water and some cereal bars. And factor-fifty suncream. The top of his forehead stings like hell.

Nate hasn't asked him anything else about Bearmans' since their surfing trip, and Jude hopes he doesn't bring up the subject of work again. He's blocked Kathy's calls, but after they got back from Kayana last night he discovered she'd sent him an email. He'd deleted it, then labelled her contact details as spam to ensure he doesn't receive anything else from her going forward. Nate might be his oldest and best friend, but after yesterday, he realizes it was a mistake to think he could talk to him about this. Nate has moved on; Bearmans' isn't part of his life any more and he wouldn't understand.

Layla had rowed with Nate before the taxi arrived, a heated discussion in the hallway after she accused him of moving her keys, which he'd categorically denied. Sophie had offered to help her look, but Nate had said they needed to leave and he'd find them when they got back.

Layla has been unusually quiet since, staring out of the window into the darkness and occasionally biting her nails; clicking sounds that cut through the silence, setting his teeth on edge. Nate looks like he's fallen asleep in the passenger seat. Sophie had chatted excitedly for the first twenty minutes of the journey, fuelled by the double espresso she'd downed before they left, but with half an hour still to go, tiredness has kicked in and now she's dozing too, her head lolling against Layla's shoulder as the car weaves around the bends.

He isn't even sure he wants to do this hike. Nate had irritated him yesterday with his comments about showing off. Jude hadn't meant to hit him with his board, for fuck's sake. It was an accident. And if Nate had stayed in the shallows rather than buggering off further out because he wanted to chat to his other surfer mates, it wouldn't have happened in the first place.

They'd barely spoken last night at Kayana – Nate had spent all his time with the crowd who had appeared in the bar after they'd finished eating. Layla had introduced Jude to a few of them – all part of the digital nomad tribe with job titles like *content creator* and *mindfulness coach*, occupations that sound as though they're made up. He'd felt like he'd been relegated to the sidelines, half listening to cliquey conversations about rental prices, visas and bitcoin while Nate chatted away animatedly to Alex.

The taxi pulls up on a patch of scrubland illuminated by the faint glow of what look like several large mobile homes. Jude shivers, glad he's brought a fleece, and adjusts the straps on the rucksack to fit his taller frame. The instrument panel in the taxi had said it was twenty degrees, and it's the first time he hasn't felt hot since he got here. A man appears from inside one of the buildings and hands them each a headtorch.

'I am Gede,' he says, 'your guide for today. Mount Batur is one of the four sacred mountains in Bali, and it will take around two hours to get to the summit, where we will have breakfast. Do you have water?' They nod. 'Snacks?' They nod again. He shines his torch over them, checking their footwear. 'The ground is rough in places, so I lead and you stay with me, yes? No wandering off the path.'

They observe him silently in the darkness.

Gede tuts. 'You think I just say this to scare you, but I am serious. Other tourists, they have died here. One man' – he points at Jude – 'not that long ago. Slipped and fell. Broke his neck. So, you must always listen to what I tell you, yes?'

Jude turns to look at Sophie, who nods earnestly. Maybe this wasn't such a great idea. They're supposed to be here to have fun. His wife has gone a bit rogue booking this trek – he's not sure whether Layla's influence has rubbed off on her; she's the one that normally comes up with mad ideas – he should have realized how full on it was going to be and stopped them going earlier.

They aren't the only people here. The assembly area is beginning to resemble a car park; other tourists are being dropped off and met by guides handing out headtorches. Surely it can't be that dangerous if this many people do it? Gede is just trying to freak them out, ensure they do exactly what he wants to make his life easier.

Jude gets out his phone and tries to take a photo of Sophie, but it comes out blurred with red-eye, just like the ones he used to take of his friends at university. He deletes it without showing her.

The path is wide to start off with, but it quickly narrows

and he's forced to walk behind Nate, focusing on the glow from his torch. Gede tells them there's a stop halfway up the volcano. After they've been walking for around thirty minutes, Jude looks behind him to where he can see dozens of lights following them along the path. He hadn't realized it would be so busy. It's hard going, but not as steep as he'd been expecting. Gede had clearly been exaggerating.

He's seen photos of where they're going, and in them the grassy vegetation that covers the summit had looked a bit like an English hillside. Despite knowing that Mount Batur is an active volcano, it hadn't occurred to him that for much of the way they'd be walking on what looks like dried, black mud; dirt with solid lumps of cooled lava that slip beneath his feet, threatening to rick his ankle.

He pauses as Layla stops in front of him. It's still cool, but his physical efforts have made him start to sweat, and he looks ahead to where Nate is helping Sophie peel off her fleece. Something flickers inside him as he watches them, her dimples appearing as she smiles. Nate holds up her fleece, then hands it back to her so she can tie it around her waist.

He remembers all the times at Bearmans' when Nate had taken over one of his projects, and the flicker inside him ignites into a small flame. He wipes a line of perspiration off his forehead, tells himself not to be ridiculous. Nate is happy with Layla. And even if he wasn't, Jude can comfort himself with the fact that he knows something about Layla that Nate doesn't.

Something Nate wouldn't be very happy to discover about his girlfriend at all.

17. Layla

Layla has to remind herself that the beams of light she can see bobbing around below her in the darkness are actually attached to something. It seems as if they are floating in mid-air, about to fall off the edge of the mountain at any moment – and it makes her redouble her efforts to concentrate on exactly where she's putting her feet.

Her headtorch illuminates Nate in front of her and picks out the purple bruise on his arm. It's bigger than she thought it would be, a dark aubergine swirl of colour. She feels bad now about accusing him of being a hypochondriac when he'd complained about it. Jude must have hit him pretty hard. No wonder Nate left him on his own last night while he went to talk to Alex – the one person she wishes hadn't turned up at all. She'd successfully managed to avoid him for most of the evening, had focused on talking to Sophie and Harmony, but had felt a flush spread over her skin when she'd caught him staring at her across the bar.

They've been walking for an hour before the path levels out to a large, flat area where other tourists are standing around with their guides, drinking from bottles of water or buying something from the food stall set up by a few of the locals.

Nate and Jude join the queue, but Layla doesn't feel like eating. Her stomach has been in a tight knot since she left the villa, her brain attempting to remember her exact movements after they got in from Kayana last night. She'd put her keys in the bowl on the shelf by the front door, before getting a bottle of water out of the fridge. She's sure she did. More than sure. Convinced.

She shuts her eyes briefly, pictures her brown leather fob dropping into the bottom of the bowl on the shelf next to her hair scrunchie. She *had* done that. But then she thought she'd bought three geckos in that shop – one in each colour – and now there are only two. And Nate might be able to blame the housekeeper for moving them, but Ni Nengah wasn't even in the villa last night so she can't possibly have touched Layla's keys.

Stop thinking about it. They'll be on the kitchen counter when you get back.

It's not a disaster; Nate has his. And she'd remembered in the taxi on the way here that he'd mislaid those the other day, so has no right to have a go at her for doing the same thing. But her subconscious continues to prod and poke at her brain, quietly whispering that sane people don't hear things that aren't there, and that the place she was in a year ago isn't as far away as she thought. Those thoughts terrify her far more than a set of lost keys.

'You OK?' Sophie comes over holding a cup of black coffee.

Layla nods, remembering how they'd used to joke about how Sophie could survive seven days without food but couldn't manage one without caffeine.

'Want some?' Sophie holds out the cup.

The knot in her stomach tightens. 'No, I'm good.' She

runs her thumb across the top of her nail, which still feels rough where she'd bitten it in the taxi.

Sophie frowns. 'You sure?'

She nods. 'Just thinking about where I could have put my keys.'

Sophie takes another sip of coffee. 'I wouldn't worry about it. I'm sure they'll turn up. Nate has his, doesn't he? It's not like you're locked out.'

'No. I know that. It's just I was so sure I'd put them in the bowl on the hall shelf.'

Sophie finishes the last few drops and throws the plastic cup in one of the bins on the ground beside her.

'After the burglary, I kept losing things,' she says. 'I had to make a list before I left the flat or I'd forget something. Classic anxiety symptoms. That and not being able to sleep.' She hesitates. 'Are you still stressed? About the noises?'

Nate and Jude reappear with a couple of bottles of water and two bananas.

'Who's stressed?' Nate asks.

'No one,' Layla says quickly.

'We were just talking about the burglary,' Sophie says.

Nate takes a swig of his water. 'Everyone says Bali is still a developing country, but I feel way safer out here than I did in Streatham. The police at home just hand out a crime number and leave you to claim on the insurance.'

'It was a complete violation of our space, somewhere we'd created so many memories,' Sophie continues. 'Do you know what I mean?'

Layla nods, wondering how they've managed to change the subject from her losing her keys to the burglary. She shouldn't be nodding. She doesn't know how Sophie feels. She's never been burgled – thank God.

'I threw up when I got to my neighbour's,' Sophie adds. 'I think it was the shock, but I also just couldn't get over the fact that someone had deliberately wrecked something that had taken us so long to get right.'

Jude goes to put his arm around her shoulders, but she sidesteps out of the way.

'Don't! You're all sweaty! I'm over it now,' she says, 'but we're going to look to buy somewhere nearer Jude's office when we get back. Wimbledon to Canary Wharf is too long a commute.' She touches Jude's arm with her fingertips. 'Aren't we?'

Jude nods, briefly, then throws his empty bottle of water in the air and catches it again, squashing the plastic so it crackles before aiming it at one of the rubbish bins and missing. Nate picks it up and hurls it in, raising his arms in triumph.

Jude turns to Gede.

'Shall we get going?'

Gede nods as Nate stuffs his fleece into his rucksack. 'It's going to get harder from here,' he says. 'Much steeper and more slippery.'

'He's quite the harbinger of doom, isn't he?' Jude mutters under his breath, and Layla can't help giggling, until she sees the look Sophie gives her. As if she's been caught doing something she shouldn't.

A chill spreads through her insides as she suddenly realizes what Sophie really meant when she was talking about wrecking things. She hasn't forgiven her for what happened at the wedding at all.

18. Nate

'We need to decide which route to take,' Gede says. 'One is easier but with more people, the other is steeper but less busy.'

'How steep?' Nate shuffles from one foot to the other, his hands clenched in his pockets. He'd checked his emails while they were at the rest stop and discovered Nyoman hasn't replied to the one he'd sent yesterday asking why the doors and windows still haven't gone in. Yet another unavoidable delay. He's absolutely seething, but there's no point in trying to call him; Nyoman won't answer.

'Quite steep,' Gede says. 'Either way, it's not like the path we've just walked up. It's much more slippery – you'll be walking on gravel made of lava rock.'

'But manageable, yes?' Jude adjusts one of the straps on his rucksack. 'I mean, we're all fit enough, we're not under any time pressure, and it would be nice to do the next bit without hundreds of other people, wouldn't it?'

'I think we should go the easy way,' Nate says. 'You and Sophie aren't accustomed to the heat out here yet, and none of us has done this before. Why risk it when we're going to end up at the same place? Both routes take about the same amount of time, right?'

Gede nods. 'About an hour. The steeper way is shorter, but we have to go slower. Either way we'll be there before 6 a.m. to see the sunrise.'

There's an awkward silence where no one says anything.

Nate looks at Sophie and Layla. 'What do you guys think?'

Layla takes a swig out of her bottle of water and shrugs. *Thanks for the support, Layla.* She's still pissed off with him after their argument earlier. How is he supposed to know where her fucking keys are? Or any of the stuff that she keeps losing at the moment, for that matter. He loves her, but sometimes he wishes she'd get her shit together, be more like Sophie, who always seems to be on top of things.

'I agree with you,' Sophie says. 'Let's just take the easier route.'

'Oh, come on.' Jude throws his hands up in the air and turns towards their guide. 'It's not like we're doing bloody mountain climbing. We don't need ropes, and we're not geriatrics. How about we split up and meet at the top? YOLO.'

Gede shakes his head. 'No. We need to stick together.'

Nate runs his hand over his hair, feels the bruise on his arm begin to throb. Why does Jude always have to push things? It's hard enough as it is to see anything in the dark. Surely the aim is for them all just to get up safely. The nearest hospital is miles away if anything goes wrong.

'Mate, do you not remember what happened when we were surfing? We don't want any more injuries.'

Jude looks at the ground, scuffs his trainers as he kicks at the dirt.

'Fine,' he says eventually.

Nate can tell from the tone of Jude's voice that he's not fine, but at this point, he honestly doesn't care. Jude is behaving like a fucking five-year-old. What the hell is wrong with him? None of them has any idea how difficult the climb is going to be until they start doing it, but Jude seems to be on some kind of a mission to prove himself and is treating everything like it's a competition.

Nate glares at him, the memory of opening their bathroom door at university sliding into his head before he can stop it. He blinks, tries to push it back down where it came from, but the moment replays in his head – turning the handle, the crack widening into a small gap and then refusing to go any further – followed by his dawning realization that there was something terrible behind it.

Jude stares back, and Nate wonders if he ever thinks about it. Whether he wakes up in the middle of the night, pulse racing, sheets drenched in sweat, dreaming he's back there, seeing that horrific shape lying on the floor.

Layla stumbles slightly and rubs her temples.

'You OK?' he asks.

She nods. 'Got a bit of a headache. Let's just get to the top, shall we?'

They follow Gede in single file. Anger pulses around Nate's veins, pushing him up the steep incline. Their guide was right; this part is more difficult, even if it is the easy route, but he knows Jude still won't admit he's wrong. There aren't many other hikers and all he can hear is the crunch of trainers on gravel and the occasional loud scraping noise whenever someone's foot slips from underneath them. He tries not to think about what would happen if any of them lost their balance. At over five thousand feet up, it's a long way to fall.

He glances up ahead to where he can see the lights

from Layla and Jude's headtorches bobbing in the darkness side by side. Maybe Jude can help her find her bloody keys. Nate's Apple Watch tells him that his heart rate has reached a hundred and fifty beats per minute, and he can feel it galloping in his chest. It can't be much further. His calves ache with the effort as he catches up with them as they stand by a large sign with gold letters engraved in the rock.

MOUNT BATUR – 1,717 M

'Almost there,' Gede says.

Nate notices Layla's hands tremble as she takes her torch off her forehead and rubs at the indented mark before putting it back on again. She shines her light on the words written around the edges of the stone. '*Since the year 1804, Mount Batur has erupted 26 times,*' she reads. '*The most devastating explosion was in 1926.*'

Gede nods. 'It destroyed the village of Karang Anyar and killed one thousand five hundred people.'

Layla looks at him. 'Would you get a warning if it was going to erupt again?'

'The last time was twenty-five years ago,' Gede says. 'On the opposite side of the volcano from the climbing track.' He smiles. 'I think we are quite safe; you do not need to worry.'

Nate glances at Jude, who turns away. He's clearly not going to apologize for his earlier tantrum. There have been so many times over the past year when Nate has seen something and wanted to tell Jude about it, has imagined Jude delivering one of his trademark sarcastic responses; his dry humour that makes Nate laugh more than anyone else he knows. Sharp needle pricks that served as a painful reminder of his best friend's absence. But now he's beginning to remember the things he hasn't missed. They've always been there, but it's like a spotlight has been directed on to all the good stuff, distracting him.

Jude wants to get his own way just as much as when they met seventeen years ago. He still refuses to take responsibility for his mistakes; a trait that had drawn them together at university as, back then, Nate had been just the same. But unlike Jude, he's changed.

And despite Gede insisting they shouldn't worry, when he looks over at Jude helping Layla with her rucksack, he can't help remembering the expression on his best friend's face when they'd seen what was behind that bathroom door – the beat of hesitation before Jude's surprise – and there's a part of Nate that begins to wish he hadn't agreed to come on this hike at all.

19. Sophie

When they finally reach the peak, the lights from the hikers' headtorches shine like tiny stars in the darkness. Gede leads them into a small hut where corrugated-metal sheets form the walls on three sides, the fourth left open for people to look out over the valley below. Jude sits down next to Sophie at one of the tables and Nate and Layla squeeze themselves on to a bench on the opposite side. Sophie shivers, conscious of the drop in temperature now she's stopped walking, and pulls her fleece back on.

She can feel Jude's leg jiggling against hers and puts her hand on his thigh under the table to stop him. He shoots her an irritated look. He's still grumpy about her siding with Nate over which route to take. Her husband resents being told what to do, he always has, but he can't expect her to take unnecessary risks. She's not that kind of person, not any more, anyway.

She thinks of Jess in London and of the last time she saw her – of how Jude had been quieter than usual when she'd come home, how he'd pursed his lips when she'd told him where she'd been. She knows he's not keen on her spending time with her sister, even if he doesn't explicitly say so. After one particularly painful visit, he had refused to go with her again. Although she knows he's got her best interests at heart and is just trying to protect her, he needs to let her deal with it. Jess doesn't mean to upset her – sometimes she just can't help it.

Gede puts four cups of tea down in front of them, and Sophie takes one, relishing the warmth of the liquid as it spreads through her chest.

More hikers appear and the places to sit fill up until there is no more room inside the hut and new arrivals are forced to sit on one of the bamboo benches outside on the mountaintop. The darkness gradually dissolves into a misty pastel sunrise and she finally gets a sense of how high up they are. The ground slopes away to one side and thousands of feet below she can make out the roofs of houses: small, coloured rectangles beside a vast lake; the silhouette of Mount Agung rising up in the distance on the other side of the valley.

Layla pulls out her phone and takes a few photos. Having already scrolled through the posts on her grid, Sophie can imagine the hashtags: *#Blessed #NewBeginnings #LifeIsGood #InnerCalm.* Saccharine phrases that Sophie knows are the exact opposite of feeling humble. People want what they can't have, and this is a way of shoving it in their faces while pretending to be grateful. Do people really believe that stuff? Why is it in any way helpful when you're dissatisfied with your own life to start scrolling through other people's? Surely that just makes you feel worse?

As far as she's concerned, the whole life-coaching business seems like a scam – a role dreamed up by people like Layla to show off their incredible lifestyles while telling others that if they just follow a few tips, they can achieve the same thing. None of them mentions the inheritance or trust fund, or the home that they're renting out on Airbnb that pays for their lifestyle over here. It's as disingenuous as the work she does in PR – but at least she's honest about the fact she's trying to sell something. She thinks of her mother in her care home, unable to string a sentence together; of her sister still in Wimbledon. No amount of Instagram posts or online 'coaching' will help them.

Gede finishes the last of his tea.

'Shall we go?' he says. 'We're going to cook eggs for breakfast.'

She hangs back, waits for Nate to fasten his rucksack, while Jude follows Layla and their guide out of the hut and along the path.

'I'm sorry if Jude has been a bit of an arse,' she says. 'I think not getting that promotion at work has affected him more than he's letting on.'

Nate hoists the rucksack over his shoulders.

'I didn't know about the promotion,' he says. 'He should have told me.'

Sophie hesitates. 'You made it to vice-president three years ago,' she says finally. 'I think Jude would feel humiliated, accepting sympathy from you. His dad always used to tell him he was a failure and, although he won't admit it, I think it's stayed with him.'

A look of confusion passes across Nate's face.

'Oliver said that?'

'Not Oliver,' Sophie says. 'His biological dad.'

'Oh ... Jude never really talks to me about him,' Nate says.

'Well, he hasn't seen him since he was thirteen, when

his mum walked out and took Jude with her. He hardly ever talks about it to me either, to be honest, other than to say he never wants to end up like him.'

Nate grimaces as he picks up the empty cups and throws them in the bin.

'Families,' he says. 'Always tricky to navigate.' He pauses before he steps out of the hut on to the mountain and turns towards her.

'I haven't had a chance to say it since you got here, Soph, but I'm sorry again about what happened at the wedding. So is Layla, more than you realize. You know she wasn't herself.'

Sophie deliberately avoids making eye contact and gazes out over the valley. 'Do you think she's better now?' she asks quietly.

He frowns. 'You can see she is.'

Sophie takes off her headtorch and zips it into the pocket of her fleece, suddenly aware of how intensely Nate is looking at her. She remembers the darkness of the other night, the shape of his silhouette against Layla's, and feels a flush spread across her cheeks.

'She told me she can hear noises in the villa,' Sophie says, keen to get the words out before she changes her mind about telling him at all. 'She thinks someone is moving her things around. Look at how she was this morning with her keys.'

Nate's brow creases.

'Anyone can lose their keys,' he says. 'I couldn't find mine a few weeks ago. Spent three days looking every-where for them, was about to get the locks changed, then discovered I'd left them at the building site.'

Sophie bends down to retie the laces on her trainers, her face hot.

'You know what I'm talking about,' she says. 'I'm not saying she doesn't seem better than she did before you guys left London – but let's face it, Nate, things couldn't have got much worse. Not many brides can say they don't have any photos from their wedding reception, not to mention what she—'

'She apologized for all that.'

'I know.' Sophie stands back up. 'And I'm trying very hard to put it in the past. But don't pretend she's totally fine now, when you know as well as I do that she isn't.'

She can see she's hit a nerve from Nate's pinched expression as he walks out of the hut to where the others are waiting, standing on the edge of the crater that runs around the vent in a circle, like the rim of a mug – one side drops down towards the valley below, the other into the volcano itself. The clouds have cleared, floating across the valley below like balls of cotton wool.

The view is breathtaking – the sun a fiery line of bright orange and yellow that stretches across the horizon in a completely clear blue sky. It feels as if she is standing on top of the world. She shuts her eyes briefly, wishes Jess could be here to share this with her.

'It's beautiful,' she says. 'Definitely worth the trek to get here.'

Jude already has his phone out and is taking dozens of photos. He focuses on Layla, who goofs around while posing for the camera, holding up two fingers on both hands in peace signs.

Gede leads them along one of the paths off the top of

the crater to where steam is pouring out from a gap in the rocks. He crouches down and digs a small hole in the earth.

'Hold out your hands,' he says. They move them to where he's pointing, feeling the heat from the wet steam of lava that churns beneath the surface. Gede reaches into his backpack, takes out a few eggs and lowers them into the hole.

'We wait ten minutes,' he says, 'and then they will be cooked.'

'That's awesome!' Layla crouches down and films their guide covering the hole with dead grass just as there's a sudden swell in the noise from the crowd further along the path. Gede stands up and looks at the hubbub of activity. People are holding their phones in the air on selfie sticks, filming what's ahead of them.

Layla walks along the path and stands on tiptoes.

'What is it?' Sophie shouts over. 'Is someone hurt?'

'No,' Layla says. 'But you've got to come and see this.'

20. Jude

Jude follows Sophie over to where Layla has joined a group of tourists who are all staring at a naked man who is waving his arms in the air and dancing on the spot, his clothes discarded in a pile. A girl kneels on the ground a few feet away from him, filming him with her phone, while a music track with a heavy beat blares out from a portable speaker.

'What the fuck is he doing?' Jude slides his rucksack off his back and lowers it on to the dirt as he blinks. The sun-cream he put on before they left has mixed with his perspiration and stings his eyes, but he daren't wipe it off in case his forehead ends up more burnt than it already is.

'Dunno,' Nate says. 'Maybe it's a publicity stunt? You'll probably see it all over social media in the next few days.'

'He looks off his face,' Jude says. 'Who does a climb like that while they're high? He must have taken something when he got up here.'

Nate doesn't answer, and Jude senses the awkwardness between them, like they have pulled an elastic band too tight and are now hoping it doesn't snap. He knows he should apologize for losing his temper earlier, but resentment continues to ooze from the very heart of him when he thinks about being in Kayana last night, of how Nate had virtually ignored him as soon as Alex had arrived.

'That man has no respect for our culture,' Gede says,

shaking his head. 'This mountain is sacred to the Balinese. What he is doing is highly offensive. Tourist behaviour is getting worse – eighty-five people ended up being deported from our country last year. The locals are getting fed up. They want to see something done about it. The government will end up banning everyone from visiting sites like this because of people like him, and I'll have to find another way to make a living.'

Jude watches someone pick the man's jeans up off the ground and tell him to put them on, but he ignores them and carries on dancing.

'If there wasn't such an obsession with social media, he wouldn't do it in the first place,' Sophie mutters. 'It's only because he's hoping his reel will go viral.'

Layla frowns. 'You don't know that.'

'It doesn't take a genius to work it out,' Sophie continues. 'It's a cry for attention. I mean, just look at him.' She points to where three guides are holding up a blanket to protect his modesty, while someone else attempts to stop the woman filming.

'Are you suggesting that what I do is just for attention?' Layla asks.

Nate tilts his head. 'Sophie didn't say that.'

Layla ignores him. 'Well, are you?'

Jude sees his wife fold her arms across her chest. Before the burglary, Sophie had rarely got angry, not in public, anyway. She was like a swan – calm on the surface even if she was paddling away frantically underneath. But in the past month, it hasn't taken much to irritate her. And he wants to tell Layla not to push her luck, not unless she wants to get into a full-on argument.

Nate turns away from the dancing man and looks at Jude in a silent plea for help to defuse the growing tension. For the first time since Jude arrived here, he feels useful: Nate actually needs him for something.

The naked man stops dancing, his bottom half now swaddled in the blanket while he pulls his T-shirt back on over his head.

'I think Sophie just means that you can't believe everything you see online,' Jude says carefully, tightening his grip on his wife's shoulder as she opens her mouth to respond. 'So much of it is curated, isn't it? She's not saying that's the case with your posts, but loads of people on social media pretend to be something they're not. Photos might capture a moment, but they never show the whole picture, do they?'

Before Layla has a chance to reply, one of the monkeys sitting on the side of the path snatches Jude's rucksack and drags it away behind them. It slides across the ground, accompanied by a series of thuds as it bumps over a couple of rocks.

'Hey!' A burst of adrenaline explodes inside his chest as he runs forward and stamps down on the loose strap slithering over the dirt.

Gede laughs. 'They'll try to take anything.'

'You should have warned us,' Jude's voice is tight – he almost just lost his phone and their guide seems to think it's funny. He retrieves his rucksack and the monkey chatters loudly then slopes off to join the rest of the troop.

'If you don't keep an eye on your things,' Sophie says, 'you'll end up losing them. And I think the monkeys are cute. Macaques, aren't they? Look at that one – she's got her baby hanging on to her chest.' She watches as the monkey nibbles on a piece of mango someone must have given it. Jude stares at her. That fucking burglary has a lot to answer for. Sophie never used to be so quick to criticize him.

Layla gives him a sympathetic smile as he brushes the dirt off his rucksack.

Jude unzips the pocket of his bag and checks his phone, feels a prickle of relief when he sees it's still functioning, before slinging the rucksack back over his shoulders.

'Shall we eat?' Gede says. 'I think our breakfast should be ready.'

Jude follows him back down the path to where they left the eggs cooking but can't help noticing the way Nate keeps glancing back at the man who was dancing. And how the man – now fully dressed and sitting on the path beside one of the guides – raises his hand very briefly when he sees Nate looking at him. A gesture that Jude can only describe as acknowledgement.

21. 2007

The water level of the river is way above where it should be.

A sudden shriek comes from behind me and I turn around to see Ashley frantically shaking her hand as she starts to run down the steps.

'Don't run!' I shout. But she doesn't listen. I can see her begin to panic, and she pushes Buddy, the teenage boy ahead of her, out of her way. He loses his footing and staggers, but manages to grip on to the metal railing and stay upright.

'Ashley, stop!' I frantically climb back up the twenty or so steps between us. 'Stay calm. What's the matter?'

Her panic is infectious and the rest of the group are now hurrying down the steps, the noise of their oars banging against the rocks as they pass me.

'Something burned me!' Ashley shouts.

Her eyes blur with tears as she holds out her hand and I see the red welt that has risen up on the back of her skin.

'There was a beetle on the railing,' she says. 'A brown-and-orange one.'

'Probably a tomcat,' I say. 'They're common here. We just need to wash it to make sure we've got rid of any poison. Come down carefully.'

The others have already reached the bottom of the steps. Dan leans on his oar, mumbling expletives in his American accent. He breathes heavily as he looks at his wife, who starts to undo the chin strap of her helmet.

'Keep it on, please, Jen!' I shout.

If one person messes around with their equipment, the whole lot of them will start.

I take mine off, lean over the riverbank to fill it with water and stick Ashley's hand into it, watching her wince as she rubs the skin several times then wipes it on her T-shirt.

'Will it scar?' she asks, looking at the purple mark.

I shake my head. 'We'll keep an eye on it, but it should be OK. Tomcats give a nasty sting, but we've caught it quickly so the poison shouldn't spread.'

Mia puts her arm around Ashley's shoulders as she looks at the river uncertainly.

'Does it always flow this fast?' she asks.

I pretend to consider her question. If we turn around and go back now, Kadek won't have had time to unlock the minibus and clone the customers' credit cards before replacing them. We've perfected our system over the past couple of tourist seasons and everything has always gone without a hitch. We're careful. We don't take any physical valuables like mobile phones or watches, tempting though it is when someone happily hands over their Rolex. All customers' belongings are returned at the end of the trip, which means I'm not considered suspicious when they later discover money missing from their account.

The noise of the water is so loud Jen-babe has to raise her voice to be heard.

'Are you sure it's safe?'

I nod, but Mia doesn't look convinced, and now Kristin and James are frowning as they look at the rapids further downstream, where the water froths in white peaks over the rocks.

'The first part of the journey isn't difficult,' I say. 'And halfway down we stop at a waterfall. We can always get out and walk along the riverbank at that point — I can pick the boat up later.'

'Sounds like a plan,' Dan drawls. 'You up for it, babe?'

Jen nods and lifts her chin to get her husband to tighten the strap on her helmet again. She'll go along with whatever he suggests. I wouldn't have thought Dan would be the one to agree with me, but I suspect he'll do anything to avoid trekking back up hundreds of steps.

'James?' I say. 'Is that OK with you?'

Get him on my side and everyone else will fall into line. Give Kadek enough time to do what he needs to do.

James takes another look at the water, and then at the boat. The red craft is made of high-strength fabric coated with urethane to help it slip over any rocks. Three inflatable tubes run across the inside for the clients to sit on, loops fixed to the floor into which they can jam their feet. He peers further down the river.

'You're sure a couple of boats have gone out already?' he asks.

I nod, displaying a level of certainty I don't feel. There are usually five boats here, so I'm assuming two must have left, although I'm surprised anything has set off with the river like this.

'Then let's do it,' he says.

Relief swills around my stomach before I look up at the dark clouds and offer a silent prayer that the rain holds off.

'Are we going to get wet?' Kristin asks.

'Mum?!' Buddy rolls his eyes. 'We're going down rapids. What do you think?'

'If there's anything you want kept dry that you didn't leave in the minibus,' I say, 'give it to me now and I'll put it in the water-proof bag.'

Mia hands me her camera. Dan gives me his mobile and a packet of tablets with a prescription label stuck on the front. I'm not going to ask what they're for.

The others shuffle towards the boat, lining themselves up beside where they want to sit while trying not to make their intentions too obvious. As I go to put my Nokia away, it pings at me. A text message from Kadek that makes my blood run cold.

We have a big problem.

22. Layla

Layla watches the others peel the shells off their boiled eggs and discard them on the ground. The thought of food still makes her nauseous and she passes hers to Nate, who raises his eyebrows questioningly. She nods, and he doesn't need to be told twice before stuffing it into his mouth. Nate is like a human dustbin – back in London, given the chance, he'd eat almost anything, but he's made a huge effort to be healthier since they got out here.

Her headache does seem to have eased since they got to the summit – belladonna always does the trick; she doesn't know why Nate is so quick to dismiss it. Her neck itches and she feels a twinge of disappointment as her fingers run over a small scaly patch on her skin and she realizes her eczema is back. She thought it had gone for good. It had flared up constantly in London but had completely disappeared after they got out here. A sign she needs to relax more and look after herself.

She uploads one of her sunrise photos to Instagram with the caption 'What do you want to achieve today?' and adds the hashtags *#MountainMornings #Blessed #LifeIsGood #InnerCalm*.

Gede has brought Balinese cake and she watches Jude help himself to a slice. He clearly needs the energy. Below the strip of sunburn across his forehead, his face looks even paler than usual, but the hike up here has taken it out of all of them; she doesn't imagine she looks that great either.

Sophie flicks cake crumbs off her trousers, her French-manicured nails still immaculate, the monkeys eyeing her from a safe distance, waiting to move in. The female carrying her baby looks so sorrowful that Layla takes one of the uneaten boiled eggs, gets up and walks closer to her before rolling it towards her. The monkey grabs it out of the dirt and runs away with it along the path.

'I guess you have to take your chances when you can in life,' Jude says with a laugh. 'Every monkey for himself, and all that.'

Layla turns around. She hadn't realized he'd followed her.

'Glad to see your sense of humour is back,' she says. 'I thought you'd lost that along with your rucksack.'

Jude rolls his eyes. 'Very funny.'

Gede clears his throat and presses his hands together in prayer.

'When we come to Mount Batur we offer up prayers to Antaboga,' he says, seeing them staring at him. 'He is a serpentine god who existed before the beginning of time who lies under the volcano, and when he shakes his head, the volcano erupts.'

'Well, if you can ask him not to do that today, we'd all appreciate it.' Jude grins and gives Layla's shoulder a friendly squeeze.

The sun rises higher above the horizon, burning off the last remnants of cloud covering the valley and revealing the view below with pinpoint sharpness. Jude takes some more photos as Layla stands beside him, feeling the warmth on her face. Nate always complains they can't go anywhere without her needing to get a picture, but Jude seems to take more than she does.

'Shall we get going, then?' Nate asks. 'It's going to take a couple of hours to get down, I guess. Or is it quicker on the way back?'

Gede shakes his head. 'Most people find it tougher. We'll take it slowly.'

Sophie chooses to walk beside her, and Layla wonders why she doesn't wait for Jude, feels her heart flutter as if it senses something is wrong and is trying to warn her.

'How's the headache?' Sophie asks.

She nods. 'Better, thanks. I think the belladonna did the trick.'

She's always found Sophie slightly intimidating. One of those women who she isn't sure if she'd ever have continued to be friends with long term if it weren't for Nate and Jude's relationship. Looking back, she sometimes wonders whether they only ever had such a good time when they met up in London because every outing was accompanied by at least a couple of bottles of Whispering Angel. There had been occasional moments of true connection over the years – possibilities that had appeared like chinks of light in a dark room, but even before the wedding, she couldn't always be sure whether Sophie was just making an effort with her for Jude's sake. Now she's convinced that's the case.

The path, which is relatively flat around the rim of the crater, begins to drop steeply away in front of them. The ground here consists of a thick layer of black gravel – like a coal-mining slag heap – all the grassy vegetation has been worn away and is now growing only on the edge beside the steep drop.

Gede slides down the slope, the cooled lava crunching beneath his feet. She can tell he's done this many times before; he doesn't seem to be worried about falling, despite the fact he has to run to keep himself upright.

'Makes it seem easy, doesn't he?' Sophie says.

He stops on a flat area before the next steep descent, waits for them to catch up. Layla looks behind them to where Nate is standing fifty or so yards further up the mountain, laughing at something Jude has said, relieved the earlier tension between them seems to have been resolved.

'Look at it as a challenge,' Sophie says. 'It'll push us out of our comfort zone. I mean, that's what we're here for, isn't it? To do stuff we'd never do at home.'

Layla can't tell whether Sophie really means what she's saying, or whether she's just trying to convince herself. She's never been that keen on heights herself, had stupidly only worried about whether she could manage the climb up; hadn't thought about how they were going to get down. She takes a few steps forward, feels herself start to slide and stops, a spurt of fear shooting through her gut. It's too unstable. She's going to wait for Nate and Jude.

'Do you want me to go in front?' Sophie fiddles with her wedding ring, twisting it around her finger.

Layla doesn't reply, her eyes drawn to the platinum band. It matches the one Jude has, just slightly thinner.

'How come you two have never tied the knot?' Sophie suddenly says, catching her looking. 'I thought you would when you came out here. A wedding in paradise, and all that.'

Layla's skin prickles. Ever since Sophie arrived, she's felt as if she's been standing on a railway track with a train hurtling towards her, unable to get out of the way, waiting for that inevitable moment of it crashing into her at full speed. She wishes Nate would hurry up.

'We've never felt the need,' she says.

'You could have had it on the beach at sunset,' Sophie says. 'Something a bit different. Like ours was, in the end.' She hesitates. 'Although, obviously, we hadn't planned it that way.'

Layla looks at her. 'I told you I was sorry.'

Sophie's eyes narrow. 'You messaged me a few times and sent a letter from Bali. We never talked about it properly.'

'What do you want me to say?' Layla says. 'I was grieving.'

'You don't have a monopoly on grief, Layla.'

'My parents had just *died*, for fuck's sake.'

'What happened to your parents was a tragedy,' Sophie says quietly, 'but terrible things happen to other people and they don't choose to wreck someone else's wedding. You could have made the decision not to come. Instead, you ruined our day.'

'I really am sorry.' Layla's eyes well up. Nate hadn't spoken to her for almost a week afterwards. She'd never seen him so angry – she hadn't been sure that he'd still go to Bali.

Sophie points just above her eyebrow. 'I'll always have a scar. It might have faded, but it's still there.'

Layla buries her nails in her palms as she senses the

barely controlled anger bubbling just beneath the surface of Sophie's skin. She wants to tell her that she can't remember anything after they got to the hotel reception and started drinking. A couple of glasses that had turned into entire bottles, and then anything she could lay her hands on. That whole afternoon is just a blur. She'd wanted to curl up and die the following morning when Nate had told her what she'd done. Her insides had shrivelled up with humiliation as she'd retched over the toilet seat with the worst hangover of her life.

'You told everyone I'd been convicted of shoplifting and then you threw up all over the top table,' Sophie says. 'I wanted to die with embarrassment. My mum didn't even know. No one listened to the speeches, everyone was too busy discussing what I'd nicked. One stupid mistake I was cautioned for sixteen years ago.'

'I'm so sorry,' Layla repeats.

'So you said,' Sophie says tartly. 'Why tell everyone something I'd told you in confidence? And even after you'd done that, I still don't understand why you were so desperate to speak to Jude.'

Layla can feel her cheeks burning.

'I tried to explain in my letter; I have no idea. I was completely hammered.'

Sophie's nostrils flare. 'Well, it must have been important. Worth pouring an entire glass of red wine over my dress.'

Layla glances behind her, but Nate hasn't moved. 'Please,' she says. 'Let's not do this now. Let's just concentrate on getting down this mountain.'

Sophie clenches her fists as she turns away and shuffles

forward, holding her arms out either side of her in an effort to balance as she sets off down the slope. The gravel makes a horrible crunching sound every time she moves.

Layla knows she's going to have to follow her. She wishes she could change what happened. The guilt is bad enough, but she hates having to lie. She knows what she was trying to tell Jude, she just can't tell Sophie. Can't risk Nate finding out.

She steps forward tentatively and feels the ground slip beneath her feet. Sophie turns, glances behind her, and Layla sees her eyes widen. Before Layla really understands what's happening, Sophie's legs are in the air and her back is on the gravel, stones scattering across the steep incline.

Layla hears her scream, sees her hands claw at the dirt, unable to establish a grip, her body gathering speed as it slides towards the edge of the slope.

23. Nate

Jude is mid-sentence when Nate hears the shriek, and feels his stomach plummet towards his feet.

He can see Layla crouched motionless near the top of the slope while Sophie slips down the steep incline towards the edge, her arms flailing. His muscles freeze and time loses its usual steady rhythm, becomes relative, dozens of memories flashing through his brain in a fraction of a second, leaving behind a whirlwind of emotions and a wave of nausea.

All that is in the past. He is no longer that person.

Jude moves before he does, his gangly figure, all arms and legs, scrambling down towards Sophie and Layla. Nate fixes his eyes on Gede, sees their guide hurrying up the gravel slope, trying to reach Sophie, who is still sliding, now dangerously close to the edge. Below there is nothing, just rocks and scrubland hundreds of feet down.

'Sophie? Sophie?!' Jude shouts his wife's name repeatedly as if his voice is an anchor that will slow her down. Nate's legs come back to life and he hurries after him across the uneven terrain, wishing he could move faster.

Why doesn't Layla do something, for fuck's sake? She's closest – she was just behind Sophie when he heard her shriek, but at the moment she's just squatting on the ground with her arms wrapped around her knees.

'Sophie?' Jude screams her name as he reaches the top of the incline and doesn't hesitate before sliding down towards his wife. Gede reaches her just before him, manages to grab hold of Sophie's arm to bring her to a halt. The awful crunching ceases.

'Are you hurt?' Jude pants.

Sophie pulls herself up slowly into a sitting position and coughs as the dust settles around her. Jude goes to embrace her, moves her straggled hair away from her face.

Nate slithers down to join them. He'd moved straight past Layla, a chill passing through him when he'd seen the way she'd looked at him blankly, as if she hadn't even recognized him.

Sophie wipes the dirt off her hands on to her T-shirt.

'I'm OK.' Her voice is shaky. 'I think I've scratched my cheek.' She turns to one side for Jude to look at it. 'Have I cut it? It feels sore.'

He traces his fingers gently over her skin.

'I can't see anything,' he says. 'It's probably just bruised. Are you sure your arms and legs feel all right? Nothing broken? You took a hell of a tumble. You must have slid about fifty feet.'

She stretches out her arms, wiggles her fingers and slowly bends her knees.

'Everything seems to be working,' she says.

Gede reaches into his rucksack and passes her a bottle of water as Layla slides down beside them.

'Have a drink,' he says. 'Pour some on your hands to get rid of the dirt. We should get you checked over. I can call down to my colleagues for help, ask for someone who has medical training to come up and meet us?'

Sophie shakes her head. 'I don't need anything like that. I'm fine. Honestly.'

Her hands tremble as she holds the bottle.

'Fucking hell, Soph,' Nate says. 'You gave us such a fright. Thank God you're OK.'

She swallows a few gulps of water, wipes her mouth on her sleeve and hands the bottle back to Gede.

'I don't know what happened,' she says.

'Your feet just went from under you,' Layla says.

Jude takes off her fleece and examines her forearms for damage as Sophie brushes gravel from her knees. Nate can see a pale pink line where she's stripped the top layer of skin off her calf.

He points at it. 'You're going to need some antiseptic cream on that.'

'I'll be fine,' Sophie says. 'Maybe we should move some-where a bit less steep before someone else falls over?'

She points to where the dark gravel flattens off and more grassy vegetation covers the ground, and they half walk, half slide down the slope towards it. Nate sees the way Sophie clings to Jude's arm, her knuckles white.

Gede's face visibly sags with relief once they reach flat-ter ground. Nate knows a serious accident would put him straight out of business.

'I was trying to be careful,' Sophie says. She glances at Nate as she pulls the elastic band out of the bottom of her hair and holds it in her mouth while gathering the blonde strands back into a ponytail and securing them into place. 'I guess I should be grateful – it could have been a lot worse.'

Jude's arm is firmly around her waist, but Nate finds it

hard to ignore the way she looks at Layla over her shoulder. Sophie's earlier words run through his head — *don't pretend she's totally fine now.* He remembers tracing the letters carved into the back of Layla's wardrobe and suddenly has a horrible feeling Sophie is trying to tell him something.

Layla shuffles closer to him and holds on to his hand more tightly. He studies her face; she's lost that blank look she had when she was crouched on the slope, but her cheeks are flushed and he thinks she might be about to cry.

Something sharp slices at his heart. He's seen her like this before; knows her too well to ignore the guilt that is written all over her face.

24. Sophie

Sophie feels Jude tug gently on her hand, a sign he wants to get going, but she's not sure she's ready. Her legs are still shaking.

'I'll stay beside you,' he says reassuringly. 'Make sure you're OK.'

She smiles at him, suddenly grateful that he's here with her. Jude might have his faults, but he's never let her down when she's needed him; always makes her feel she's his number-one priority.

They follow Gede, who keeps carefully to the middle of the path, despite it having flattened out considerably after that first steep descent. She can't bring herself to tell Jude that it's not just getting down the mountain that she's concerned about. Since the burglary, she can't get rid of the ball of anger that's been sitting in the centre of her chest. A tight, hard knot that has spread like a cancer, eating away at her insides.

She wishes Jess was here. She'd been the one who'd helped her last time she felt like this. Only a year younger than her; everyone said they were more like twins than sisters – the colour of their hair the obvious physical difference between them. The only person who has ever truly understood her; the only person who believed her when she'd told her what had happened at school and everyone, including her mother, had accused her of lying.

She thinks back to standing in their garden in Wimbledon, looking at Jess's bedroom lit up against the night sky, remembers the feel of the heat against her face, and for a second, she feels like she's choking. The ball inside her chest rolls around a little, expanding with rage.

She glances behind at Layla, can see her gripping Nate's hand. Before they'd started down that slope, she'd hoped that a face-to-face conversation might shed more light on Layla's behaviour at the wedding. But she hadn't offered any more of an explanation than the excuse she'd given in her letter – that she was so drunk she couldn't even remember doing it. The tiny grain of doubt – or hope – that has been stuck inside Sophie's brain, allowing her to think that she might have got this all wrong, has begun to disappear. She needs to know. Once and for all.

By the time they reach the bottom of Mount Batur, her knees ache with the effort of holding herself upright. Nate and Layla are still following close behind, but interaction between the two couples has been restricted to the occasional warning of loose rocks. Everyone has stripped off their fleeces, and Sophie thinks she might need to put on more suncream; her face feels as if it's starting to burn.

Gede and Jude go into one of the huts beside the car park to find a medical box for Sophie, and Layla goes off to buy some water.

'Does it hurt?' Nate asks.

Sophie looks down at her leg. 'Jude is just being over-cautious. You know what he's like. Protective to the last.'

Nate crouches down to inspect the cut.

'How did you . . . I mean, the way you looked at Layla after you fell, it made me think . . .'

142

Sophie hesitates, rubs her forehead and feels a lump where she must have hit it. 'We had a few words, that's all. About the wedding.'

An expression of relief crosses Nate's face as he runs his hand over his hair.

'And how she wrecked it,' Sophie adds.

Nate shakes his head. 'I know what she did was awful, but don't you think it's time to move on? Please? I get that she ruined your day, but you know how much of a mess she was back then. She's apologized, and she's changed.'

'Has she, though?'

Sophie's voice comes out shrill, and she winces. High-pitched hysteria doesn't command respect. She's attended enough presentations on how to win clients and has had enough experiences of her own to know that men don't respond to desperation. They simply tune it out and ignore it. *Lower and slower* are the buzzwords that are supposed to make a difference.

Nate frowns at her. 'Have you seen her drinking constantly since you got here? Blacking out? Crying all the time?'

Sophie hesitates, then shakes her head. 'No. I haven't. But I have heard her say she can hear things that aren't there, and she insists someone is hiding her things in the villa.'

Nate looks at Mount Agung on the other side of the valley.

'Sometimes people do terrible things,' he says, 'but everyone deserves a second chance, don't you think? I'm sure you've done stuff that you regret.'

Sophie doesn't reply. How can Nate defend Layla? Can't

he see what's right in front of him? Layla's unstable; Sophie knew that before she even got out here. Her Instagram posts about her 'journey of self-discovery', as far as Sophie is concerned, only serve to reinforce that.

She heads over to wait in the makeshift reception area, sits down on one of the mismatched chairs. A pool table takes up most of the floor space and the corrugated-iron sheets that cover the roof provide only partial shade from the sun. Layla can stand outside if she feels like it, but Sophie needs to escape from the heat that has wrapped itself around her face. She's so relieved to be off the mountain – she wishes she hadn't booked this trip in the first place. Her body seems to have absorbed the sensation of falling down that slope and her brain can't stop replaying it on a loop. She pulls off one of her trainers, tips it upside down and watches the stream of fine dirt pour out on to the ground like black icing sugar.

Nate and Layla are outside talking to Gede as Jude comes back with some antiseptic wipes, then tells her he's going to find the gents or a bush, whichever he comes across first.

A couple of Balinese policemen with their distinctive beige shirts and black berets watch the tourists milling about, waiting for taxis to collect them. Sophie smiles at one of the men when he looks at her, but he doesn't smile back, and she catches a glimpse of black metal in his belt as he turns away.

A shiver runs down her back despite the heat – the revolver is a stark reminder that she is no longer in England, and despite the laid-back atmosphere and party vibe, things are very different out here.

As if to emphasize this sudden realization, another guide appears at the bottom of the trail with his group. She recognizes one of the tourists as the man who was dancing naked on the top of the mountain. He's walking beside the woman who was filming him; their arms wrapped around one another's waist.

One of the policemen says something into his radio and then goes over to the group and starts a conversation in Balinese with the guide. Sophie watches the verbal exchange that ensues, the previously naked man gradually becoming more agitated until a scuffle breaks out, ending up with him in handcuffs and the woman shrieking hysterically beside him.

Calm down, Sophie thinks. *Lower and slower.*

The policemen hold the man's arms as they walk him over to their car. The woman carries on shouting, telling them they've made a mistake and need to let him go, but they act as if they can't hear her.

As they walk past where Gede is standing, Sophie sees Nate turn away and look in the other direction. The man spots him and stops struggling for a moment, opens his mouth as if he's about to say something, then shuts it again.

She continues to watch as he's pushed forward across the stony ground. The woman's shrieks reach a crescendo as he approaches the car, but the policemen ignore her. The man disappears inside, the door slams and they drive away, leaving her kneeling in the dirt.

25. Jude

As Jude enters the small concrete toilet block, he wishes he had found a tree instead. The acrid stench of stale urine sits in the back of his throat as he empties his bladder as fast as he can before zipping up his trousers.

He puts his hand out to flush the chain but whips it away again as it touches something soft and sticky. Looking closer, he realizes there is a large web stretched across the back wall of the cubicle, a huge spider in the middle of it. He peers at the creature that is currently sitting motionless – it's the size of a small dinner plate, each of its shiny black legs divided into three sections, the joints marked by yellow dots, its body the shape of a blunt rectangle, painted with two parallel yellow stripes.

He fishes around in his backpack for his phone and takes a couple of photos, has to open the door and stand back to fit the whole thing in. A decades-old memory flashes into his head – his dad holding his old Minolta Maxxum 7000, walking back and forth across their lawn at home trying to line up the perfect shot. Jude worries, not for the first time, that his interest in photography has been passed on from his biological father. Oliver has no interest in the hobby, so is it in his genes to be drawn to it? If he allows himself to believe that, then he has to face the fact that there are other things he could have inherited, things that would make him more like his father than he ever wants to be. He hopes, instead, that it's simply something he started doing subconsciously in an effort to make up for the absent connection. Which is ridiculous, as his father has no idea he even does it.

Sophie would go nuts if she saw this. She hates spiders – says their erratic movements remind her of grabbing hands – she can't even stand the small ones they get in their Wimbledon flat, with their tiny bodies and legs like threads.

He's contemplating prodding it with something to see if it moves when the door to the outside opens and Gede walks in. Jude steps back and turns on the small tap on the basin.

'I wouldn't go in that one,' he says as Gede heads towards the cubicle he's just vacated. 'There's a massive spider on the wall.'

Gede peers inside. 'A giant wood spider.' He looks at Jude. 'I'm surprised you're still in here. Most tourists would have run out screaming.'

'You know they have three-hundred-and-sixty-degree vision?' Jude says. 'And can see colours that we can't? I find them fascinating, as long as they aren't poisonous.' He hesitates. 'It's not poisonous, is it?'

Gede shakes his head. 'There aren't any poisonous spiders in Bali. Just large ones.' He starts to push open the other cubicle door and then stops.

'I'm sorry about what happened to your wife.'

Jude turns off the tap, shakes his hands, decides not to go anywhere near the grubby towel hanging from a hook on the wall and wipes them on his trousers. For a moment he wonders if Gede is only saying this in case it affects his tip, but then feels bad for jumping to conclusions.

'Sophie's fine,' he says. 'At least she didn't break anything.'

Gede nods, starts to say something but then stops.

'What?' Jude asks.

Gede hesitates. 'I saw what happened before she fell.'

Jude blinks, Gede's words taking a couple of seconds to sink in.

'I don't want to cause any trouble,' Gede continues. 'As you say, your wife is fine. So maybe it's better just to leave it.' He glances down at the ground and then back at Jude. 'And it all happened very fast. I wouldn't swear that—'

'What did you see?' Jude says sharply.

Gede picks at a loose thread on his T-shirt. 'From where I was standing,' he says eventually, 'it looked like Layla pushed your wife down that slope. I saw her hand on Sophie's shoulder.'

When Jude emerges out of the concrete building he can see Nate and Layla talking to a woman who has just finished the hike, her rucksack on the ground by her feet as she swigs from her water bottle. What was that Latin quote his father had framed on his study wall? *Everything we see is a perspective, not the truth.* Layla wouldn't have pushed Sophie. He's certain of that. Isn't he?

He walks over to where his wife is sitting on a bench watching a couple of other tourists playing pool on an ancient table, the green baize worn down to stringy beige patches in several places. She stands up and he gives her a hug, feels the familiar gesture of her hands sliding down into the back pockets of his trousers. He waits for her to squeeze his bum through the lining material as she always used to, but she doesn't.

'Nate has just got to take a work call,' Layla says as she walks over.

Jude glances behind her to where he can see Nate talking into his Apple Watch.

'About before,' Layla says to Sophie, 'I know you're still pissed off with me about the wedding, but I really do want to try and make it up to you. As you said back at the villa, we need a fresh start. I am truly sorry about what happened.'

Her eyes well up. Jude prides himself on being able to spot when someone is lying, but he can't tell with Layla. She seems genuine. But then so had Gede.

Before he can gather his thoughts, Sophie breaks away from him, steps forward and embraces Layla in a slightly awkward hug.

'Let's forget about it,' she says. 'Go back to the villa, chill out by the pool and go out somewhere nice later.'

Nate reappears behind him and clears his throat.

'Tide would be a good place to go – I'll book one of the cabanas overlooking the beach. You'll love it there.'

Layla smiles as the hiker she was talking to earlier walks past and waves.

'She's off to see the city of the dead,' she says.

Sophie frowns. 'The what?'

'It's a trip you can go on from here. You catch a boat across the lake to Trunyan, where there's an open-air cemetery. People take their dead relatives there and leave them in these cages made of bamboo.'

Sophie pales. 'That's horrific. You can't just leave a dead body outside to rot.'

'Grim, isn't it?' Layla shudders and looks at Nate. 'I've never even seen a dead body,' she adds, her voice catching. 'Have you?'

Jude watches Nate shake his head, squinting at the car that has just pulled into the area of land used as an unofficial car park.

'I think that's our taxi,' Nate says. He walks away, avoiding eye contact as he strides ahead of the others. Jude knows why. Nate is lying. He has seen a dead body.

They both have.

26. Layla

Tide Beach Club is already packed by the time they arrive. They're shown through to the VIP area, where Nate has booked one of the deluxe beds overlooking the ocean. Each one has a minimum spend attached, and Layla is beginning to get annoyed that Nate is acting as if money is no object. The building costs are escalating faster than either of them expected and it won't be long until her parents' inheritance is wiped out completely.

Nate keeps telling her not to worry, that with his contract and what she brings in from life coaching, they've got enough to manage, but she can tell he's worried too. Yesterday she'd discovered another invoice for the new villa that he'd hidden under the pile of magazines in the living room.

Sophie walks ahead of her, and Layla feels a prickle of sweat slide down her back as she notices the graze on Sophie's calf; a bubblegum-pink raw patch where the skin has been scraped away by the gravel.

She watches Nate step forward and exchange pleasantries with their Balinese hostess, radiating confidence, as always. When they first came out here, she'd relied on him to always take the lead, but he still does it automatically, and sometimes it grates. She wonders if she should make more of an effort. The hostess guides them past dozens of identical loungers covered in white cushions, each one shaded by a navy-blue umbrella with luxurious matching cushions and towels. They walk around the infinity pool, which has *VIP* emblazoned in giant blue letters on the bottom, visible through the ripples on the surface of the turquoise water. The beach stretches away ahead of them as far as she can see in either direction, the sea calm and flat today, no sign of the usual surfers.

She reaches for Nate's hand, but he moves away before she can get hold of it. Was that deliberate? She can't tell, but the rejection brings a lump to her throat. He's been off with her ever since the taxi picked them up at Mount Batur, barely spoke a word on the journey back, and disappeared straight into their bedroom when they got home, saying he needed a shower and a quick nap.

While Jude and Sophie sunbathed by the pool, she'd spent a futile hour searching for her keys. They seemed to have vanished into thin air, along with an elephant ornament that she could have sworn was on one of the shelves in the living room. Now she's not so sure. Had it been there? Or had she moved it into Sophie and Jude's room? Perhaps Nate broke it and hasn't told her – she's lost track of the number of wine glasses he's accidentally smashed since they've been together. Clumsy doesn't cover the half of it. She daren't ask him – she doesn't want another row.

The Tide hostess points towards their giant bed: a huge mattress covered in scatter cushions with a small wooden tray table in the centre.

'You can choose small plates and sharing platters on the menu using our app,' she says. 'Would you like something to drink?'

'Can we get four mojitos to start with?' Nate says.

'Sure.' She smiles. 'I'll bring them over.'

Layla scratches her neck; wishes Nate had asked what she wanted before ordering for them all. She doesn't want an afternoon of heavy drinking – she's knackered from the hike, even if he seems to have managed to bounce back, in his usual fashion. She shuffles on to one end of the bed and adjusts the cushions behind her.

'I'm just going to visit the gents,' he says. 'Back in a sec.'

He saunters off and she watches Sophie strip off her cover-up to reveal an olive-coloured bikini that she's sure she's seen in a magazine recently – possibly Melissa Odabash? It suits her; all Sophie's clothes suit her. She's got a great sense of style: upmarket classic high street with the odd designer piece thrown in. If Layla hadn't already known, she'd guess Sophie worked in fashion. Jude reaches out and strokes his wife's leg, and Layla experiences a twinge of envy.

'There's a great view of the sunset from this spot,' she says. 'Though you won't be able to move in here later. The DJs really pull in the crowds – they had Fatboy Slim at the New Year's Eve party; he was incredible. Took me right back to being a teenager, begging my mum to let me go and see him with my schoolfriends in Brighton.' She taps Sophie's foot. 'Were you into him?'

A shadow slides across Sophie's face as she reaches in her bag for a hairclip.

'Not really,' she says. 'I didn't do stuff like that at school.'

Their hostess returns with four drinks which she places on the wooden tray table, sprigs of mint poking from the top of each one. Layla takes a sip, the cold condensation dripping on to her chest a welcome relief from the heat. Nate had actually got it spot on – mojitos were the perfect choice.

Half an hour later, Sophie and Jude are stretched out sunbathing, but there's still no sign of Nate. The ice cubes in his glass have melted, the mojito threatening to spill over the rim of the glass. Layla tries calling him, but it goes straight to voicemail.

Where r u?

No reply on WhatsApp either.

She fixes a smile on her face as she looks around, tries to ignore the buzz of conversation and shrieks of laughter coming from the other loungers, sucks the last few drops of diluted rum out of her glass with her straw. The toilets aren't that far away. What is he doing, for heaven's sake?

She quietly hums an out-of-tune version of 'Happy Birthday', joining in with a group of people who are celebrating a few loungers away as she slips her dress back over her head.

'I'm just going to see where Nate has got to,' she says.

Jude holds up his thumb but doesn't move from his reclined position. She takes a couple of deep breaths as she edges off the bed and slides her feet back into her flip-flops, the rubber hot against her skin. She knows she's probably being ridiculous, but she has a squirming feeling in the bottom of her stomach that tells her something is wrong.

This section of the beach club can hold up to a thousand people, and it's already almost full. Maybe there's just a queue for the toilets; maybe Nate has bumped into someone he knows – both are perfectly plausible explanations, but it doesn't stop the writhing feeling in her guts. Ever since her parents' accident, her brain hurtles towards the worst possible scenario whenever someone is late. Her therapist had managed to stop her full-on panic attacks, had given her strategies to cope, but she can feel her anxiety building, crawling up her legs and squeezing her lungs.

She checks her phone again. Nothing.

Maybe he went out on to the beach? She scans the sand as she walks around the pool. Why would he do that, though? He'd just ordered a drink. She squeezes herself into the narrow gaps between the dozens of loungers, glancing at their occupants, trying not to be too obvious, but still can't find him, so heads back towards the reception area.

Just as she can feel herself beginning to hyperventilate, she spots him perched on a lounger talking to the guy who works in the surf shop at Echo Beach, whose name she can't remember. Relief floods over her like a wave. Bryce, that's it. An Aussie who'd come over on a gap year and ended up staying for much longer. As so many of them do. He's been to their villa a couple of times recently after taking Nate out for surf lessons. She starts to walk towards them but hesitates as she sees Nate open up his rucksack, take something out and hand it to Bryce, who slides it into his bag.

Her body freezes.

What the fuck?

The exchange only takes a couple of seconds, but she's seen similar happen enough times outside Streatham station to know what she's just witnessed.

No, she must have got it wrong.

Nate wouldn't do that.

He might have smoked the odd joint in London, but he's never been into drugs and, anyway, he's not that stupid. He knows if he's caught doing that out here, the punishment won't just be a slap on the wrist – he'll get a death sentence. They'd both read the newspaper articles about firing squads and the Bali Nine before they got out here.

Nate wouldn't do that.

If she repeats the words to herself enough times, she can persuade herself it's the truth.

Maybe she should pretend she hasn't seen it. Go back to her sunbed, tell herself it never happened. She turns to walk away, and it's then that she sees him. A thin figure standing about twenty feet away by the side of the pool, staring intently at Nate and Bryce. She is struck by an overwhelming feeling of dread that the man has just witnessed exactly what she has. She thinks of the folded-up piece of paper she'd hidden in the bottom of her chest of drawers and realizes she's failed to deliver what he asked for. With only one day left until his deadline, she's about to run out of time.

And as if he can read her mind, he turns his head and looks at her, the grin spreading across his face confirming her worst fears.

27. Nate

Nate stands up and high-fives Bryce before zipping up the pocket of his rucksack and slinging it over his shoulder. His fingers tingle as he walks back towards the VIP area – the euphoria brought on by an adrenaline rush. That was so much easier than he thought it would be. He should have taken up Alex's offer earlier – after all, it's not the first time he's done it.

They'd met in ConnectZen a few months ago. Alex had an accent that Nate couldn't place and seemed to vary depending on who he was talking to. He'd claimed his family had moved around a lot when he was growing up and that he'd arrived in Bali fifteen years ago – before it was considered cool, and long before the recent influx of digital nomads. They'd struck up a conversation after he'd caught Nate admiring the tattoo of a Balinese Om symbol on his arm; had given him tips on the best trainers to use in the gym and the best masseur to visit afterwards.

Nate had watched him in action – being asked by others in ConnectZen for cryptocurrency trading tips and casually showing them screenshots on his phone of the profits he'd made. Having worked for an investment bank, Nate was used to pushy salesmen camouflaged in flash suits, but Alex wasn't like that. Nate never had the feeling he was trying to sell something or show off, just a sense that this charismatic guy had chosen him as a confidant.

When Alex casually dropped into conversation the fact that his profits had allowed him to invest in Kayana, Nate had suddenly realized just how much he was making and had expressed a desire to get involved.

Initially, Alex had been reluctant to pass on any tips, which had made Nate even more desperate. By the time he'd realized cryptocurrency wasn't the only thing Alex traded, Nate had already agreed to help him with the odd favour. Dropping off an occasional package. Picking up another. Nate is grateful for what he gets paid for doing it, but it doesn't quite offset his crypto trading losses. Alex's tips haven't proved anything like as lucrative as he'd hoped.

Alex had phoned Nate just after they'd finished the Mount Batur hike. Had asked if he knew Lachlan, who worked for him occasionally. Nate had told him he didn't, but then realized who it was he'd seen dragged into a police car. Alex said he'd always thought Lachlan was a bit of a dick but had just had his suspicions confirmed by a call from his police contact saying the idiot had been arrested for dancing naked on a sacred mountain and maybe Nate would like the job Lachlan was supposed to do today instead? He just needed to pick up a package from inside one of the lockers in the VIP reception area at Tide and deliver it to a guy called Bryce who works in the surf shack on Echo Beach. Did Nate know him?

Nate had hesitated, weighing up the consequences. He knew Alex always got others to deliver for him, wouldn't risk getting caught with anything himself. Layla would kill Nate if she found out, but then he'd always been careful. Plus, when he thought of the words she'd carved inside her wardrobe, of how she'd shouted at him this morning when she'd lost her keys, of the scene she'd caused at the wedding, he realized that he was fed up with having to deal with her ever more erratic behaviour. The job would only take a couple of minutes and he'd get his usual commission of fifteen per cent, plus another two for stepping in at the last minute.

Nate had found the locker but had wanted to wait until the area was empty before he plugged in the code Alex had given him. Finding a gap among the constant flow of guests had taken longer than he'd expected, but eventually there had been a lull in activity and he'd found the plastic bag, small enough to hold in his fist without being noticeable. He'd put it into his rucksack, but not before tipping out a couple of grams for himself, sealing the white powder inside a piece of clingfilm he'd bought with him. Something to make the job more worthwhile. A quick bump could add a bit of spice to the party he wants to go to next week – enough for him and Jude to share, and Alex would never have to know.

Doing Alex the odd favour helps to plug the gap in their finances until Layla's life-coaching business takes off. He knows a few of his friends are doing it too. An easy way to earn a bit of extra cash that he can use to pay Nyoman to finish their fucking villa so they can move in and Layla can stop going on about hearing noises.

He feels his phone vibrate in his pocket as he heads into Tide's reception area and texts Alex with a single thumbs-up emoji. Less than two minutes later, he logs into his bank account and can see that his balance has increased by twenty million rupiah. He calls Nyoman.

'Hello, Nate.'

His site manager doesn't sound surprised to hear from him. But then Nate suspects Nyoman always knew he'd find a way to get him what he owes.

'I've got the money.'

There's a silence on the other end of the phone.

'Thanks for not saying anything about it in front of Layla and my friends the other day,' Nate continues. 'I've moved what I owe to your bank account, plus another million Indonesian rupiah extra.' He hesitates. 'As a . . . thank-you. I presume this means we can finally get things moving.'

There's a pause before Nyoman replies.

'I don't accept bribes, Nate. You shouldn't assume everyone in Bali is corrupt. I just want the amount we agreed that I'm owed. I'll return the extra. And then I'm sure we can have the doors and windows fitted in the next couple of weeks.'

Nate flushes. It wasn't supposed to be a bribe. Just something to show his appreciation of Nyoman not making a bad situation any worse than it already is.

'Fine,' Nate says. 'Whatever you say.' There's another silence, then he swallows.

'I hope there are no more cashflow problems going forwards,' Nyoman says.

The line goes dead and Nate resists the urge to throw his phone on the floor and stamp on it. He doesn't have a solution to this problem other than to keep giving Nyoman cash and hope he finishes the job as fast as possible. As much as Nate wants to sack him and hire someone else, there's no point. He'll lose the money he paid up front, the build will be no further forward and he'll still have to pay someone else.

Right now, he needs a miracle. If they can just get the villa to the point where at least the shell is complete, then he and Layla can do the decorating themselves. Jude and Sophie will help and he'll hire the trades he needs on a day rate if he has to.

He glances at his messages. One from Layla asking where he is. He hates lying to her; he knows the damage that keeping secrets does, but he can't tell her about this. He tries not to think about what happened on the hike; the guilty look on her face he's still convinced he saw. He's going to have to say he bumped into someone he knows from HiveHub, got chatting and lost track of time.

He steps out of the reception area and threads his way through various groups of people standing beside ice buckets of champagne, dancing to the music that is pumping out of the speakers. He makes his way back to their cabana, running through names of possible candidates from HiveHub in his head – someone Layla doesn't know that well and who they are unlikely to see in the next few weeks.

Sophie and Jude are stretched out immobile on the cabana, making the most of the last hour or so of sunshine. Nate shoves his rucksack underneath the bed and sits down.

'Where's Layla?' he asks.

Sophie bends her head forward and peers over the top of her sunglasses.

'She went to find you.'

Nate frowns. 'I didn't see her.'

Sophie shrugs as she lies back down. 'She left about fifteen minutes ago. You must have passed each other. Your mojito is on the table, but all the ice has melted. It might taste a bit grim now.'

Nate bends down and takes a couple of sips so he can pick up the drink without it spilling. He glances at his mobile, sees a missed call from Nyoman. His heart sinks as he dials his voicemail, expecting to hear a message from his site manager complaining that the funds haven't arrived, or a request for more money.

He presses the phone against his ear so he can hear properly, but the message isn't from Nyoman. It's from Patrick. His old boss at Bearmans'.

What the hell is Patrick calling him for?

At first, he listens to Patrick asking whether he'd be interested in doing some contract work, and relief washes over him; he could really do with the extra money right now. But as Patrick continues talking, Nate finds himself turning to look at Jude, who is lying motionless on the bed, and feels a prickling sensation on the back of his neck.

His best friend has been lying to him. Jude isn't here on a sabbatical. He no longer works at Bearman Brothers; he was sacked five weeks ago, just before Nate agreed he and Sophie could come out and stay.

28. Sophie

Sophie watches Nate from behind her sunglasses, sees him frown as he takes his phone away from his ear and puts it back into his pocket. She raises herself up on to her elbows, tucks a strand of her blonde hair behind her ear and takes another sip of the Sex on the Beach she'd ordered, her tongue smarting from the tartness of the cranberry.

'What's the matter?' she asks. 'Is it Layla?'

He shakes his head.

'Just our site manager,' he says, after a pause. 'He's still having issues with the windows.'

Sophie stretches her arms and rearranges the cushions behind her.

'Sounds like things aren't any better here than in London. Building work always takes ten times longer than you think it will, and inevitably goes way over budget.' She picks up one of the towels from the bed. 'I'm going to have a swim.'

Jude mumbles something inaudible from his horizontal position beside her in response.

'If I see Layla, I'll tell her you're back,' she says to Nate. 'Do you want me to get any more drinks?'

He nods. 'Can you get me a vodka? Double, neat with ice.'

She raises her eyebrows. He's not messing around.

'Sure,' she replies.

She slings the towel over her shoulder and winces as her grazed calf brushes against the side of the bed. Nate sits down opposite Jude as she heads over to the pool. If he's expecting a conversation, he'll be disappointed. Sophie knows better than to disturb her husband when he's trying to doze.

The sudden drop in temperature as she enters the pool is an exquisite pain that makes her gasp. The water swallows the heat of the sun as it edges up her body and forces her to take short, sharp breaths. She braces herself before lowering her hands in, makes herself keep going despite the urge to yank them straight back out, then pushes off from the side and pulls herself along in long, languid strokes.

She remembers her mother taking her and Jess swimming in Tooting lido after school – she'd clung on to the rusty metal steps, delaying the inevitable moment of getting in for as long as possible. The water had been freezing – even in the height of the British summer she'd come out with her arms covered in goosebumps, hairs standing on end, desperate to wrap herself in the thick towel that she'd laid out on the grass to warm up.

Jess had loved it. The cold hadn't bothered her – she'd always jumped in, usually with a run-up off the side first, tucking herself into a ball and clutching her knees as she entered the water. The resulting giant splash meant she'd always encounter filthy looks from those in the vicinity, her mother included – ladies of a certain age doing lengths of breaststroke with their heads firmly out of the water to avoid getting their hair wet.

Sophie floats on her back and smiles at the memory, blocks out others that threaten to intrude on her trip into the past. She's not going to think about those. Not right now. The awful moment of realization she'd had after walking into their flat in Wimbledon and seeing her precious things lying in pieces on the floor seems a million miles away. Out here, she can almost persuade herself that it never happened at all. She turns her face towards the sun, lets the brightness dissolve the vignette of images on the inside of her eyelids until they burn away, leaving behind nothing but white.

It doesn't take her long to cool down. She climbs back up the steps and out of the water. Her graze has stopped throbbing, but her bikini bottoms have ridden up and she pulls them back down, suddenly self-conscious. Thirty-five isn't old, but it's the first time she's started to notice that the other women around her all seem to be younger; the ones she can see in the pool and standing by their loungers are toned, with svelte figures and tanned, unblemished skin that isn't starting to sag or droop.

She grabs her towel and buries her face in it, wrapping it around herself as she pulls her stomach in, ironing out the creases to make it match the others she can see; totally flat, not even a hint of a roll over their bikini bottoms. She wonders whether Nate ever fantasizes about curvy women – like her – before his and Layla's silhouettes merge together in the dark; whether it would make a difference to her sex life with Jude if she had Layla's without-an-ounce-of-fat body type.

She squeezes the water out of the ends of her hair, hoping the chlorine doesn't turn it green, then spots Layla sitting on one of the loungers. At least she thinks it's Layla. The woman has her back to her and is talking to a Balinese man, but Sophie recognizes her blue-and-white batik print maxi dress. Her brain contracts as she attempts to match the man's face to a place; she knows she's seen him before, she just can't remember where. HiveHub. That's it. He had been leaving just as she and Nate had arrived. Layla had claimed he'd been asking her about life coaching, but the intense discussion they're having now suggests they definitely know each other.

Layla's gestures become more animated and her hands make jerky movements in the air as she speaks. The man's face darkens and he suddenly leans forward and grabs Layla's wrist. Sophie feels as if someone has turned down a volume button. She's at school, thirteen years old again, staring at someone who has hold of her wrist in exactly the same way as this man is holding on to Layla's. Terrible words she doesn't want to hear are whispered into her ear and, as they sink into her brain, dread rises up out of the rug on the floor and buries its claws into her legs, anchoring her to the spot.

She lowers herself on to the lounger beside her, ignoring the woman who leans over her to retrieve her drink. She should go and help Layla, but she can't move.

Get up. She can hear Jess saying the words to her in her head, swears she can feel someone wrap their arms around her shoulders like her sister used to do, leaning her chin on the top of Sophie's head. She takes a deep breath, digs her nails into the palms of her hands and shuts her eyes. When she opens them again, Layla is standing in front of her and the man is nowhere to be seen.

'Good swim?' Layla asks.

Sophie glances over at the now empty lounger. 'Who was that man you were with?'

'Which man?'

'The one you were just speaking to. I saw him grab your wrist. I thought he—'

She breaks off as she can see the way Layla is staring at her.

'I wasn't talking to anyone,' Layla says. 'I've just come out of the ladies. There was a bit of a queue.'

Sophie looks across the loungers towards the reception area, then over by the pool. The man seems to have vanished. A wave of confusion washes over her. She had seen him. She knows she had. Hadn't she?

Layla squeezes her arm. 'Shall we go back to the boys?'

Sophie nods slowly, then follows behind, still scanning the people around her as if the man is suddenly going to reappear. Her flip-flop catches on the strut of one of the loungers and she staggers forward, just manages to stop herself falling at the last second.

Layla reaches out to steady her, and it's then that Sophie sees the red marks on her wrist. Four perfectly shaped ovals, evenly spaced, where someone has clearly pressed their fingers into Layla's skin.

29. Jude

Jude feels something touch his foot.

'Get off,' he mumbles. 'I'm trying to sleep.'

Nate prods him. 'Mate, we need to talk.'

'Later. I'm knackered. That bloody hike has finished me off. I just want to chill out for a bit.' He yawns and pulls a towel over his face, doesn't want to risk getting burnt again. The skin on his forehead is already peeling off in small strips. 'Wake me up in an hour or so? I'll be ready for a few espresso martinis then.'

Nate's prods turn into a shove and Jude bends his knees, moves his legs further up the bed so Nate can't reach them.

'Chill out, bro,' he says.

'Wake the fuck up, Jude.'

Nate's tone of voice makes him open his eyes, pull off the towel and frown as he squints at the figure at the opposite end of the bed, a silhouette against the sun.

'Jesus. What?'

Nate leans over the side of the daybed, pushes his rucksack further underneath and then shuffles towards him. 'You need to tell me what's going on.'

As the expression on Nate's face becomes visible, Jude is suddenly acutely aware of how pissed off he looks.

'I haven't got a fucking clue what you're talking about.'

'I just got a call from Patrick,' Nate says.

Several drops of perspiration slide down Jude's back. *Fuck.*

'As in Patrick, our old boss,' Nate adds.

Jude swallows. 'I know who you mean.'

'He left a message offering me some temporary contracting work. Apparently, they're short-staffed at the moment. But then he asked if we'd been in touch since they let you go five weeks ago.'

Jude looks up at the teak spokes of the parasol, his heart thudding in his chest. Bloody Patrick. He hadn't ever considered he might call Nate.

'Jude?' Nate barks out his name, making him jump. 'Why didn't you tell me you'd been fired?'

'Keep your voice down.' Jude bites his lip. The heat is making it difficult for him to think coherently.

Nate rubs his forehead. 'You haven't told Sophie, have you?'

Jude hesitates, then shakes his head.

'She had enough to deal with after the burglary. I am going to tell her; I'm just waiting for the right time.'

Nate covers his face with his hands. '*The right time?* Jesus, mate. Don't you think your wife deserves to know that you've lost your job and you're not swanning around Bali on a sabbatical?'

Jude glances at the various groups of people in the VIP area, who all seem to be having the time of their lives, their smiles exposing their bright white teeth; oblivious to this conversation. He wishes he was one of them, their buzz of conversation bubbling with excitement as the DJ turns up the music.

He'd mentally left Bearmans' behind the minute he and

Sophie boarded the plane and has no desire to dredge up everything all over again. Does it really make that much difference whether he's on a sabbatical or between jobs? Either way, he's still out here and is supposed to be having a good time. If and when he decides to tell Sophie is none of Nate's business. But he doesn't want him saying anything to her right now.

'They kicked up a ridiculous fuss over nothing,' he says. 'You know what Bearmans' is like – Patrick and I fell out, so he started nitpicking about things he said I'd done, and then they fired me.'

Nate frowns at him. 'Patrick's always clashing with people in the team. Why didn't they do what they normally do – make you redundant and pay you off?'

Jude blinks and wipes a line of perspiration off his forehead.

'I guess it was an HR call. I honestly don't know.' His palms are slippery; the linen cushion on their daybed feels damp when he touches it.

'They must have given you a reason.' Nate's voice is hard. 'They can't just fire you for nothing. They're such bastards. You should get in touch with an employment lawyer. You might be able to sue them. Threaten to, at least. I know a few people out here who have good contacts – I'll have a word and get you their details.'

Jude picks up his almost empty glass and swirls the dregs around in the bottom before putting it down again. 'Thanks for the offer,' he says. 'I really appreciate it, bro, but you're making this into a bigger deal than it actually is. You know how much I hated working there. I'm better off out of it. The news just didn't come at the best time, that's all. I didn't tell Sophie in case she changed her mind about coming out here. She needs this break. The burglary really shook her up – imagine coming home and finding a stranger in your bathroom, for fuck's sake.'

There's an uncomfortable silence.

'What do you want me to say to Patrick?' Nate asks finally. 'I said I'd get back to him but I didn't tell him you were staying with me.'

Jude feels his face flush. There's no way he can let Nate talk to Patrick. He daren't think about what will happen if the truth slides out without him being able to stop it.

'Mate?'

Jude opens his mouth to reply when he feels something cold drip on to his shoulder and looks up to see Sophie holding two cocktails. He takes one, beyond grateful for the distraction from the conversation, and feels the alcohol burn as he swallows a couple of large mouthfuls.

'Why are you both looking so serious?' Layla asks.

'We're not.' Jude keeps his eyes firmly on his drink and away from Nate. As soon as he gets a couple of minutes on his own, he'll send Patrick an email. Threaten to sue him if he so much as mentions the fact he fired Jude from Bearman Brothers to anyone else, let alone the reason for it.

30. Layla

The sun disappears below the horizon, pulling with it the deep blue of the afternoon. Layla looks up at the star-sprinkled velvet darkness that's appeared in its place. The humidity is softer at this time of night, a warm sultriness rather than the searing heat of a few hours earlier.

She tries to breathe it in, appreciate the calmness, but her stomach churns as she watches Nate from the daybed. He's in his element as he throws various shapes on the dance floor – holding his arms up in the air among the crowd of people, keeping in sync with the DJ's beats.

He'd lied when she asked him where he'd been. Said he'd bumped into some guy from HiveHub she's never heard of and hadn't mentioned Bryce at all.

She turns away, watches the waves as they slip up the beach under the full moon. How can he have been so stupid? He's supposed to be the bright one, the one with all the qualifications – he'd worked for an investment bank, for fuck's sake. Surely he understands the insane risk he's taking. And for what? A few quid more to blow on nights like this?

Sophie is out in front of the DJ as well, keeping her distance from Nate, who has dragged Jude into the middle of the action. Layla had seen Sophie looking at the red marks on her wrists and hopes to God she doesn't mention anything.

Layla wants to go home. She can't relax enough to connect with the music and, ever since their argument about her keys, she knows Nate's been off with her. The longer they stay here, the more hammered he'll get, and she has a horrible feeling that one of them will say something they later regret.

She should have known Wayan Santi would come and find her – if she's learned anything in the past couple of months, it's that he's persistent. She'd told him she still had until tomorrow to deliver what he's asked for, that until then, he could fuck off and leave her alone. He hadn't mentioned anything about seeing what Nate had passed to Bryce. But then he wouldn't, would he? Wayan would relish keeping something like that to himself and then declare it when it benefitted him most. The thought of it sends another wave of nausea swilling around her stomach.

She runs her fingers over her wrist, traces over where he'd dug his fingers into it. The bruises will start to show tomorrow – she'll need to remember to cover them with make-up. Something else along with the thin lines of bone-white scars that she doesn't want anyone to see.

'You coming to dance?' Sophie emerges out of the crowd, her face glowing.

Layla shakes her head. 'I'm OK here.'

'Come on, you need to check Nate out. I haven't seen moves like that for a long time. He just took a cherry out of my drink to try his famous party trick of tying a knot in the stalk with his tongue – but we were laughing too much and he couldn't do it.'

Sophie's drunk. Layla can tell by how friendly she's

being. She wonders if Nate sent her over to get her. She holds up her glass.

'I'll come after I've finished this.'

Sophie's eyes flicker to Layla's wrist and she puts her arm down by her side. 'Do you want to make a move? We can head back to the villa if you've had enough.'

'I'm fine, honestly.' Layla smiles as she says it, but it feels tight and forced.

'I don't think Jude will need much persuading,' Sophie says. 'He looks knackered – but Nate won't let him sit down. Hang on a sec and I'll go and get them.'

Layla opens her mouth to protest, but Sophie has already disappeared back into the throng of pulsing bodies. Layla watches her, experiences a stab of envy that she still looks so elegant, her blonde hair moving as one smooth sheet even after being on the dance floor for so long. She feels like a sweaty mess, frizzy bits of damp hair plastered to the back of her neck.

'You wanna go home?'

Nate slurs his words as he staggers over towards the daybed. Layla can't quite bring herself to meet his eyes as he picks up his rucksack. If he knew how furious she was with him right now, he wouldn't be trying to talk to her at all.

'Only if you're happy to,' she says coldly. 'I don't want to spoil anyone's fun.'

He holds up his hands, sways slightly from side to side.

'If you want to go, you just need to say.' He hesitates. 'But I'm not actually sure you know what you want, Layla.'

'What's that supposed to mean?'

His eyes are unfocused, flickering away from hers.

'You're all over the place at the moment.'

He's right. Everything feels as if it's starting to fall apart. Losing her keys is just a symptom of a much bigger problem. She's scared she's sliding back into the person she was when they first came out here, and knows Nate is thinking the same thing but can't bring himself to say it.

She glares at him. 'And you're fucking hammered, so I guess we both have a few issues to deal with, don't we?'

Nate opens his mouth to say something, but Jude puts his arm around his shoulders.

'Come on, bro, let's just go back to the villa. It's been a long day and we're all knackered. Let's quit while we're ahead.'

Layla follows Jude as he leads Nate through the maze of loungers towards the exit, wishing that he and Sophie had never come out to Bali, that they hadn't come to Tide tonight, that Nate wasn't such a fucking idiot sometimes. She wants to be able to start today over again; if she could just go back and find her keys, perhaps everything would play out differently. She doesn't want to be here, but she doesn't want to go back to the villa either. The thought of lying awake in the darkness listening to noises that might actually be coming from inside her head fills her with terror.

She opens the Gojek app on her phone and orders a taxi as they walk away from the dance floor. They join the queue in the reception area – dozens of people standing in a long line, snaking towards the exit doors.

Sophie leans against the wall while Layla stands on tiptoes, trying to see what's causing the hold-up. When they've been here before, they've always just walked straight out.

They shuffle forwards, until finally she can see what's causing the issue. Two policemen are standing by the door, checking everyone's bags and patting them down before allowing them outside. A third policeman is positioned on the other side of the corridor, watching the queue.

Her blood roars in her ears as she sees a young guy ahead of them being asked to turn out his pockets, beads of sweat gleaming on his forehead under the lights.

Fuck.

She looks at Nate, but he's too pissed to register what's going on. His rucksack dangles from the crook of his elbow, the strap having slipped off his shoulder, and Jude is practically having to hold him up.

There's a sudden commotion over by the doors and Layla watches with horror as one of the policemen holds up something that looks suspiciously like a joint and begins to shout something in Balinese, his face a few inches away from the man whose pocket he has taken it out of. The policemen don't waste any time as they grab his arms and force them into handcuffs behind his back while he protests his innocence: faltering sentences that turn into pleas of desperation as he is ushered out of the door.

Layla swallows. She can feel her face burning, presses her cheek against the wall to try and cool it down. The altercation seems to have finally stirred Nate from his drunken reverie and she watches him gape in horror at the spot where the man was standing just a few seconds ago.

The policeman tells everyone to move forward and resumes his search. Nate turns to look at her, then glances at his rucksack, and she knows without having to ask what he put in there, and what the police will do if they find it.

31. Nate

There are eight people ahead of them. A group of four, then two couples, all in their twenties, one girl with a large snake tattooed across her tanned shoulder. Nate swears he can see it moving, slithering, backwards and forwards, wave-like, across her skin.

They're all laughing, and he recognizes that hyped-up, end-of-the-night feeling – the temptation to carry on, go somewhere else and keep drinking, make things last that little bit longer. He's usually the first to suggest it, but not tonight.

He fights the urge to step out of the line and walk back into the beach club, knows the policeman standing at the side of the wide corridor is watching him. Seeing that young guy handcuffed was like a sharp knife slicing straight through the warm fuzziness in his brain, but his thoughts are still jumping from one thing to another, unable to form any kind of logical order.

His rucksack is a lead weight on his shoulder. He mentally runs through its contents – suncream, sunglasses, Chilly's water bottle, Sophie's purse, which she'd given him to look after earlier, some chewing gum and, yes, Officer, that is approximately three grams of coke wrapped up in clingfilm.

A package not even a quarter of the size of his phone, but impossible to disguise or get rid of. There's absolutely nowhere in this corridor to hide anything – no rubbish bins, not even one of the large terracotta pots containing a palm tree that sit in other areas of the beach club. The only accessories are a few framed pictures on the walls and some giant neon signs with 'Tide' and 'Welcome!' glowing in pink and white lights.

Think, for fuck's sake.

He can't. His brain seems to have turned into a mass of synapses that are firing randomly in panic. He can't leave the line to go to the gents – the policeman will ask to search him. Could he pretend to faint? Take out the wrap and swallow it? If he turned around, the policeman might not see. Is that even possible, or would he choke? Or collapse from an overdose? Various options flash through his head, each dismissed one after another. He's been in Bali long enough to hear the horror stories of Kerobokan. Dozens of men crammed into a single cell, razor wire around the bars, nowhere to sleep, infested with rats. And that's if he's lucky enough to get a prison sentence. He can't bring himself to contemplate the alternative.

He glances at Layla and sees her face flush, before she turns away. He knows he was out of order with her before, his frustrations amplified by too many cocktails. They need to sit down and have a proper conversation – talk about what he saw in her wardrobe and discuss whether she needs to go back to her therapist, but he can't do that right now.

If they'd just stayed on the dance floor a bit longer, this might not have happened. He's never seen police at Tide before. Not in the entire time he's been in Canggu. Chances are, they'll only stay long enough to be able to tick a box on a form, saying they've carried out a random check. Unless they're looking for something specific. He thinks of how keen Alex had been for him to do this job and something icy and cold slithers across his chest and down through his insides.

Fuck. Has he been set up?

The two policemen finish searching the last of the big group in front and wave them through the exit on to the street. Nate's heart squeezes into a knot, missing a beat. Only four more people to go.

'You all right, bro?' He realizes Jude is staring at him.

He doesn't reply. He thinks if he opens his mouth he might be sick.

'You've gone really pale.' Sophie frowns. 'Here, give me your rucksack and sit down for a second. Put your head between your knees.'

He holds on to the strap on his bag as Sophie leans across to take it. For a fraction of a second he considers not letting go, because he knows what is inside, and how can he possibly hand over a ticking bomb of his own making to anyone, let alone his best friend's wife? But then time slips in his head and he remembers the person he once was, the one who did let go, because when it comes down to it, people do what they need to in order to survive.

After all, Jude wouldn't behave any differently. Nate knows, because he's seen him in that situation before.

He shuts his eyes briefly, opens his hand and feels the strap slither through his fingers. Sophie slings the bag over her shoulder as he sinks to the floor and rests his head on his knees.

'Up!' The policeman monitoring the queue from the other side of the corridor points at him.

Jude holds out his hand. 'Our friend isn't feeling well. Can you just give us a minute?'

The policeman shakes his head and points again.

'You!' He makes an upward motion with his hand. 'Up!'

Jude helps Nate to his feet, and he leans against the wall for balance, welcomes the coolness of the concrete that seeps through his T-shirt. Tells himself to keep breathing, that somehow this will work out, that the pain in his chest isn't his heart splitting into pieces.

The first couple after the group are through.

Last chance.

The final two tourists have their bags out on the small table; Nate can hear the sound of zips being opened. Sophie smiles at him, his bag dangling from her shoulder.

'You feeling any better?' she asks. 'We'll be out of here in a minute and you can get some air.'

The last tourists ahead of them disappear through the large wooden doors and he and the others are beckoned forward.

One of the policemen points at the rucksack and Sophie puts it on the table. The other man pats Nate down, then does the same thing to Jude, asks them to turn out the pockets of their shorts and take out their phones, wallets and keys. Nate tries to look anywhere other than at the rucksack. Sophie smiles as the policeman starts to unzip the various pockets and dump the contents on to the table.

A tube of suncream, sunglasses case, water bottle. The pain in Nate's chest is now so acute he thinks his heart might stop.

Please don't look in the side pocket.

He offers up a prayer to any god who might be listening, promises to sell his soul if they can all just walk out through those double doors, but then remembers he made that bargain once before. And no one gets the chance to do it twice. The policeman starts to unzip the side pocket and Nate has to clamp his jaw shut to stop his teeth chattering.

Sophie is still smiling as the policeman hesitates, then looks up at her.

Nate shuts his eyes.

When he opens them again, the policeman is in the process of putting the items back inside the bag. He hands it to Sophie and she slings it over her shoulder.

'Shall we go?' she says.

Nate nods, unable to speak, and holds out his hand for his rucksack. She passes it to him, a look of concern on her face, before walking out of the club and on to the street, Layla by her side.

He follows, half expecting to hear a shout from behind them, demanding they come back. The relief of being out of the club hits him like a physical blow and he stumbles towards the taxi, his vision blurring. He doesn't understand what's just happened. Had the policeman missed it? That's impossible. That clingfilm wrap was the only thing in the pocket of his bag.

The girls get in one side of the taxi, and Jude gets into the front. A humming noise vibrates in Nate's head and his legs don't seem to want to do what he's asking. He trips as he steps off the kerb, overwhelmed by the smell of exhaust fumes and cooking aromas from the late-night takeaway stalls. He staggers around the back of the taxi to the driver's side, the guilt of what he just did to Sophie sliding around like something greasy in the bottom of his stomach.

He doesn't even see the scooter.

It hits him as he opens the taxi door, the bike skidding out from underneath its driver. A horrible squeal of brakes and, for a significant part of its journey along the carriageway, Nate's body, caught in the front wheel by the straps of his rucksack.

Mercifully, Nate isn't aware of it. He is only conscious of the initial blow to his ribs, forcing every ounce of oxygen from his lungs in a silent scream, before his world spins upside down and everything turns black.

32. 2007

My heart stutters as I read Kadek's message again.

'Everything all right?' Dan seems to have finally got his breath back.

No, I want to say. It's not. The same feeling of unease I'd had earlier swirls around in my gut. Kadek thinks someone is watching the minibus. I text back and tell him to wait a bit longer before he lets himself in. He's being paranoid. It's probably nothing.

'All fine,' I reply, a smile fixed on to my face. 'Before we get going, there are a few things you need to remember. Firstly, you always need to listen to me when I'm speaking. When I say paddle, you paddle. If I say stop, you stop.' I hesitate. 'Buddy, is there a problem?'

The teenager is having a conversation with Mia while I'm talking and despite me shooting him a few glances he hasn't taken the hint. He finally shuts up when Mia turns her back on him.

'If you fall out of the boat,' I continue, 'swim towards it and grab one of these safety lines.' I point to the two ropes attached to the sides of the inflatable, threaded through a series of metal rings. 'We'll pull you back in.'

My phone buzzes again. It's another text from Kadek.

The two boats that set off earlier had to stop. Too dangerous.

Shit.

The group looks at me, waiting expectantly for me to continue. I look at the frothing rapids, at the dark sky overhead, and take a deep breath. *All my instincts tell me that we should turn back. I open my mouth to tell them, but then think of how many months' rent Kadek and I could cover if our plan works out. If we can just get to the waterfall, we'll stop there, and Kadek will have had enough time to do what he needs. I close my mouth and text three words back.*

We're still going.

I swallow my misgivings, stick my phone in the waterproof bag and hold up my paddle.

'The handles of these are shaped like a "T" for a reason,' I say. 'Keep one hand on the top bar, and another on the shaft. It will give you a better grip and stop you knocking yourself out. And keep your helmet and life vest on at all times.'

'Can we get in the boat now?' James asks.

I nod, feeling my heart rate increase as he climbs in. There's a voice in my head, screaming at me to get him out and walk back to the van, but I refuse to listen to it. James holds out his hand to Kristin and looks around for his son.

'Buddy? Come and sit with us, mate.'

The teenager shakes his head. 'I'll sit in the middle with Ashley and Mia. It'll balance the boat better. You and Mum stay at the front, Dan and Jen can go behind us.'

I untie the boat and push it away from the side, then sit on the back of the inflatable, raised up, to get the best viewpoint. My phone chimes from inside the bag, but it's too late to look at it now.

The current grabs hold of us from the moment we set off, and suddenly I can imagine how a rat feels when they are caught and shaken by a dog. Water hits the boat in violent sprays and the group gasp in shock — a temporary relief from the tropical heat that sticks to our skin and buries itself in our throats.

'Paddle!' *I yell in the few brief seconds before we hit another set of*

185

rapids, but despite everyone doing what I tell them, it feels as if we are trying to move a tank using tablespoons. The jungle foliage, a dense mass of green on both banks, slides past at a dizzying speed. Thunderflies hang in clusters over the water and birds screech a warning from the trees above.

My shoulders are on fire after the first four kilometres. The water is like treacle and there is a heaviness in my chest, reminding me each time I take a breath that we shouldn't have come.

Every bend in the river looks the same. Where's the waterfall? Surely we should have reached it by now? The boat jolts as we hit another set of rapids, steeper this time, and I can feel us being pulled towards the rocks.

'Paddle!' This time my voice is edged with panic.

But the boat doesn't move fast enough and, for a few seconds, the front disappears below the frothing water. When it resurfaces, Kristin is screaming. The seat beside her is empty, and James is nowhere to be seen.

33. Sophie

Sophie prays silently that the ambulance taking Nate to the hospital has got there quicker than her and Jude's taxi. They've crawled along at an agonizing pace, Jude's foot tapping impatiently. She clings desperately to the hope that Nate has continued to breathe after the paramedics' CPR, but the sick feeling in her stomach tells her that everything could have changed on that journey. Layla's screams echo in her head, and when she blinks she can still see the dark patches Nate's body left on the tarmac, wet and shiny under the glare of the streetlights.

When they finally pull up outside Siloam Medika, Sophie's eyes are drawn to the giant sign by the entrance: *24 HOUR EMERGENCY* written in large white capital letters on a red background. The words send a shiver down her spine. She hates everything about hospitals: their squeaky linoleum flooring, the too-bright lights and the smell of chlorine; the inability to control anything that happens inside.

Jude shoves a bundle of rupiah notes at the driver as they scramble out.

The hospital isn't like the monoliths she's used to at home with their vast car parks, multiple different departments and ambulances lined up outside. This building is much smaller, set just a few feet back from the road, crammed in between tyre shops, motorbike dealers and a guesthouse. If it wasn't for the sign on the wall, she could almost have mistaken it for an office.

She stops and grips the metal railing as Jude walks ahead towards the set of sliding glass doors.

'What's the matter?' he asks.

'I'm not sure I can go in.'

He walks back and puts his arms around her, but her body is stiff and unyielding. His chest presses against hers as he looks down at her.

'Your heart's racing.'

'You know how much I hate hospitals.' She swallows, wants to hide the crack in her voice.

'Nate isn't your dad, Soph,' he says gently.

She nods, but can't bring herself to tell him that she's not thinking about her father's fatal heart attack, her mind has taken her further back than that; to the sound of sirens and flashing lights, to people kneeling in front of her on the damp lawn behind their house, asking her the same question over and over again until she'd put her hands over her ears, squeezed her eyes shut and refused to answer.

Where did you last see her?

Jude touches her arm, and she flinches. In the silence that follows, she looks down at the paving slabs, moving her feet so that each one fits inside the herringbone pattern without touching the lines. He's the one person to whom she's confessed what happened, and he has never judged her for it. A connection that holds them together more strongly than any of the bonds usually associated with marriage. Something she can't break.

'It's OK, Soph. You don't have to come in if you don't want to,' he says.

She rubs at a mark she thinks she can see on the back of her hand, then blinks and realizes there's nothing there – just a rawness, as if she's been burned. Can Jude tell what she's thinking? Sometimes she feels as if he can read her thoughts like words on a page; all the secrets she hides from everyone else. She thinks about Nate and Layla, of their movements in the dark, of the physical ache she'd felt watching them, and then looks at her husband, wonders if what constitutes their marriage is stronger than that.

'What if he's dead?' she whispers. She thinks of Nate laughing, of all the nights the four of them have spent together, of the solidity of his presence, of the way he and Jude mess about, taking the piss out of each other. He can't be dead. He just can't.

Jude glances at his phone. He's had it in his hand all the way here, checking it constantly for messages.

'Layla would have called us,' he says.

Sophie isn't so sure. And she doesn't want to go in and find out. Doesn't want everything to change for ever.

Jude holds out his hand. 'I can always stay here with Layla and you can go back to the villa if you want.'

She shakes her head. 'I'm not leaving you to do this by yourself.'

Inside, the hospital feels just as alien as outside. There aren't dozens of metal seats crammed full of people waiting for hours to be seen. This place is immaculately clean, with only a handful of people sitting on sofas in the reception area. She and Jude are directed to the emergency centre by a sleek and efficient woman sitting behind a desk.

'It's so quiet,' Sophie says as they head up a set of glass stairs. 'Can you imagine A&E being like this in London?'

Jude doesn't answer, is too busy striding ahead towards another desk, where he mentions Nate's name, and someone points them towards the end of a wide corridor.

The sick feeling in her stomach swirls as she walks beside him, her flip-flops slapping against the floor. The air-conditioning means it's much cooler than outside and she wishes she had a cardigan.

Layla stumbles from her chair and lets out a sob as Jude puts his arms around her. Sophie looks around the small room – a water fountain stands in one corner; a gold plant pot with fake orchids sits on top of a polished wooden coffee table. She's reassured by the fact that it's spotless, wants to believe it's a sign that Nate is getting the best possible care.

'Any news?' she asks.

Layla sits back down and rubs her temples. 'They're most worried about his head injury, but they're also not sure how bad his leg break is; whether he'll need an operation as well as a skin graft.' Tears slide down her cheeks. 'I just don't understand what happened. All he was doing was getting into the taxi.'

Sophie puts her arm around Layla's shoulders. She glances at the rucksack lying on the floor with its broken straps and has a flashback to Nate's body being dragged along the ground, the shrieks of horror from other tourists watching from the pavement.

'Let's just wait to see what the doctors say,' Sophie says. 'You know he's in the best place.'

Layla nods. 'Thank fuck we've got insurance. The local

hospitals are . . . very different.' Sophie doesn't say what they're clearly both thinking. The Balinese man riding the scooter had been taken to one of those.

There's a knock on the doorframe and Sophie looks up to see a woman with long dark hair dressed in blue scrubs with a stethoscope around her neck.

'Layla Matthews?'

Layla nods.

'I'm Dr Purwanta, one of the team treating your partner, Nate Osbourne. The good news is that we've managed to stabilize his bleeding and the X-ray suggests he won't need an operation on his leg. The main issue currently is that the MRI shows his brain has swollen as a result of the accident, so we have had to put him into an induced coma. We're currently monitoring him until we decide what to do next – we need to see if the swelling gets any worse. There's not much more I can tell you at this stage, but we'll let you know as soon as we have any more information.'

Layla's eyes well up.

'Do you know when that's likely to be?' Jude says.

'It's difficult to say,' Dr Purwanta replies, 'but we'll keep you updated.' She hesitates. 'Something else I should mention,' she adds, 'is that apart from Nate's obvious physical injuries, our tests have shown that he is suffering from methanol poisoning.'

'Methanol poisoning?' Jude repeats.

Sophie remembers how Nate had slid down the wall and on to the floor while they were queuing to get out of Tide. She'd assumed he was drunk.

'It's not uncommon in Bali,' Dr Purwanta says. 'It's

often due to bars using cheaper local alcohol which hasn't been brewed correctly. It's tasteless, so Nate wouldn't have known he was drinking it, but it may have caused him to be confused and uncoordinated. There have been several cases recently of tourists dying after consuming it – but in Nate's case, we've picked it up quickly so hopefully we can treat it.'

She looks at Layla. 'Ironically, getting hit by a scooter may actually end up saving your partner's life.'

34. Jude

'Can she see him?' Jude asks.

Dr Purwanta doesn't answer.

'Please?' Layla says. 'Just for a minute?'

'OK,' she says finally. 'But your friends will need to wait here.'

Layla nods. Jude squeezes her hand briefly before she follows Dr Purwanta out into the corridor.

The sound of a baby crying floats in through the open door and Jude feels himself tense as he perches on the edge of the chair. Sophie glances in the direction of the noise, then pours herself a cup of water from the fountain and knocks it back in one go, like a shot of tequila.

The doctor's words spin in his head. How can Nate have been poisoned? Surely that kind of thing doesn't happen in a beach club? Should they call Nate's parents, or wait for more news? Jude doesn't want to worry them unnecessarily, but they're going to need to know.

'I still don't understand,' he says. 'Did Nate trip getting into the cab? Or did the scooter just plough into him?'

'I didn't see what happened,' Sophie says. 'He went around to the other side of the taxi and then I just heard that awful screech of brakes. It wasn't until the scooter slid further down the road that I realized Nate was—'

She breaks off and pours herself some more water.

Jude runs his hand through his hair, his fingers encountering knotted tufts, stuck together after sweating on the dance floor, and he yanks at them, frustrated.

'I should have noticed something wasn't right. He looked hammered when we were queuing to get out of Tide, but I never thought . . . Fuck, what a mess.'

Sophie blinks away tears as she puts her hand on his knee. 'I've seen him in worse states when he's been drunk. We couldn't have known. He's getting the best treatment. You heard the doctor.'

Jude rubs his hand over his beard. 'I hope so.'

'Now I get why he seemed so out of it,' Sophie says, glancing towards the sound that continues to float in from the corridor. 'He was a bit all over the place when we were dancing, as well. Kept saying I needed to talk to you about your job.'

Jude takes off his glasses and wipes the perspiration off the bridge of his nose before putting them back on as he shifts uncomfortably in his seat. What the fuck had Nate said that for?

'He was clearly off his face,' he says, his cheeks flushed. He thinks of his oldest friend lying in a coma. Had Nate betrayed his confidence? They'd agreed never to give up each other's secrets. A pact made back at university. But then he remembers the stab of hurt he'd felt at being sidelined in Kayana, of Nate laughing with Alex about things that Jude wasn't involved in. Maybe he and Nate have drifted more than he's realized.

His wife continues to stare at him, and he feels as if her eyes are boring into his skin, studying all his secrets; the ones he doesn't tell anyone about, not even her. She throws the paper cup in the bin and crosses her arms, her eyes glistening. He hates seeing her upset. Loves her so much that it sometimes feels as if the intensity of it will suffocate him.

'There are rumours of redundancies at work,' he says after a pause. Better to offer a half-truth, make it sound more convincing. Her blue eyes widen. 'Nothing's certain,' he adds, 'and I don't even know if it will affect our division, but it's something we should probably prepare ourselves for. A worst-case scenario.'

She blinks. 'Why didn't you tell me?'

'I was worried you wouldn't want to come to Bali,' he says. 'And you really needed this break. You were so stressed after the burglary.'

'You should have told me.' Her voice is cold.

'I know. I'm sorry.' The baby's cries become louder, drowning out the end of her sentence. He walks over and shuts the door, muffling the noise.

'I presume if the worst happens, Bearmans' will give you a good reference?' Sophie says tightly.

He swallows. 'I'm sure they will.'

'Because we need your income, Jude. Especially if we're looking to buy a place. We'll never get a mortgage on just my salary.'

'I know.'

'You promised that coming away on a sabbatical wouldn't change our long-term plans. Look at what Layla and Nate have got out here – isn't that the kind of thing we want? A proper home?'

The baby's cries finally tail off, leaving them in silence. He glances at the door.

'And we definitely can't have one of those if you don't have a job,' she adds.

He looks at her. 'I'm aware of that, Sophie. But we also can't have a baby without actually having sex, and that isn't something you seem particularly keen on at the moment. Especially not since the burglary.'

He regrets saying the words the moment they've left his mouth. He's been trying to give her space, knows how traumatized she's been, but the stress of Nate's accident has made him lash out. She glares at him as the sound of footsteps in the corridor gets louder and Layla walks back in, tears running down her cheeks. Sophie leads her over to a chair as Jude passes her water and a tissue.

'Drink this,' he says. 'And breathe slowly.'

Layla holds the cup, her hands trembling, and takes a few sips.

'Nate just looks like he's asleep,' she says. 'Apart from all the tubes. They're going to move him into ICU and said I can go and sit with him.' Another tear trickles down her cheek.

'The doctor said he'd had a call from his friend at the local hospital,' she continues. 'The man riding the scooter died. He'd lost a lot of blood, and they didn't have enough in the hospital where he was to give him a transfusion.'

'God, Layla, that's terrible,' Sophie says.

'I know it was an accident' – Layla gazes blankly ahead – 'but that doesn't make it any better. What if Nate stepped out in front of him? What if it was his fault?'

'You don't know that, though, do you?' Jude pats

Layla's knee, notices the four red marks on her wrist as she takes another sip of water then throws the cup in the bin. 'What if it was the scooter driver's fault?' he says. 'What if he swerved and hit Nate?'

Layla buries her head in her hands.

'You two should go back to the villa,' she says.

Jude frowns. 'I don't think you should be here on your own. One of us should stay with you.'

She shakes her head.

'No, you go back. I'll be fine by myself. I'm not leaving him, and I don't sleep well at home anyway.' She laughs bitterly. 'Especially not without Nate. At least here I'll know what the noises are.'

She fishes around in Nate's rucksack and gives his keys to Jude. 'Go and have a shower, get some sleep, then maybe you can sort out some stuff for Nate and come back in the morning? There's no point in all three of us being here. There's nothing you can do, and they'll only allow me into ICU tonight with him anyway.'

She points at the green sweatshirt she's wearing. 'They lent me this for now – it's cold with the air-con. Beach-club attire doesn't really work in intensive care,' she says, attempting a smile.

Sophie twists the thin gold chain around her wrist. 'I'm happy to stay if you want me to.'

Jude knows that's a lie. Sophie hates hospitals, and he completely understands why. Watching her dad die had been awful for her.

Layla shakes her head more firmly.

'No, I'm OK, honestly.'

Jude squeezes Layla's shoulder.

'We'll be back after we've had a sleep. WhatsApp us if you need anything at all.'

He glances at Sophie, who is already on her feet, and tries to think of ways to avoid discussing Bearmans' or redundancy on the twenty-minute taxi ride back to the villa.

the digital nomad community. They're going to have to pray Bryce doesn't get caught by the police, although she'd bet he's already on his way out of the country. She daren't even think about Wayan Santi and what he saw.

She opens Nate's rucksack and takes out his phone. The screen has been smashed across one corner, a spider's web unfurling across the glass, but it jumps into life when she touches it. Something inside her lifts when she sees it's working – if his phone can survive being dragged across tarmac under the wheels of a scooter, then surely so can he. She enters his passcode, but the phone vibrates in her hand and asks her to enter it again. She frowns. Has he changed it? She types the number in slowly, but the phone buzzes at her again. He must have changed it.

And not told her.

The pendulum in her brain, previously swinging between a plethora of emotions, lands on anger. She picks up his rucksack, checks around the small room to make sure she hasn't left anything behind and heads out past reception towards the intensive care unit, his phone heavy in the pocket of her dress.

Dr Purwanta isn't in the ICU, but a nurse is looking at the various machines that are monitoring Nate's vital statistics and keeping him tethered to life. She tells Layla to leave the rucksack on a shelf at the side of the room and puts a chair next to the bed for her. Layla lets go of the bag reluctantly, tucks up the broken straps so they aren't trailing on the floor before she sits down.

'You can hold his hand.'

The nurse gives her Nate's leather bracelet.

'We had to remove this when he came in. And you can

talk to him – we don't know if he can hear you, but patients who wake up after being in a coma often say they can remember things relatives said to them.'

Layla squeezes the plaited strip of leather strip in her palm, overcome by a desire to fasten it back around Nate's wrist. A way to make the shaven-headed stranger in the bed more recognizable. She swallows. His shoulder and upper arm are covered in a layer of gauze bandages – she presumes to stop any infection getting into the grazes caused by sliding along the tarmac – but there's a small section of his forearm where the skin remains unblemished. Tanned, with a sprinkling of dark hair. She lowers her hand gently and slides it down to his wrist, reassured at the steady beat of his pulse just below the surface of his skin. She presses the lotus flower she'd had tattooed on to her wrist against his – they'd had them done together when they'd arrived in Canggu – and wills him to feel all the things it represents – strength, rebirth, resilience.

Wake up. You need to wake up.

She communicates her desire silently, despite what the nurse said, reluctant to say anything out loud in case she disturbs the beeping regularity of the machines. Is it good that they're beeping? She doesn't want to ask in case they say no. The turquoise charm on her pendant rests on Nate's hand as she entwines her fingers between his and pretends she can feel him moving in response.

Wishing won't make it happen.

She knows this too. She tried that before with her parents. Tears prick at her eyes. She can't cope if anything happens to him, even if he is a fucking idiot.

The nurse taps her gently on the shoulder. 'Would you like a cup of tea?'

Layla nods. 'Thanks. That would be great.'

As the woman walks out of the room, Layla reaches into her pocket and takes out Nate's phone. She hesitates, swipes the screen up, holds it about ten inches away from his face and prays it works with his eyes shut.

At least give me this.

The screen springs into life. She breathes a sigh of relief, offers thanks to whichever power just manifested that for her, and opens his messages. Bryce's name comes up first, but the two brief texts he exchanged with Nate yesterday don't tell her what she needs to know.

Am at Tide, followed by a thumbs-up emoji from Nate in response.

She continues to scroll down until she spots what she's looking for: Alex's name, with his familiar profile picture beside it – his professional pose, flashing a glimpse of his perfect white veneers. She taps on his name, reads down the thread of messages exchanged between the two of them and then looks at Nate lying motionless in the bed.

'You really are a fucking idiot,' she says.

She puts his phone back in her pocket and gets out hers, scrolls through her contacts to find him. She's got Alex saved under a different name, just in case Nate ever looks through her phone, hasn't been able to bring herself to delete all the messages they've sent each other. She types out a brief text and presses send.

I think we need to talk, don't you?

36. Sophie

Sophie can feel the resentment sitting like a brick wall between them in the back of the taxi. She can't believe Jude didn't tell her there could be redundancies at Bearmans', but they've barely had any sleep these past couple of days and she doesn't want to say something now that she'll regret later. She can see how worried he is about Nate – his body is hunched in on itself as he gazes out of the window in silence.

Even in the early hours of the morning, the roads are full of traffic – scooters weave past their car, the occupants wearing thin, short-sleeved T-shirts or dresses with spaghetti straps. She keeps remembering Nate's body sliding across the tarmac and shivers, despite the heat.

Strings of fairy lights have been wound around the palm trees and greenery outside the local restaurants, and the tiny bulbs wink in the darkness. Sphere-shaped lanterns hang above empty tables in long rows. The frenetic atmosphere that fills these places in the scorching heat of the day has disappeared; the shops are shut, mannequins gaze blankly out of lit-up windows, their turquoise and orange outfits passing by in a blur of colour.

She can hear stray dogs barking above the ever-present hum of traffic when they reach the villa and pay for the taxi, and her pulse speeds up – the line between civilization and chaos feels thinner here than it does in London.

Something fragile that doesn't follow familiar rules and can easily be broken. Jude presses the key fob against the panel to open the villa gates and she has to control her urge to tell him to hurry up.

'Did you see those marks on Layla's wrists?' he asks as the gates start to open.

She nods, her face flushing as she looks down at the thin gold chain around her own, remembering the feeling of being gripped and unable to move as if it was yesterday.

'They weren't anything to do with you, were they?' Jude asks slowly.

''Course not,' she says angrily. 'Bloody hell, Jude, do you really think I'd hurt Layla?'

She notes the beat of hesitation before he shakes his head, and the brick wall she'd felt in the taxi rises up again between them. How can he think she'd do something like that? The answer comes almost before she's formed the question. *You know why.* Well, fuck you, Jude. She presses her lips together – there's no point in trying to explain – he won't believe her anyway.

Jude doesn't say anything while they wait in silence for the gates to swing fully open. He kicks off his shoes when they get inside the villa and puts the keys in the bowl on the hall shelf.

'I'm going to jump in the shower,' he says. 'Try and get some sleep before we go back. Christ, I still can't believe it. Poor Nate.'

Sophie nods, her anger draining out of her. 'I'll be along in a minute. I'm just going to grab some water and put the TV on for a bit. I need something else to focus on – I can't get the images of him under that scooter out of my head.'

Jude takes off his glasses and rubs his eyes. His pale skin has a grey tinge to it as he steps towards her, embraces her in a hug and kisses the top of her head.

'I'm sorry I didn't tell you about Bearmans',' he says. 'And I know you wouldn't hurt Layla. You're the most important thing in the world to me, Soph.' He steps back, strokes her cheek with his finger. 'I love you. Don't stay up too long.'

She walks into the kitchen and takes a bottle of water out of the fridge, the automatic night lights creating a soft glow. What Jude had said in the hospital about having a baby circles slowly round her brain. She hears him turn on the shower, thinks about how in the past she might have gone in and joined him.

She walks quietly down the corridor towards Nate and Layla's room and steps into the soft blackness, pushing the door closed so only a small crack of light filters inside. The smell of Nate's aftershave lingers faintly in the air and their duvet lies rumpled on the bed. She remembers watching their silhouettes in this room and her heart flutters. She can't believe Nate's not here – he's so full of life that everything feels smaller without him. She waits for her eyes to become accustomed to the dark, doesn't want to switch on any lights in case Jude sees her, just like she can see him in the bathroom opposite, a blurred figure behind the glass.

She opens Layla's bedside drawer and experiences a visceral thrill at the thought of being somewhere she shouldn't. She hasn't got long to find what she's looking for. A tangled cluster of gold necklaces, a blank notebook, a couple of pens and a few business cards from various restaurants, other life coaches and a tattooist.

Nothing there.

She moves across to their fitted wardrobe and slides back the doors that stretch from floor to ceiling. Layla's dresses are hanging up and she runs her hands over them, her fingers encountering linen and silk. All white and cream, with just the odd splash of colour; everything is long and floaty – nothing like the kind of thing she'd buy – Layla has her own distinctive style, mostly pieces she seems to pick up from market stalls. Sophie wishes she could do that. She spends a fortune on clothes but has to copy things she's seen other people wearing to get the look she's aiming for.

She spreads the hangers back out to make it look as if nothing has been touched and catches sight of something etched into the wood.

The bathroom light on the opposite side of the villa goes out and she stands very still, waits to see if Jude will come out to see where she is, but he doesn't, and their bedroom remains in darkness. He must have got straight into bed. She switches her phone torch to its lowest setting and shines the light inside the wardrobe.

It was my fault.

She peers closer.

I am a bad person.

Dozens of words have been carved into the back panel with a knife.

The sound of a door shutting makes her jump. She switches off her torch, stands still in the darkness and waits. Was that Jude? Her ears strain to pick out sounds in the silence. A prickle runs down her spine as she imagines a hand reaching out to touch her. She tells herself not to be ridiculous. She doesn't believe in ghosts. Once you're dead, you're dead – that's it. You can't come back. Layla might think she can hear noises, but they're all in her head. There is no one else here.

She slides the wardrobe shut and walks past the chest of drawers, stopping to pick up one of Layla's tortoise-shell butterfly claw clips that's lying on the surface. Jess used to own one like this. She remembers kneeling behind her sister on her bed in Wimbledon, brushing her hair then fastening the front section with a clip that had ended up half buried among Jess's red curls. She can still smell the herbal scent of her sister's Timotei shampoo.

She misses her more than she can possibly articulate. The butterfly clip feels heavy in her hand, and she catches a glimpse of herself in Layla's mirror – the dark, smudged outline of her face seems to move, like the shimmer of a heatwave, as if someone is standing behind her, their two faces merging into one.

She shivers.

Jess isn't here.

Jess is back at home, in Wimbledon. Sophie had gone to see her before she came out to Bali to tell her about the trip. To say that she wished she was coming too. She'd spent an hour with her, had cried when she'd had to leave, and had walked around the Common for ages before heading back to the flat to give her puffy, bloodshot eyes a chance to calm down. Jude hadn't wanted her to go in the first place, doesn't understand why she puts herself through these visits when it's clear they only upset her. But her husband is an only child and finds her and Jess's sibling bond incomprehensible.

Jude would never say it, but she thinks he resents Jess. Doesn't like the amount of time Sophie spends with her. And a part of her understands that.

He can never compete with someone who's dead.

Sophie had stood in the same place she always did when she talked to her, on the patch of immaculately cut grass beside the grey headstone, her sister's name carved in capital letters – something that always made her feel like a stranger was buried in the plot. Her sister had hated being called Jessica, had only ever answered to Jess. But her mother had insisted on Jess's full name being engraved and, at thirteen, Sophie hadn't been in a position to argue. Twenty-two years without her and she still can't believe she's gone.

A shiver runs down her back as the air seems to whisper something. A soft hiss that doesn't sound human and makes her dizzy with fear. She turns on her iPhone torch again, her hands clammy, not caring whether Jude sees her now. One reflection gazes back at her, her pupils wide in the bright light.

There is no one else here.

She fights the urge to run as she walks out of the bedroom towards the living room; thinks about the words Layla has carved into the back of her wardrobe and tells herself that she's found the confession she was looking for.

37. Jude

Jude wakes up before sunrise and watches the blackness outside gradually rinse away, replaced by pastel pinks and yellows. He'd been too knackered to shut the blinds last night, and clearly Sophie had been too, although God knows what time she'd come to bed – he'd been out cold almost as soon as his head touched the pillow.

He runs through a mental list of things he needs to take in for Nate. Should he even bother with pyjamas or a T-shirt? A toothbrush? Will someone brush his teeth for him? Can they even do that if he's intubated? He decides to pack everything; the nurses can decide what they need.

He looks across at Sophie, still fast asleep, her blonde hair trailing across her pillow, and feels a twinge of dread when he thinks about the email he'd discovered last night before he got in the shower. From the Met police in London, requesting he get in touch. He's deleted it, but how on earth he's going to keep that from her, he isn't sure.

He'd stepped under the stream of running water, hoping that somehow he'd imagined it, but the email had still been there in black and white when he got out. He'd assumed Bearmans' wouldn't escalate things after he went abroad, but it looks like he was wrong. The longer he can persuade Sophie to stay out here, the better. At least he hadn't told her what Gede had said about Layla pushing her on Mount Batur – Sophie would insist on leaving the villa if she knew that, and if they lose their free accommodation, they won't be able to afford to stay in Bali.

He studies their beautifully decorated room, with its stylish vases and diffusers, remembers what Sophie said last night about wanting something like this. His wife has always been ambitious, it's one of the things he loves about her, but sometimes he wishes she wouldn't push quite so hard. He hates the feeling that he's letting her down, doesn't know how to tell her that he's not her father, that they won't ever end up in a house like the one she grew up in. He's sure that's what she's secretly hoping for, that this sabbatical will give him a chance to recharge his batteries and attack the corporate ladder with renewed vigour when he gets home, but that's just not going to happen. He knows where his real talents lie, and it's not in banking.

In many ways, they are closer than any other couple he knows, including Nate and Layla, but there is still a small piece of him that he wants to keep to himself. Perhaps that's the case for everyone. Something they don't share with anyone else; something that reveals who they really are. His father flashes briefly into his head before he pushes him out again. Maybe he's more like him than he wants to admit.

Sophie has trusted him with secrets that he's certain she hasn't told another living soul, but there are things she doesn't tell him too. He'd been surprised when he'd opened her bedside drawer last night and seen Layla's things in there. Surprised, but not shocked. After all, he knows what his wife is capable of.

She opens her eyes.

'Morning, sleepyhead.'

He leans over and gives her a kiss. She smiles, and he realizes for a fraction of a second that she's forgotten the events of last night. Then she blinks and her smile fades.

'I texted Layla an hour ago, but she says there's been no change,' he says. 'I'll get some things together for Nate. Do you want to do the same for her?'

She sits up and yawns.

'Should we take her in a towel? Maybe there are showers at the hospital she can use.'

'Why don't you WhatsApp her and ask?' He hesitates. 'And see if she's remembered where she left her keys,' he adds, 'we could take those in for her too.'

Sophie looks at him, her blue eyes wide, her pupils fixed. A picture of innocence. 'I think she's got more important things to be worrying about right now than her keys, Jude.'

She slides out of bed and smooths the sheet behind her before plumping up the pillows, makes no mention of the fact that Layla's keys are sitting in her bedside drawer. 'Give me a few minutes to jump in the shower and then we can go.'

Sometimes, he thinks, his wife is almost as good at hiding things as he is.

The taxi takes them inland, out of Pererenan and away from the coast. Through the back-seat window, Jude can see horned cattle knee-deep in lush green fields peering out over the grass. The road acts as a dividing line; the view out of the driver's side of the car towards Canggu is like looking at a different country. Restaurants, shops and buildings are crammed in next to one another, stretching away into the distance. Every so often they pass an area on the same side as the fields where the ground has been stripped bare and is covered in piles of logs, concrete slabs and metal rods.

'So many new developments,' Sophie says.

The taxi driver points at Kayana as they drive past.

'That hotel was only finished a few months ago,' he says. 'Owned by foreigners. They take away business from the homestays and warungs, but the profits don't get invested back into our country.'

Jude exchanges glances with Sophie, but neither of them says anything. It hadn't occurred to him to consider the impact on the Canggu economy on their night out, and when he thinks about all the places where they've spent their money since coming here, he feels slightly uncomfortable before shaking it off – he's here to have a good time; it's not his responsibility to prop up local enterprises.

They hover at the entrance to the ICU until Dr Purwanta shows them inside. Jude can see Nate is the only person in the room, his arm covered in bandages, surrounded by machines. Layla is sitting beside him and smiles when she sees them, but Jude can't help noticing the dark circles under her eyes.

'Did you get any sleep?' he asks.

Layla shrugs. 'A bit. They gave me a blanket and told me to go and lie down on one of the sofas for an hour.'

'We brought some clothes and washing stuff for you both.' Sophie puts the bag on the floor. 'How is he?'

'The same. Dr Purwanta has just been doing some more tests. Do you want to stay with him while I go and freshen up, and then we can go and get something to eat? There's a café downstairs.'

'I'll nip to the gents before we grab a coffee.' Jude follows Layla out of the room and down the corridor. 'How are you holding up?' he asks. 'Is there anything we can do?'

'I don't think there's anything anyone can do.' She squeezes his arm, and he notices her nails aren't painted, unlike Sophie's; hers are always perfectly manicured. 'But thanks for asking.' She hesitates. 'I feel I owe you. You're always rescuing me – just like you did in London.'

Jude places his hand on top of hers. 'I'm not doing anything Nate wouldn't do if the situation was reversed.'

She steps forward and gives him a hug before pulling away and disappearing into the ladies. He watches her go and, for a moment, doesn't move, senses a heaviness in the air, as if something has been left unfinished between them. He waits, hoping she might come out again, but she doesn't.

He gets back to the ICU before she does. Sophie is leaning over Nate's bed, wiping his face with one of the flannels he'd packed in Nate's washbag.

'Do you think we should call his parents?' she asks.

'Let's wait to see what Dr Purwanta says.'

The entire situation feels surreal. Less than twelve hours ago they were drinking cocktails and dancing in a beach club. How the hell have they ended up here?

When Layla comes back, they head downstairs to the café, the nurses smiling as they walk past. The place has more in common with a flash hotel than a hospital.

The café is larger than he expected; a dozen or so white melamine tables and dark wooden chairs arranged in the middle and a counter at one end of the room with four large refrigerated units containing a variety of sandwiches and snacks.

Sophie and Layla sit down while Jude goes up to order. He returns with coffees and a packet of sandwiches and starts to unwrap the plastic packaging, not hungry in the slightest. Layla's ringtone trills and the colour drains out of her face as she answers her phone.

'It's Nate,' she says, getting up. 'Something's happened.'

38. Layla

Dr Purwanta is standing by Nate's bed, two nurses either side of her, the machines beeping loudly as the numbers flash red.

'What is it? What's wrong with him?' Layla's words are garbled as they spill out of her mouth.

Please let him be OK. I don't care if he's a fucking idiot. Just don't let him die.

'Nate is fine,' Dr Purwanta says. 'It looked like there was a problem with his breathing, but it turns out one of the tubes connected to his oxygen had become loose.'

Jude frowns. 'How can a tube become loose if he isn't moving?'

'It happens occasionally,' Dr Purwanta says. 'It may have become dislodged while we were doing our tests, but I can assure you there is nothing to worry about. The machines alert us immediately if there is an issue. I think one of my nursing colleagues was a little overzealous in calling you.'

She turns to Jude. 'It might be better if we just have one person in here with Nate at a time. I know you all want to be with your friend, but there really is nothing you can do for him right now. The drugs we're giving him will keep him in an induced coma until we know whether the swelling on his brain is going to get any worse. I suggest you all go home and get some rest. We'll call you immediately if there's any change.'

Layla looks at Jude.

'She's right,' she says. 'There isn't anything you can do. You and Sophie should go back to the villa.'

'You need a break too,' Jude says.

Layla's phone buzzes and she glances at the screen, then shakes her head and ignores the message that has arrived from Alex. She can't deal with it now, needs to wait until Sophie and Jude have gone.

'I'm fine, honestly,' she says quickly.

Sophie touches her arm and Layla sees her eyes well up. 'None of us are fine, Layla. I hate seeing Nate like this too, but you heard Dr Purwanta. Nate might have to stay in here for a while. You need to look after yourself, or you won't be able to look after him.'

Layla shivers. The thought of sleeping by herself in their king-size bed fills her with horror. Waking up in the pitch-dark and hearing noises is bad enough when Nate is there; she's not sure how she'd cope if he isn't.

'I'll come back a bit later,' she says. 'I'm going to call Nate's parents and let them know what's happened.' She hesitates. 'Maybe you could say a prayer for him, if you believe in that kind of thing.'

She watches the two of them walk away, a curdled mix of guilt and relief swilling around her insides. They've only just arrived and now she's sending them home again. Having Sophie here makes her nervous, like those first few visits to Nate's parents when she didn't know them very well and felt like she had to be on her best behaviour. And although she knows it's selfish, part of her wants to keep Nate all to herself. Spend every minute she can with him. Make sure she understands exactly what's going on at all times.

She gets out her phone, opens Alex's message.

You wanted to talk?

She types a thumbs-up emoji back, followed by *Give me two minutes*. She kisses Nate's wrist, then gets up and walks out of ICU to the end of the corridor by the toilets and calls Alex back.

'I didn't expect to hear from you again,' he says.

She swallows. 'I'm in hospital. Nate was hit by a scooter.'

There's a short silence.

'Is he OK?'

'Don't pretend you care,' she says. 'What did you get him to do for you?'

Another pause.

'If I had any business with Nate,' he says, 'it stays between the two of us.'

Yes, she thinks. I bet it does.

'After what happened last time, I thought I made it quite clear that I didn't want anything to do with you.'

He laughs. 'You did. Crystal. And I haven't. My dealings have all been with Nate. I did warn you there were risks with crypto at the time. Don't forget that.'

She swallows her anger. There's no point in going over old ground. He'd been so persuasive, had sounded so knowledgeable when she'd met him eight months ago. Had reeled her in, made her feel special, had flirted with her outrageously during their various clandestine meetings, and then she'd watched as half her inheritance had vanished into thin air. They'd had a row outside HiveHub so furious that other people had turned to watch them, their Beats headphones slung round their necks.

She hadn't told Nate. She had been too ashamed to

admit how stupid she'd been, trusting Alex with her money. And it wasn't just that. She still cringed every time she thought about how ridiculous her behaviour had been – how she'd believed Alex had actually fancied her. She'd been horrified a few months later when Nate told her he'd met someone called Alex at ConnectZen who traded cryptocurrency.

'I gave you an opportunity to earn back your losses,' he says. 'You were the one who chose not to take it.'

'Maybe because I didn't want to get involved in something that carries a death sentence,' Layla snaps back.

'Well, Nate clearly sees things rather differently,' Alex says. 'I don't know what you've said to him, but I need to talk to him, and he's not answering his phone. Can you pass on a message?'

'Not really,' Layla says flatly. 'He's in a coma.'

There's another silence.

'Well, you can help me out while he's indisposed, then,' Alex continues. 'You might be aware that a mutual friend of ours, Bryce, met up with Nate last night. I asked him to let me know the exact weight of the bag Nate gave him.' He pauses. 'It was three grams less than I expected.'

Fuck.

There's a silence, and then she hears Alex let out a sigh.

'I take it that doesn't come as a surprise to you,' he says. 'And to be honest, it doesn't to me, either. Reputation is everything in this business. I had a feeling Nate had been ripping me off for a while – a few grams here and there – I presume he thought I wouldn't notice, but it all adds up. And this time I made a point of double-checking what Bryce came out of Tide with to be absolutely certain Nate was the one responsible. The minute he's out of hospital, we'll be having a chat about how much he owes me, but to give you a heads-up, I reckon it's at least thirty million rupiah. Plus interest. A lot of interest, by the way. We're looking at double that figure at least. I don't like being taken for a fool, Layla, so in order to not piss me off any more than I am already, let's start by you giving me back what Nate took last night.'

Her skin prickles as he goes silent again.

'I'll come round to the villa later this evening,' he says, finally. 'And I expect you to have it ready. Otherwise, I'll be forced to pay Nate a visit. And I don't think either of us want that, do we?'

39. Sophie

Sophie has been sitting in the garden for most of the afternoon, scrolling through social media and checking WhatsApp for any messages from Layla. She doesn't want to sunbathe – how can she do anything vaguely enjoyable when Nate is lying in a coma? She's staying in the shade, slipping into the pool to swim a couple of lengths when the heat gets too much to bear.

Her mind plays back images of Nate's body sliding across the tarmac, over and over on a loop in her head. She feels she should be doing something but doesn't know what. She hates just sitting around, can't cope with this wait-and-see-what-happens approach.

What if he doesn't regain consciousness?

She wonders whether Layla will completely fall apart again. Judging by the words carved into the back of her wardrobe, she's already closer to the edge than people realize. And as much as part of Sophie wants that, as much as she thinks the life coaching and spiritual stuff is all a load of bollocks and that Layla is still lying to her about what she did at their wedding, she can't help feeling sorry for her. Nothing compares to the emotional devastation of losing someone close to you.

She looks across at Jude, who is draped over an inflatable alligator in the pool, his body too long to fit on it properly.

'Why don't we go out and get something to eat?' she asks. 'Get an early dinner.'

He slides off, swims to the side and pulls himself out before rubbing his hair with a towel.

'Shouldn't we wait for Layla?' he asks.

'She said she's going to grab something at the hospital, and I'm hungry now.'

'Still no news on Nate?'

Sophie checks her phone again and shakes her head. 'We could walk up the road to that Italian place?'

Jude nods. 'OK. Let me just get changed.'

They head up the scruffy main road that has no pavements, taking refuge behind palm trees when the occasional scooter flies past. She blocks out flashbacks to the screech of metal and the smell of petrol, flinches when a driver sounds their horn. Ten-metre-tall bamboo poles, the tops arched over in a curve, stand at the side of the road every fifty or so yards. Each one is covered in ornate decorations made of fruit, rice and vegetables.

'I keep seeing those everywhere,' she says.

'Nate said they're called penjor,' Jude says. 'Something to do with one of the festivals they have out here.'

Sophie raises her eyebrows. Festivals and hand-clapping stuff is more Layla's kind of thing than hers. Jude takes a few photos, then checks his phone for messages.

'You know she'll call us if there's any news.' Sophie wants to reassure herself as much as Jude but is just as desperate for an update as he is.

The restaurant, Bottega Italiana, is a white building set a few feet back from the road; giant ceramic pots filled with bright pink flowers sit on the steps outside. Glass doors stretch across the front of the building, and a pergola has been constructed at the front, the roof covered in bamboo canes to provide shade, the rectangular stone patio underneath filled with half a dozen painted wooden tables and chairs.

'In or out?' Jude asks.

'Out,' Sophie says. She's had enough of being blasted by air-conditioning at the hospital.

A Balinese waiter brings them over a couple of menus. She chooses *cotoletta* – pan-seared chicken breast with cherry tomatoes – and orders a large glass of Gavi, while Jude has *frutti di mare* with pappardelle and a beer. Small terracotta pots filled with overhanging greenery are suspended from the canes of the pergola above them.

'It doesn't feel right to be here without them, does it?' Jude says. 'I just keep wanting to go back to when we left Tide and do it again, but this time make sure Nate just gets straight into the taxi.'

'At least they picked up on the methanol poisoning,' Sophie says. 'If we'd made it back to the villa, no one would have even realized. Do you think his parents will come out?'

Jude looks at her. 'Wouldn't you? If it was your child?'

Sophie nods but doesn't answer. Children are a razor-sharp topic between them that they've rowed about too many times before. She knows how much he wants them; he knows she wants to wait. At the moment there is nothing left to discuss. She's told him it all comes down to finances; to the fact she wants them to have a place of their own and enough savings to feel secure, but it's more complicated than that. She isn't sure whether she even wants a baby. The relationship she has with her mother isn't one she wants to inflict on anyone else; doesn't want to risk repeating history.

The waiter comes back with the drinks. Jude takes a mouthful of his beer and then gets up.

'Should have gone before we left, won't be a sec.'

He leaves his phone on the table and Sophie picks it up as she takes a sip of her chilled white wine, enlarges the photo he'd taken of the penjor and wonders how long it took someone to bend coconut-palm leaves into those shapes. She can't imagine anyone taking the time to do something like that at home. She might not believe in God, but she recognizes that there's a spiritual element to life out here that's lacking in London – the sense there's something bigger than themselves. She'd felt it walking up Mount Batur as well.

She goes to put Jude's phone down but changes her mind and opens his email instead, feeling a twinge of guilt as she does so. They never look through each other's phones, but he's so touchy about the whole redundancy thing, it's a good opportunity for her to see if he's heard anything from Bearmans' without her having to ask. At least then she'll know what she's dealing with. Can put out a few feelers with recruitment agents in the City without him being any the wiser.

There's nothing in his inbox, so she checks his trash, scrolls past dozens of spam messages until she sees one from a sender which makes her stop.

J_carson@met.police.uk

Why is Jude being sent emails from the Met Police?

She goes to open it when she feels a hand on her shoulder and the phone is snatched from her.

'What are you doing?'

She flushes. 'I was just looking at the photos you took of the penjor.'

'You were going through my emails.'

She takes another sip of her wine, decides it will make things worse if she lies.

'I wanted to know if Bearmans' had said anything else about redundancies.'

'Why didn't you just ask me?' he snaps.

'Because you're so bloody stressed about Nate. I hate not knowing what's going on, Jude. We might not have anywhere to stay if Nate's parents come out here, and if we have to go back to London sooner than we planned, I need to know what's happening with your job.'

'I haven't heard anything,' he says quickly.

She studies him from behind her sunglasses. Her husband, who she had once thought she shared everything with.

'Why have you got an email from the police?'

'Jesus, Sophie. Is this some kind of interrogation?' He runs his hand through his hair as he sits down and takes another mouthful of beer.

'Just answer the question. Why are the police emailing you?'

He doesn't reply. She can feel her heart thumping below her ribs.

'It's about the burglary,' he says finally. 'They've decided not to investigate it any further. I didn't want to tell you as I knew you'd be upset.'

She looks at him, the salt-and-pepper colouring in his hair more obvious in the sun. Why does she feel he's not telling her the whole truth?

'Show me,' she says.

'What?'

'The email. Show it to me. I won't be upset.'

She sees his knuckles turn white as he grips his phone more tightly.

'Don't you believe me?' he asks.

What he's said makes sense, and she desperately wants to believe what he's telling her, but there's something in his eyes that makes her think he's lying, and she can't bring herself to answer. Her silence seems to ignite something inside him and he pushes his chair out from under the table.

'Fucking hell, Sophie. Why can't you just cut me some slack? If you can't trust me after everything we've—'

He breaks off and picks up his bottle of beer. 'Actually, forget it. I'm going for a walk. Call me if Layla has any news.'

He takes his wallet out of his pocket and throws a handful of rupiah notes down on the table.

'You can eat on your own. I've lost my appetite.'

40. Jude

Jude stomps back down the main road, the heat the only thing stopping him from breaking into a run. Tiny flies buzz around his face, churned up in the dust by the scooters that speed past, close enough for him to want to shout at the drivers to be more fucking careful unless they want to kill someone. No wonder his best friend is lying in a coma.

He opens up his phone, deletes the email from the police from his trash and curses himself for not doing it before. If Sophie asks to see it again he's not sure what he's going to say. Tell her he got rid of it as he didn't want to be reminded of the break-in.

Maybe he needs to bring up what he found in her bedside drawer. That should be enough to distract her. He thought she'd forgiven Layla for what happened at their wedding, but he should have known how long his wife can hold a grudge.

If only Nate hadn't said anything to Sophie, this would never have happened. What if he's been careless with their other secrets? Have they slipped out in a moment of indiscretion too? Has he told Layla? He just has to hope those are buried too deep to reach. If Nate would just wake up, he could talk to him about it. A sudden memory of them both messing around in the pool after he arrived in Canggu flashes into his head and he has to swallow the lump that rises up in his throat.

Perhaps he should just tell Sophie he's been made redundant. Rip off the Band-Aid and get it over with. The seed has already been sown; it's not as if it will come as a huge shock.

You know why you can't do that.

She'll ask to see the letter from Bearmans', will insist on running it past a solicitor who specializes in employment law to check the terms are fair. She'll want to go back to London and start lining up appointments with recruiters, who will take one look at the reason his job was terminated and tell him they can't help. He slaps his arm as he feels one of the flies biting him, misses it and swears when he sees a raised red lump on his skin.

He needs to stick to the plan he'd made before they arrived in Bali. Make Sophie fall in love with the lifestyle out here; show her everything they could benefit from as digital nomads, compared to living in London.

Nate ending up in hospital has really thrown a spanner in the works. Something he couldn't have anticipated. Sophie's right – if Nate's parents do decide to fly out, he and Sophie will have to find somewhere else to stay. And now he's no longer got a salary, that's not going to be feasible for long.

He passes the entrance to the villa, the large wooden double gates shut tight, and keeps walking, welcoming the shade that envelops him as he ducks beneath the banana-palm leaves overhanging the road. He can see several penjor and a few dozen scooters parked at the end of the road which leads straight on to the beach. More rustic-looking cafés with thatched roofs, mismatched tables and chairs, chest freezers full of ice cream and vending machines dispensing cans of Coke and Pepsi line the road, along with street vendors sitting beside food carts beneath tatty garden parasols.

The long beach stretches away in both directions. Surfers are out in force, riding the large waves beneath the setting sun. For a few seconds Jude finds himself looking for Nate among them before he remembers and the hole in his chest expands again. He checks his phone as he walks across the black sand and plonks himself down on one of the beanbags, but there are still no messages from Layla. Or Sophie.

He knows he can't stay here for long, that he's going to have to go back and face his wife. He's normally good at controlling his emotions, compartmentalizes everything into boxes, but Nate's accident feels like a bomb has exploded and scattered his feelings all over the place. He takes a deep breath, lets his worries dissipate as he gazes out over the ocean. Bearmans' can't touch him out here – he shouldn't waste valuable energy even thinking about them.

'Jude?'

He feels a tap on his shoulder and looks around, but doesn't recognize the man standing beside him.

'Yes?'

'It's Nyoman Santi. Nate's site manager. We met when you came to visit the building site.'

'Of course.' Jude shakes the man's outstretched hand. 'I remember.'

There's an awkward silence as Nyoman smiles at him.

'How's the villa coming along?' Jude asks. He's here for some peace and quiet, doesn't want to start a conversation.

'It's progressing well.' Nyoman hesitates. 'I was hoping

to speak to Nate about a few things actually. I've called and left messages, but he hasn't got back to me.'

Jude frowns. 'Oh shit, sorry. Of course, you don't know – there was an accident. With a scooter. Nate's in hospital.'

Nyoman frowns. 'Nate got run over?'

Jude nods. 'He's in a coma with a serious head injury.'

There's another silence.

'I'm so sorry to hear that,' Nyoman says. 'My questions about the build can wait. Can you let Layla know I am thinking of her? Tell her I will make an offering for Nate. Good people do not deserve bad things to happen to them.'

'No, they don't,' Jude agrees. 'And of course I'll tell her.'

Nyoman nods again, then walks away across the beach, leaving Jude sitting on his beanbag. His phone buzzes. A WhatsApp from Layla.

Leaving hospital now. Dr says they might try reducing his sedation as MRI shows brain function is good and swelling seems stable. But she's still worried about possible kidney damage from methanol. See you in a bit x

He sends a thumbs-up emoji in reply, then types a message to Sophie.

I'm sorry. Everything with Nate has really stressed me out. Heading back to villa now. Will make it up to you x

He watches the surfers for a bit longer, wonders how long it took them to get to this point. Whether it becomes effortless, or whether they are always learning. Is it the same with every hobby?

It isn't until he's off the beach and back on the main road that what Nyoman said really sinks in. *Good people do not deserve bad things to happen to them.* He has a flashback to him and Nate walking down the corridor in their university house. Of Nate opening the bathroom door and them both flinching in horror.

Is Nate really a good person?

And, for that matter, is he?

41. 2007

'James?' Kristin's shrieks are swept away by the noise of the rapids.

I scan the water and spot his red helmet bob up a few feet away. He splutters as he breaks the surface. The boat turns on the spot, caught in an eddy, and for one terrible moment I think he's going to be swept straight past us, but his fingers manage to grab on to the safety line and we haul him back in. Kristin is still crying as she scrunches up the sopping-wet hem of his T-shirt in her fist and refuses to let go.

I should have cancelled the trip as soon as I saw the water levels. Made Dan trek back up the steps and told Kadek to abandon the job.

James rearranges himself on the seat, wipes his face with his hand and adjusts his grip on his paddle.

'Are you OK?' I ask.

He nods. 'I'm fine.'

The others stare at him, and I wonder if they can hear the same tremble in his voice that I can, despite his efforts to hide it.

He pats Kristin's leg. 'Honestly, I'm OK. I've been in rougher scrums on a rugby pitch.'

Dan lets out a guffaw and James grins, the colour returning to his face. Mia and Ashley exchange looks as, finally, the waterfall appears.

The muscles in my legs spasm as we paddle into the sheltered area. The stream of water gushes down through the vegetation in the canyon above our heads, then falls over the rocks which jut out over the edge of the pool. James continues to grin inanely and won't stop talking – I can't work out whether he's still in shock or high on adrenaline.

Buddy jumps into the water – luckily it's shallow enough to stand up in, but I wish he'd checked with me first. The others follow, Kristin still gripping James's T-shirt. I'm relieved Ashley has her hand in the water as the backpackers splash each other. I didn't tell her before we set off, but tomcat stings can leave a nasty scar – I just hope we caught hers in time.

I retrieve my phone from the waterproof bag and pick up a voice-mail from Kadek. He sounds breathless, like he's been running; I have to listen to the message twice for my brain to properly process the words.

Police came. Had to run.

Shit.

Shit.

'Shall we get going, then?' Buddy climbs back into the boat and shakes himself dry like a dog, looking over at Mia to make sure she's watching as he flexes his muscles.

I hesitate, conscious of the cramping in my shoulders and the frustration that all this has been for nothing now Kadek has abandoned the van.

'I think we should get out here and walk back,' I say. 'The current is stronger than I thought it would be, and that first stretch was hard enough.'

Buddy frowns. 'But we've come this far. I think we should finish.'

'I don't think that's a good idea,' I say.

He shrugs. 'You said two boats have already done it today. If they can manage it, there's no reason we can't. Don't start going all health and safety on us.'

He looks over to where Mia and Ashley are still laughing under

233

the waterfall and I experience a brief twinge of sympathy for his desperation to impress.

'Guys!' he shouts. 'Shall we make a move?'

The others start to wade back towards the boat.

'I don't think we should go any further,' I say.

'Come on,' Buddy says. 'Don't be a killjoy.'

'The other boats had to stop a bit further downstream,' I blurt out. 'It wasn't safe.'

Buddy hesitates. 'Why didn't you say anything before?'

I swallow. 'I only just found out.'

He stares at me.

'Really?'

I nod, but his raised eyebrows make it clear he doesn't believe me.

James has now clambered back into the boat and is listening to our conversation. There's no way I can show them Kadek's texts unless I want them to know what we've been up to. I grip my phone more tightly.

Buddy holds out his hand and pulls Mia back on board, making a big show of his efforts.

'Are we going, then?' she asks. 'Ashley says her hand is still hurting.'

'I don't think it's safe,' I repeat quietly.

Buddy looks at Mia, who frowns in confusion, and then at his father. In James's expression, I can see all the traits he's passed on to his son. The arrogance that comes from wealth and a sense of entitlement.

'I fell in and was fine,' James says. 'It's all part of the experience, isn't it? I think we should carry on to the end.'

'Maybe we need to—'

Kristin starts to speak, but James holds up his hand and she stops, mid-sentence.

'We're not quitters,' James continues. He turns to the others, dismissing me. 'How about we vote? Who wants to give it a try?'

'We can't give it a try, James,' I say. 'Once we start, we can't stop.'

He scrutinizes me and the gap between us widens. 'It's a turn of phrase,' he says tightly. 'My family are up for carrying on. Who else is?'

Mia looks at Buddy, who winks.

'I am,' she says.

'Good girl.' James turns to Dan. 'You're not going to back out on us now, are you?'

'What d'you think, babe?' Dan says.

Jen shrugs. 'I'm in if you are.'

'So that's a majority.' Buddy can't disguise the triumph in his voice. He leans towards me and puts his face a couple of inches away from mine.

'I think we should go now.'

He hands Mia her paddle and then slaps me on my shoulder, making it throb worse than ever.

'Don't stress, mate. Might be a bit of a rougher ride than you're used to, but trust me, we're going to be absolutely fine.'

42. Layla

Layla unfastens her talisman pendant and wraps it around Nate's wrist so that the turquoise eye faces outwards. She struggles to do up the clasp – it's too fiddly for her stubby nails to get a proper grip. The nurses will probably take it off, but she wants him to wear it overnight while she can't be here. Something to ward off the negativity she can sense hovering in the corner of the room, waiting for her to leave so it can lie down beside him and run its fingers over his shaved head.

This is her fault. It's always her fault. Terrible things happen to the people she loves because she is a bad person. She should have learned this by now – she'd thought that by coming to Bali, by starting afresh, by helping others, things would be different. But she's beginning to think she doesn't deserve to be happy. People with a guilty conscience never do.

She checks her phone, but there are no more messages from Alex. She sends a WhatsApp to Jude and Sophie to let them know she's on her way back, kisses Nate's bandaged arm and picks up his rucksack.

As she heads out of ICU towards reception, she unzips the side pocket of the bag and feels around for the cling-film wrap, hopes none of it has fallen out. She'd have a problem explaining that to Alex.

It's not there.

The pocket is empty.

A clammy sweat prickles across her chest.

She must be looking in the wrong place. She stops, puts the rucksack down and crouches beside it, unzips every pocket and searches through all of them, her efforts becoming more and more frantic. It's not there.

It's got to be there.

She forces herself to take a few deep breaths, then repeats the process, her hands shaking as she runs them around the inside of the fabric, feeling right to the very bottom.

It's gone.

Fuck.

What the hell is she going to tell Alex? Nate already owes him three grand – which they can't afford – there's no way she's admitting she's lost what he took yesterday. She clasps the bag against her chest as she heads downstairs to reception. She doesn't understand. She's had Nate's rucksack with her the entire time since they got to the hospital. The clingfilm wrap can't have just disappeared. One of the nurses must have taken it. Or one of the cleaners?

Fuck. Fuck. Fuck.

She walks out through the glass doors and orders a taxi before looking up to find a familiar face grinning at her. The man she wishes they'd never met.

'What are you doing here?'

'I thought I'd come and see Nate,' Wayan Santi says. 'Everyone's talking about what happened.'

Half the people who frequent HiveHub and Connect-Zen would have been in Tide when they were there. It doesn't take long for word to get around.

Wayan looks at her. 'How is he?'

'He's in intensive care. You won't be allowed in.'

She knows why Wayan has come here, and it's not to visit Nate. Three days. She'd completely forgotten.

'Yours?' Wayan asks as she glances at her taxi as it pulls up. 'We can go back to Pererenan together. Sort out what you agreed to get me on the way.' He walks over to the car and opens the door, waits for her to get inside.

She clings tightly to Nate's rucksack and hopes that, somehow, what Alex wants will be in there the next time she looks.

The driver pulls away and they sit in silence.

'It's blackmail, you know,' she says, finally.

'It's my land,' Wayan replies.

'We bought it off you.'

'Foreigners can't officially buy land in Bali,' he says. 'You know that. You can't own land or property under the Hak Milik title.'

Layla frowns. 'I know that *now*. But when your solicitor introduced us and you agreed to act as our nominee, he told us it wouldn't be a problem, and so did you. We've always been up front with you. You knew we were going to build a villa on the plot and we paid the full amount you asked for. We didn't even try and negotiate on the price. I can't believe you're now demanding more.'

'You can always give the land back to me,' Wayan says.

'We've almost finished building the villa!'

Wayan smiles. 'Then you know what you need to do. And if you don't pay and I take you to court, they will enforce the law and return the land to me.' He hesitates. 'Or I could talk to Nate about it when he wakes up.'

She presses her fingers against her temples.

'We agreed you wouldn't do that,' she says.

'I'm sure Nate would be interested to see how friendly you and Alex were a few months ago.' He pulls out his phone. 'I can show you the photos again if you want?'

Layla shakes her head, remembering how Alex had leaned over the table to kiss her, how she'd pulled away, but only after a few seconds during which she'd felt her body swim with a mixture of guilt and desire.

'I'll give you the money,' she says. 'But that's everything I have, Wayan. Everything. We don't even have enough to finish the build, and I have no idea how we're going to manage to pay rent on the place we're staying in this month.'

She gets out her phone and makes a bank transfer, shows him the screen.

'Satisfied?'

Wayan nods as the taxi hits a queue of traffic. Scooters overtake them, the sound of their horns making her flinch away from the window.

'You said we could trust you,' she says. 'But you lied, didn't you? Our new solicitor told me it's one of the most common mistakes foreign investors make in Bali. And if you ask me for any more money, I'm telling you now, I don't have it.'

The taxi crawls past Kayana and she looks out of the window at the lake at the front of the hotel, her eyes pricking.

'You see that?' Wayan points to the small run-down warung beside the huge new hotel. 'That was my restaurant. My business. I am having to close it. I have had to tell all my staff to find other jobs. When Kayana opened, I couldn't make enough to stay open any more. The tourists, they flock to see the celebrity chef and drink in the terrace bar. My warung had been open for twenty years and this hotel bankrupted it in under three months. I would like the owners to suffer like my family is suffering, but they don't live in Canggu, they take all their profits abroad. Asking you for more money was not the plan,' he adds. 'But I do not have a choice.'

A hollow feeling spreads through Layla's chest as she looks out of the taxi window at the dozens of tourists walking into the hotel. She hadn't realized Wayan's situation was so dire. She'd heard rumours about locals in Canggu losing their businesses to foreign companies but hadn't really taken much notice.

She'd assumed that both she and Nate had integrated into the local community but realizes they've morphed into something more akin to expats. Same clique, just a different name. They're nothing more than long-term tourists – people who claim to be searching for a better way of life but in reality just want go abroad for however long it suits them. Who take advantage of a few hours of remote working each week to exploit the cheaper cost of living without ever giving back.

'You know Alex invested in Kayana,' she says eventually. 'He helped put the owners in touch with the right people to get it built out here in the first place.'

Wayan looks at her and she meets his eyes, unblinking.

'I just thought you might want to know,' she adds.

43. Sophie

Sophie picks up Jude's message as she's finishing the last pieces of her pan-seared chicken. She'd sent back his seafood pasta after apologizing to the waiter, saying her husband had suddenly felt unwell. He'd nodded sympathetically when she'd suggested it was probably heatstroke; too much lying around by the pool without enough sunscreen.

'It happens to so many tourists.'

'We're not really tourists,' she'd said, sipping her second large glass of Gavi. 'We're here on sabbatical. Staying with our friends who live here. Bali is such an incredible country.'

The waiter had smiled politely, but Sophie had cringed inwardly as soon as the words left her mouth. Two glasses of wine on an empty stomach had turned her into one of those people she'd despised before she came out here – someone who thinks spending a few days on holiday means they understand the nuances and culture of another country, when they haven't so much as scratched the surface.

She believes Jude when he says he'll make it up to her. He always does. She's convinced his hissy fit is nothing to do with being stressed about Nate and everything to do with that email from the police. She just needs to pick the right time to approach him. Invisible fingers tap at the back of her brain, a reminder of something she should know, but can't remember. Maybe it will come back to her.

She drains her glass and orders a taxi. It's almost seven o'clock and although it's still hot, the sun has set. She can't face the thought of trudging along in the dark, scooters scaring the shit out of her every time they go past, and doesn't want to risk an encounter with any of the street dogs that congregate in packs, even if Nate maintains they're harmless.

When she pulls up outside the villa, another taxi is driving away. For a moment she thinks she can see someone sitting in the back seat, but as Layla is already standing by the gates, she dismisses it as a trick of the light – the moon casting shadows and creating familiar shapes in her imagination.

'How's Nate?' Sophie asks as she climbs out of the taxi.

'He seems the same . . . I guess we'll know more when they start reducing his sedation.' Layla frowns. 'Where's Jude?'

'He didn't feel well,' Sophie says quickly. 'We went out to eat, but he left early and came back here.'

Layla presses the intercom and Sophie notices her hands are trembling. She really hopes that Jude is back already. There's no answer, and Layla presses the buzzer again. Sophie threads the gold chain around her neck through her fingers.

'Where is he?' Layla holds the button down, the sharp noise cutting through the silence. Finally, there's a scuffling sound and Jude's muffled voice comes through the speaker.

'Layla? Sorry, I couldn't work out how to let you in. Hang on.' There's another silence and then a click as the gates swing open.

'You not feeling well?' Layla asks Jude as she walks up the steps into the villa.

He glances at Sophie.

'I'm OK now,' he says. 'Just a bit too much sun this afternoon. How's Nate?'

'The same.' Layla grabs a bottle of water out of the fridge, takes a few gulps and wipes her forehead. 'I think one of his friends might call round this evening.'

'Do they not think you've got enough on your plate at the moment?' Sophie asks.

Layla smiles tightly. 'It's fine. They just want to drop off some headphones they borrowed. It'll only take a minute.'

'Have you eaten?' Sophie says. 'Do you want us to get you anything?'

Layla shakes her head. 'I'm not hungry. I could do with a drink though.'

'I'll get it,' Jude says. 'What do you want?'

'A gin and tonic? More gin than tonic.' She fumbles as she pulls out a bar stool. 'Thanks, Jude.'

'Do you want me to take that?' Sophie points at the rucksack that Layla is still clinging on to.

Layla shakes her head. 'No, it's fine. It probably sounds stupid, but I feel connected to Nate when I'm holding it.' Sophie knows exactly what she means. She'd slept with Jess's toy rabbit for years after she'd died, until it had fallen apart at the seams, depositing clumps of filling all over her bed.

The buzzer on the intercom sounds again and Layla

jumps up. She disappears into the hall as Jude is still pouring her drink.

'She looks awful,' he mutters quietly.

Sophie nods, trying to listen to the mumbled conversation that's taking place over the intercom. She hears the front door open. Jude brushes past her, picks up a lemon from the bowl on the windowsill, then tilts her chin up with his finger and plants a kiss on her forehead. She puts her arms around him and slides her hands into the back pockets of his shorts.

'I'm sorry,' he says.

'We'll talk about it later.' She steps backwards and puts her finger on his lips, struck by a pang of loneliness as she realizes she can't remember the last time she touched his face that intimately, then walks quietly into the hallway, following in Layla's footsteps. The front door is open and she can see Layla standing at the bottom of the driveway talking to someone beside the carved wooden gate. Their voices are muffled, but Layla is speaking faster than usual. Sophie watches her unzip one of the rucksack pockets and hold it out to show the man, who throws it on the ground and brings his face so close to Layla's that Sophie can no longer see a gap between them. If it wasn't for Layla's rigid posture, she could almost mistake it for a moment of intimacy.

Sophie flicks the switch that turns on the outdoor lights, bathing the driveway in brightness. She squints, his figure familiar. Is that Alex? She watches him recoil and shrink back into the shadows.

'I won't be a sec,' Layla shouts.

Sophie hesitates, then turns around and goes back into

the kitchen. Jude hands her a gin and tonic and she takes a large sip, having a sudden desire to forget about everything – Nate's coma, her row with Jude, the burglary, the scooter driver lying in a morgue somewhere. She rolls her shoulders as she hears the front door click shut, trying to dispel the feeling of sadness that has permeated through her skin and attached itself to something deep inside her.

Layla dumps the rucksack on the floor and scratches her neck as she climbs up on to the bar stool. She holds out her hand for the gin and tonic Jude has poured, the opal beads on her meditation bracelet clinking against the glass.

'Is everything OK?' Jude asks.

'Yes,' she says. 'There was just a bit of a misunderstanding, but it's sorted.'

'Was that Alex?' Sophie asks. 'I thought I recognized him.'

Layla takes a sip of her drink and shakes her head.

'A guy called Chris. He was one of the crowd in Kayana so he probably looked familiar.'

Sophie glances at the rucksack. 'He didn't give you the headphones then?'

Layla hesitates, then shakes her head. 'But it's fine, honestly.'

'You sure?' Jude looks sceptical.

Layla nods as she fiddles with her bracelet.

'Well, I'm going to have a shower and get an early night,' Sophie says. 'What time do we need to get going in the morning?'

'Maybe we should let Layla see Nate on her own,' Jude says. 'We're more than happy to come in if you want us to,' he continues, looking at Layla, 'but I understand you might want some privacy and we don't want to get in your way.'

'Thanks,' Layla says. 'Dr Purwanta did say she wasn't keen to have lots of people around when they're trying to bring Nate out of the coma, so perhaps it would be good to have a bit of time by ourselves.'

Sophie ignores the sharp sting of rejection. 'Whatever you think best. Jude and I can come in later, just Whats-App whenever you want. You know we're both here to support you.'

She leans in to give Layla a hug goodnight and can't help noticing the smell on her skin – part bleach, part something sour, as if fear is leaking out of her pores.

She walks down to their bedroom and sits on the bed. The low tone of Jude's voice floats out from the living room as Sophie leans across and opens the drawer of her bedside table. She looks at the squashed piece of clingfilm that she'd found in Nate's rucksack in hospital when Layla had gone to the toilet. She thinks back to being in Tide, of Nate handing her his bag when they'd been in the queue, and experiences a rush of nausea. Had this been inside it?

She pushes the drawer shut and tells herself not to be stupid. Nate is one of her closest friends. There's no way he'd do that to her. Would he?

44. Jude

'Don't do that, Soph.'

Jude sticks his hand out as Sophie takes a photo of him, tries to block her with his palm. The flash on her camera phone is so bright it burns his eyes. She lets out a small laugh, but doesn't stop, takes another and then another until the flashes blind him and he's fumbling around in a sea of whiteness, trying to find her hand to grab the phone and make her stop, but she's moved away and now he can hear a baby crying and someone is telling him that Nate's dead, but that's impossible because Nate can't be dead, he's known Nate since they were eighteen and they've been through so much together, and the sound of the baby crying is getting louder and he wants to tell it to stop, but then he realizes it's not a baby, it's a girl, and he's back at the house he shared with Nate at university in Exeter and he's walking behind him across the beige carpet with that stained patch towards their bathroom and can see the closed door ahead of them, its four panels painted in white gloss paint and its chipped handle, and he knows without a shadow of a doubt that Nate MUST NOT open it because under no circumstances do they want to see what's behind it, but a part of him already knows. He can feel it – a terrible twisting in his guts, as if someone has scraped out his insides and replaced them with snakes, and the handle on the door is opening anyway

and he can't look away and his legs just keep moving forward and—

'Jude?'

He feels someone's hand on his cheek.

'Jude!'

He opens his eyes to find Sophie staring at him.

'Are you OK? You were shouting.'

There's a slick sheen of perspiration across his chest
and under his neck that he can feel when he moves his
head. The blinds in the bedroom are still drawn and the
room is composed of different shades of grey – just light
enough to see, but without his glasses on, everything is
blurred.

'Bad dream,' he says. 'About Nate.' He rubs his eyes,
looks at the illuminated digits on the alarm clock: 07:00.

Sophie bites her lip. 'I don't think Layla should go to
the hospital by herself.'

'We talked about this last night. It's her decision,' he
says. 'We'll go in later.'

He studies her. The woman he knows so much better
than she thinks he does. Who he swore to love, honour
and cherish until death. In sickness and in health. Does
hiding things from the person closest to you constitute
a kind of sickness? He reaches for her, but she turns
away and takes a sip of water from the bottle on her
bedside table.

'Did Layla say if she'd spoken to Nate's parents?'
she asks.

'Yes. They're looking into flights, but she's going to call
them to let them know what happens today.'

He fiddles with a couple of loose threads on the edge

of the duvet, feels his mouth go dry. He's not going home. Not yet, anyway. He brushes a strand of blonde hair away from her face. 'Soph, are you sure everything's OK between you and Layla?'

She nods. 'I told you before we came out here, it's fine. I haven't forgotten what she did, but I know she wasn't in a great place, and we've put it behind us.'

Her fingers reach for the bracelet he bought her, twisting the fragile gold chain around her wrist. Sophie rarely shows her vulnerability, and he wants to protect her – it's one of the reasons he married her. He doesn't care about the physical features that other people tend to notice – her blue eyes, dimples or great body. He's drawn to the things only he sees, those things that make her so utterly unique.

He grasps her hand before she has a chance to pull away, feels for the platinum band around her finger. She lets him hold her palm for a few moments and the image of a dead fish flashes into his head; cold and limp.

'If Bearmans' are thinking about making people redundant,' she says, 'then perhaps we should go back to London so you can show them how much they need you.'

Jude swallows. 'They've put cover in place for my sabbatical,' he says. 'I don't think I can go marching back in there and tell them I've changed my mind. If we can't stay here, we can just go to a hotel or rent an Airbnb for a couple of weeks until we decide what to do next.'

'But what if—'

'Let's just take things one step at a time,' he says.

She fixes her eyes on his, and he focuses on the blue-grey colour at the centre of her iris that morphs to a dark navy around the circumference. For once, he has no idea what she's thinking. He rolls back on the pillow and stretches his arms up above his head. After yesterday afternoon in the sun, he thinks they're looking slightly more tanned, more like Nate's.

'Do you think it's too early to make a coffee?' she says. 'I don't want to disturb Layla.'

'I'm sure she's awake.'

He watches her slip on one of the towelling dressing gowns Layla put in their room and listens to Sophie's footsteps pad down the corridor into the kitchen, a sense of dread sitting in the bottom of his stomach after what he just told her about Bearmans'. Layla is already up – he hears the two of them conduct a polite morning greeting routine and then the clinking of mugs being taken out of cupboards.

He crawls across to Sophie's side of the bed, feels the warm space where her body was a few moments earlier and inhales the faint scent of pear-and-freesia perfume on her pillow. He loves that fragrance. It smells different on her than it does on anyone else. If he was blindfolded, he knows he could pick her out of a room full of women wearing it.

He hears Layla laugh and thinks back to the conversation they had last night. He's torn between desperately wanting Nate to wake up and being terrified about what his best friend might say if he does. If Nate mentions anything about Jude being fired from Bearmans', Sophie will be livid and insist they go home. And he can't have that.

He needs to have a word with Nate first, alone. And do whatever it takes to make sure he doesn't say anything.

45. Layla

He hasn't woken up.

Layla sends the WhatsApp to Jude and Sophie after Dr Purwanta leaves the ICU.

Dr P said she'll see how he is later.

She puts her cheek against Nate's chest, listens to his heartbeat, reassures herself that he's still alive and just needs more time. She's going to have to call his parents to tell them but hesitates before she dials their number, can't bring herself to destroy the hope she knows they must be nurturing right now. She'll wait. Do it later. It's still the early hours of the morning their time; she can pretend to herself that they're still asleep.

'Come on, Nate. Wake up. You can do this.' She whispers the words into his ear, runs her fingers over the bandage on his head, willing her energy to transfer itself into him.

We're coming in. A message back from Sophie pops up on her WhatsApp screen. *Be there in half an hour.*

Her stomach tightens at the thought of them all being here together in this small space, crowded around his bed. Sophie had been overfriendly this morning and it had set her teeth on edge. Dropping comments about her late-night visitor into the conversation, barbs of barely disguised interrogation that had dug into her skin.

She's told Alex she'll pay him back for the coke, but he

doesn't know she hasn't got the money. He wants thirty million rupiah plus the same again for interest and inconvenience, which takes her to three thousand pounds. Where the hell is she going to get that? She glances at Nate lying motionless on the bed, experiences a flash of rage for what he's got them into, followed by a pang of guilt. A vicious cycle of emotions that leaves her wrung out and nauseous.

She needs to get out of here.

I'm going for a drive. She messages back. *Need a break. See you at the hospital in a couple of hours.*

Nate's scooter is parked outside. She'd wondered whether to take it this morning, had thought she might get flashbacks to the accident, but driving here had been fine. Being outside and moving had actually felt liberating. She pushes her hair back out of her face and pulls her helmet on as she turns the key in the engine.

She heads out of Canggu, along the Tanah Lot bypass, past the Circle K convenience stores, the warungs, the small shops with no solid doors and frontages just a few feet wide, brooms and buckets piled up for sale on the pavement outside. She has a sudden desire to escape the noise and the traffic, to breathe in air that doesn't smell of chlorine and hasn't been filtered a dozen times through an air-conditioning system, leaving her with a headache and making her eczema itch worse than ever.

She'd done something similar after her parents' accident, back when they were still living in London. Had escaped to the Rookery in Streatham and spent hours walking around, hoping her physical exhaustion would somehow diffuse into her mind and allow her to sleep. It hadn't – the only thing that had provided some respite was vodka, bottles of it, swallowed neat until it burned her throat. She'd pass out and then wake up just a few hours later, the horror wrapped around her neck, starting to squeeze before she'd even regained consciousness.

After ten minutes of driving, she begins to leave the town behind. The shops become fewer, the spaces between them larger, filled with coconut and climbing palm trees, dark green shiny cassava bushes and jackfruit trees, their strange-looking fruit hanging in clumps like giant limes with bumpy skin.

Behind the vegetation by the roadside, paddy fields stretch away into the distance. This lush landscape is how she'd imagined Bali before she'd arrived: flowing rivers of green rice terraces cut into the hillsides. But since tourism exploded, the fields have begun to disappear, pushed further and further north by the ever-expanding urbanization that started with Kuta in the south. She wonders if at some point the development will stop, prays the country doesn't disappear completely beneath a sea of concrete.

She turns off the bypass and heads down the road towards Pura Tanah Lot, a temple supposedly guarded by a mythical snake. It stands on a rocky outcrop in the ocean which can be reached at low tide. The cave beside the temple has real snakes inside it – banded sea kraits, which are poisonous, but ones that are familiar with being handled and allegedly won't bite. It's one of Nate's favourite places. They used to come here to capture the picture-perfect postcard views at sunset. She's got the photos on her Insta grid, but today she just wants to stand and look out over the ocean. Make an appeal to whatever higher power is out there to bring Nate back to her.

She parks the scooter and walks past various stalls offering T-shirts and other souvenirs which the tourists are avidly browsing through. Giant stone pillars carved with ornate dragons stand either side of the pathway, and she passes between them, walking until she reaches the rocky beach that leads straight into the sea, the temple a couple of hundred yards further out.

She feels someone tap her shoulder and turns around to see Nyoman Suardika looking at her.

Her heart sinks. She really doesn't want company, particularly from their site manager. Nate deals with all the building stuff.

'Nyoman. What are you doing here?'

'I often come here on my days off,' he says. 'It's peaceful enough, providing you avoid the tourists.' He hesitates. 'I saw your friend yesterday. He was on the beach.'

Layla holds her hand up to shade her eyes from the sun. 'Jude? On the beach?'

Nyoman nods. 'In Pererenan. He told me about Nate. And as I said to him, good people do not deserve bad things to happen to them.'

'No,' she replies. 'They don't.'

He seems to be stating a fact rather than offering any comfort, and she doesn't know what else to say. An awkward silence follows, one which she gives in to first.

'How's the build going?'

He nods. 'It's progressing well.'

'That's great.' Her voice is devoid of enthusiasm as she

points at the rocks and dark sand – a walkable channel at low tide over to the island and the temple. 'I think I'm going to head over,' she says. 'It was good to see you, and I'll keep you updated on Nate's progress.'

'I'll come with you,' Nyoman says.

She contemplates telling him she wants to be by herself but worries that will sound rude and hopes instead that she can lose him in the gardens once they get across. Non-Balinese aren't allowed into the heart of the temple, but she isn't looking to go inside. She wants to visit the shrine, which is supposed to grant the power to heal and protect from harm. At this point, she figures anything is worth a try. They wade through the ankle-deep water, the large stones wet and slippery.

'This is one of Nate's favourite places,' she says as they reach the small island. 'He came here a lot. He used to have a real fear of the sea – someone he knew drowned when he was younger. A boating accident. It terrified him, how easily it could happen. He said he prayed for them here and it helped him come to terms with it.'

Nyoman raises his eyebrows. 'I didn't know Nate was religious.'

'He's not. I mean, not conventionally. He doesn't go to church or anything. But he said something about this place resonating with him.'

Nyoman nods slowly. 'Life does have a way of coming full circle.'

Layla winds her dark hair up into a bun to get it off her neck, ties it up with a scrunchie – she couldn't find her butterfly clip this morning – and walks over to the shrine. Two priests are blessing water from a spring, drawing symbols on people's foreheads and pressing pieces of rice on to their damp skin.

She shuts her eyes and stands very still as they carry out the same ritual on her. She thinks about Nate, wills him to wake up and get better. Willing, praying – they're the same thing. What is it some of the other digital nomads say? Manifesting. She doesn't care what they call it, she just needs it to work. Needs Nate to get better.

The priest tells her to open her eyes. He picks up a white-and-yellow frangipani flower and puts it behind her ear, and when she turns around, Nyoman has gone.

46. Sophie

Sophie is sitting by the pool with her feet in the water when the familiar ringtone of Jude's phone cuts through her thoughts. They've booked a taxi to pick them up in fifteen minutes and she wants to eke out every last moment of sunshine before they disappear inside the hospital.

She'd been desperately hoping for good news about Nate, but after Layla's message she doesn't know what to think. What if he never wakes up? She shudders at the thought of being permanently stuck in a no-man's land between life and death.

She strains to hear what Jude is saying as snippets of his conversation filter out from the living room and realizes he's talking to his mother. Sophie has what she would call a polite relationship with Sarah – they get along, but don't have much in common and aren't close. She and Oliver live on the outskirts of Nottingham and are reluctant to travel further than a few miles. She dresses in beige, never wears make-up and on the rare occasions she and Sophie see each other, Sophie comes away finding it difficult to remember anything she's said.

Jude's voice gets louder as he steps outside. She can tell from his one-word answers and the odd *uh huh* at appropriate intervals that he's already bored by the conversation. He rolls his eyes as he walks over and hands her the phone.

'Mum wants a word,' he says.

Sophie takes his mobile and he disappears back inside.

'Hi, Sarah. How are you?'

Jude's mother proceeds to tell her she's fine and that Oliver has started working as a volunteer at their local repair café, and how much he's enjoying it. Sophie wonders if Jude has told her about Nate but presumes he hasn't, as Sarah continues to talk without mentioning it. Jude is so protective of his mother, never wants her to worry. Sophie watches her husband disappear back inside, hopes he won't be long so she can give his phone back and get changed before they go to the hospital.

Just as she thinks the conversation is over, Sarah starts speaking again.

'Oh, by the way, I forgot to tell Jude,' she says, 'we've been collecting your redirected post like you asked, and a letter came from Bearmans'. It had to be signed for, so I opened it in case it was something urgent. They've sent through his P45. Oliver said it must be a mistake, so I thought Jude should know.'

Sophie feels as if she's been punched in the chest. She hears a knocking sound and turns around to see her husband smiling as he waves at her through the glass doors of their bedroom.

'I'm sure it is a mistake,' she says quickly. 'Thanks for letting us know, Sarah – I'll tell him.'

She smiles and waves back, keeping eye contact as she holds up his iPhone, watching her husband's reaction as she throws it into the middle of the swimming pool. It sinks slowly until it reaches the bottom while Jude is still struggling to open the door.

His face is bright red when he finally gets outside.

'What the fuck are you doing?'

She doesn't answer.

'Jesus, Sophie.' He pulls off his T-shirt and glasses, jumps into the water with his shorts on, retrieves the phone from the bottom of the pool and deposits it on the side before getting out again, dripping small puddles all over the stone slabs.

'I think you've ruined it.'

He squints as he looks at the screen and grabs a couple of towels off the sun loungers, wraps his phone in one of them before drying himself off quickly with the other. 'What the hell did you do that for?'

She glares at him. 'You've already been made redundant, haven't you?'

He pauses for a fraction of a second before he puts his glasses back on.

'What makes you say that?'

'Your mum just told me Bearmans' sent her your P45. She thinks it's a mistake, but it's not, is it?'

Jude walks round the pool until he's standing in front of her.

'I didn't know how to tell you.' He runs his hand over his beard. 'I'm so sorry.'

'So all that stuff about trusting you was actually just bollocks? You lost your job and just hoped that I wouldn't find out?'

'I was going to tell you,' he says.

'When, Jude? When we were on our way home? How long ago did you find out?'

He adjusts his glasses on his nose. 'They told me just before we left London.'

'Fucking hell. You should have gone to see a solicitor. It might not be legal without—'

'It is legal, Soph. You know what Bearmans' is like. Their lawyers are all over this stuff. I didn't want to tell you as I knew it would ruin our trip. There was nothing I could do about it, but I'm sorry I didn't tell you earlier.'

'Are they going to give you a redundancy payout?' she asks. 'You must be entitled to something?'

'Yup,' he says after a brief pause. 'HR are sorting all that.'

She tries to calculate the amount in her head, but she's not sure what he's entitled to. A few months' salary? At least that's something to ease the immediate pressure. And it's not like they don't have any savings, but they aren't supposed to be using those if they want to buy somewhere when they get back.

She shakes her head. 'I can't believe you didn't tell me.' She hesitates, the realization sinking in slowly. 'Nate knows, doesn't he? This is what he meant at Tide when he said I needed to ask you about your job.'

Jude looks over at the pool, then nods.

She seethes with humiliation, can't bring herself to speak.

'I'm really sorry,' he says. 'I was just waiting for the right time to tell you, and then all this happened with Nate . . .'

'I don't believe you.' Her entire body feels cold, despite the heat.

'Soph,' he says. 'Let's not do this now. We've got to get to the hospital and the taxi is coming in a minute.' He puts his hands on her shoulders, but she stands very still, her body rigid as he kisses her on the top of her forehead. 'I think we need to be honest,' he adds. 'I'm not the only one who's hiding things. We both know there are things you don't tell me.'

She looks up at him as he tucks a stray hair behind her ear and swallows.

'That's not true.'

'Isn't it?' He tightens his grip on her shoulders and she feels his fingers dig into her skin – or is she imagining it? Is she just so tense at the moment that her entire body feels as if it's one large knot?

'I told you about Jess,' she whispers. 'No one else knows about that.' A shiver runs down her spine as she remembers the ice-cold horror she'd felt when she'd realized her sister was still inside their house that night. The dampness of the lawn under her bare feet as everyone around her started shouting. How she'd heard the fire-engine sirens but had still waited for what felt like hours until they'd actually arrived.

'I know you did.' Jude strokes her hair as she leans against his chest. 'And I promised I'd never tell anyone else. I love you, Sophie. You did what you thought was right at the time. Just like I've done.'

The cicadas' chirping in the garden reaches a crescendo. They sound like someone screaming and she's desperate to cover her ears, block them out.

Jude lowers his face down so it's directly in front of hers. She can feel his hot breath on her skin.

'If we're not going to hide anything from each other,' he says, 'are you going to tell me what Layla's things are doing in your bedside drawer?'

47. Jude

Jude experiences a moment of déjà vu as he walks along the hospital corridor, his flip-flops squeaking on the linoleum floor as he smiles at the same two nurses who were here yesterday.

It feels as if someone has picked him up and shaken him – hard – and that everything has settled back down in a different place. He and Sophie rarely row; he prides himself on keeping their marriage on an even keel – anticipating potential bumps in the road and ironing them out before they become an issue – but that's twice in the last couple of days that one of them has stormed off after an argument.

He'd told her she needed to give Layla back her things, or at least leave them somewhere in the villa, if she doesn't want to explain why she took them in the first place. He understands why she'd done it. His wife clearly hasn't forgiven Layla for ruining their wedding, and taking her things was a way to mess with her head. He loves Sophie more than anything, but her vindictive streak is no secret. An ugly thing that rises to the surface when she loses control. He knows it's born out of an instinct to defend herself, and so he forgives her. It's his own fault for not paying her more attention – he should have looked after her better, protected her from herself.

He texts Sophie just before he reaches intensive care;

his phone miraculously still seems to be functioning after she threw it in the pool. He wonders if she's left the bedroom since she locked the door and refused to get in the taxi.

Will let you know if there is any news.

She doesn't reply and his fingers itch with the urge to call her. He can't bear it when she ignores him.

A nurse is standing beside the machines, writing down numbers on her clipboard, but the chair next to Nate's bed is empty and there's no sign of Layla.

'How is he?' Jude asks.

'Dr Purwanta will be coming in soon, so you can ask her,' the nurse says.

'Do people normally take a while to wake up?'

'Every patient is different,' she says. 'Nate has a very serious head injury. It's probably best if you talk to Dr Purwanta.'

She hangs the clipboard of notes on the end of Nate's bed and walks out. Jude looks at the figure lying under the white sheet, the bruising on Nate's cheek now a purple-and-yellow colour.

'All right, bro?' he says.

Nate doesn't respond. His best friend should be cracking a sarcastic retort, telling him that of course he's not all right, that his head fucking hurts and he can't wait to get out of here.

'We need to talk,' Jude continues. 'About Sophie. I can't have you telling her I was fired.'

He puts his hand on Nate's wrist, overcome by a sudden desire to prod him, see whether he'll react. Even the tiniest movement would be better than this unnatural immobility. He pinches Nate's skin between his fingers just as Layla walks in, then lets go quickly and hopes she didn't notice.

'Did you manage to clear your head?' he asks.

She nods. 'I went up to Pura Tanah Lot. Where's Sophie?'

'She wasn't feeling great, so she stayed at the villa. I've told her we'll call if there's any change.'

Layla pulls up a chair to sit beside him, looks at Nate's wrist and frowns.

'They've taken off the talisman pendant I gave him to wear last night.'

'Maybe it got in the way when they were trying to do their tests.'

Jude can't help thinking about all of Layla's things that are sitting in Sophie's drawer. What she would say if she knew what his wife had done. Layla puts her hand on his arm. Her touch feels urgent, warm, so different to Sophie's in bed this morning.

'I haven't had a chance to thank you for not telling Nate about what happened when he was away,' she says quietly.

Jude looks at her, then at Nate, his cheeks flushing.

'He can't hear us,' Layla says.

Jude moves his arm and adjusts his glasses.

'You don't know that for sure,' he says. 'There's lots of evidence that hearing is one of the last senses to remain even when someone is in a coma.'

'I know the doctors are doing their best,' Layla says, 'but what if he doesn't wake up? Ever, I mean?'

Jude can't think about that right now.

'Maybe we should go and get a coffee,' he says.

He stands up and she slides her arm under his, linking them together. As they leave the room, one of the nurses on the reception desk beckons them over.

'I need to talk to you about Nate having visitors,' she says.

Layla's forehead creases. 'What do you mean?'

'We really need to restrict anyone coming in to just family and close friends only – at least until Nate is more awake.'

Layla looks at her blankly.

'I'm sorry, I still don't understand. Jude *is* a close friend.'

The nurse blinks. 'No, I'm talking about the gentleman who came in earlier. Said he worked for you as your site manager? We found him sitting beside Nate's bed.'

Jude feels Layla's grip on his arm tighten.

'Did he say anything else?' she asks.

'Just that he wanted to pay his respects. We're not sure how he managed to slip past reception. He seemed nice enough, but he kept trying to put his hand on Nate's face. Said he wanted to pray for him.'

48. Layla

Layla lets herself back into the villa and shuts the door as quietly as she can behind her. She'd told Jude to go home earlier – this afternoon's initial excitement after Dr Purwanta said she'd felt Nate squeeze her hand had gradually ebbed away as it became clear it wouldn't happen again.

Layla had stayed until the nurse told her to get some sleep – she'd naively thought that once she and Nate were by themselves, he would give her some kind of a sign, that the connection between them would somehow force him back to life, but it hadn't, and now she feels cheated.

She had driven the scooter back to the villa in the dark, the roads unusually quiet apart from the occasional dog barking, her mind running over the conversation she'd had with Alex yesterday. How the hell is she going to get the money to repay him? She'd had a moment of panic trying to locate Nate's key fob before pressing it against the gates, wishing they would open faster, and a spurt of adrenaline had flooded her body as she'd walked up the drive, continually looking behind her, half expecting to see Alex slip in through the closing gates and stop her from ever reaching her front door.

Inside, the living room is silent. Jude and Sophie must have gone to bed. She hates the way the villa feels at night – can't wait to be out of here and into their new place. The mood lighting casts shadows over the walls, transforming everyday objects into something sinister. Plant leaves become long fingers reaching out to grab her; candles turn into faces with their mouths open in a scream.

She tells herself not to be ridiculous as she goes to get a bottle of water out of the fridge, then changes her mind and pours herself a gin instead, wincing as she opens the pull-tab on the can of tonic, the sudden release of air cutting through the silence. She waits for a few seconds to see if she can hear Jude or Sophie moving around before she picks up the glass and downs the cool liquid.

She doesn't want to be lying awake for hours, thoughts circling around her head. She's going to have to ask Jude if she can borrow some money off him – can't think of any other option. It's humiliating and she knows Sophie will kick up a fuss, but it's better than the alternative. And she's sure Jude will agree to lend it to her. He's come to her rescue before when she was at her lowest point, and he's stuck up for her despite what happened at the wedding. She'll tell him it's only a temporary loan, just until Nate gets better.

She still can't work out why Nyoman went to visit him. She'd told Dr Purwanta to make sure that, going forwards, no one is allowed into Nate's room apart from herself, Jude or Sophie. Maybe their site manager had genuinely just wanted to wish Nate better, but he hadn't mentioned visiting when she'd bumped into him at Pura Tanah Lot. And she can't help thinking about the missing pendant she'd fastened around Nate's wrist – it's not like it was worth a lot, but its sentimental value means she wants it back.

She pours herself another gin, neat this time, and downs it before heading into her bedroom. It still smells faintly of Nate. The scent of his sandalwood cologne, but also something deeper than that. His hair, his skin. Things that make her physically ache for him. She cleans her teeth, looks out across the lawn at Jude and Sophie's room opposite, but everything is pitch-black. She picks up Nate's aftershave, opens the bottle and sprays some on to a towel. Maybe she should take it into hospital with her tomorrow. Make him feel more human and less like a patient. It might help him to wake up. Or music. She needs to remember his headphones.

She curls up in bed, cuddling the towel next to her, shuts her eyes and tries to pretend he's still here. Her brain begins to feel fuzzy – the gin has done its trick – and her last conscious thoughts before she drifts off to sleep are of Nate; how in every memory she has of him, he's always smiling.

The noise wakes her. She opens her eyes as if she's been given an electric shock, can feel her heart thudding beneath her ribs.

A creak.

It sounds like one of the floorboards in the corridor outside her bedroom. The gin had helped to knock her out, but now she's wide awake, every cell in her body focused.

Is she imagining it?

She reaches for her phone to see what the time is, and her stomach sinks as she realizes she left it in the bathroom.

Nate's aftershave on the towel smells stronger than ever and she wishes more than anything that he was here. She wants to reach out and turn on her bedside light, but her limbs are frozen. She'd had night terrors when she was younger, used to wake up screaming for her mother, convinced there was something lurking in the corner of her bedroom. Something not human. It would disappear when her mother showed up in her nightdress, only to re-emerge after she'd gone while Layla hid under her duvet, sobbing quietly until she finally fell asleep.

She must have imagined it.

A nightmare which has spilled over into reality, its dark tendrils still wrapped around her brain. She'd insisted Nate get up to investigate when it happened before, but he's not here now. She thinks of Sophie, wonders how the fuck she managed to sleep in her flat after finding that burglar.

She strains to pick out sounds in the dark. The double glazing blocks out most of the noise from outside, and at this time of night there's only silence. Her ears hum with a high-pitched whine, protesting at being asked to find something that isn't there. She thinks of the words she'd carved in her wardrobe, of what she deserves, and puts her hand on her chest, tries to breathe slowly, in and out, decelerate her heart from its current manic pace.

The creak is louder this time. Closer. She isn't imagining it. She slides down under the duvet until only her nose is above the covers and peers out into the darkness. Another noise: shuffling. She knows she should turn on the light, get up and find her phone, call someone, but she can't. She can only think about Nate and whether he's died and come back, or whether Alex has somehow managed to follow her inside – is she really sure she shut the front door properly? What if this is all actually just a nightmare and she's not even awake?

The chrome handle turns on her bedroom door. She shuts her eyes as the light from the corridor creeps into the room and feels the air move as someone walks in. A barely perceptible rearranging of molecules around her. She can just make out the faint noise of feet moving carefully across her floorboards as she stays completely still. Tells herself to breathe. In and out. Like she does in yoga. Focus only on her breath. She is asleep. Fast asleep.

Whoever – or whatever – is in here stops moving. She can feel it. Knows that if she opens her eyes she will see someone or something staring back at her, their face directly above hers. There's a moment when she thinks she can't bear it any longer, that she's going to have to sit up, throw back the covers and scream, but she's certain if she does, no noise will come out. Her voice will have shrivelled away into nothing but a whisper.

Then she hears something else and has to force herself to keep breathing. She knows *exactly* what that sound is. And now she's doubting whether this is happening at all because it doesn't make any sense.

It moves again. Away from the bed. Back towards the door. She stays totally still and continues to breathe. In and out. Is it some kind of trick? She opens her eyes as slowly as she can, only the tiniest slit, in case she's wrong and whatever it is is still looking at her. But her instincts were right. The door is open wider now and there's a brief flash of light as they slip out through the gap.

She holds her breath to stop herself screaming. Even in the half-darkness, the outline of Jude's tall shape, naked apart from his boxer shorts, is unmistakable as he shuts her door behind him.

49. Sophie

When Sophie comes into the kitchen in her peach satin pyjamas the following morning, Layla is already dressed, cutting up various fruit and vegetables to fit them into the blender. She looks terrible. Puffy eyes with dark grey shadows underneath. Sophie wonders what time she got in last night.

'Morning.'

Sophie pulls a mug out of the cupboard, puts it under the Nespresso machine and sticks in a coffee pod.

'Hi.' Layla doesn't look up as she slices through the cerise-pink skin of a dragon fruit to reveal the white flesh inside, dotted with black seeds that look like frenzied dice.

'You going back to the hospital after breakfast?' Sophie asks in an effort to dispel the tension she can sense in the room as Layla's chopping becomes more frantic, the blade of the knife only narrowly missing her fingers.

Layla nods as she screws the top on to the blender and starts it, the whirring noise filling the room. Sophie wraps her hands around her mug of coffee and waits until it stops.

'Maybe you should have a break?' She reaches out and puts her hand on Layla's shoulder, feels her stiffen. 'You know they'll call you if there's any change.'

Layla doesn't answer as she pours the smoothie into a tall glass.

'Look,' Sophie adds. 'I can't imagine how difficult this is for you. I'd be going out of my mind. Let Jude and me help.'

'I can't leave Nate on his own.'

Layla's face suddenly drains of colour, and Sophie follows her eyeline to the small china elephant that she'd put on the windowsill last night. The pink liquid runs over the rim of the glass and down the side as Layla continues to overfill it. Sophie gently takes the jug out of Layla's hand and puts it on the counter, thinks back to the clingfilm wrap that is still sitting in her drawer.

'You're not going to be any use to Nate if you fall apart,' she says. 'You need a break. Come out with me for the day. We could go down the coast for a few hours, to one of the Nusa islands or something.' Layla looks at her as if she's suggested visiting the moon. 'Or we could stay here,' Sophie adds quickly. 'Whatever you want. Jude can sit with Nate so he won't be on his own and can call you if there's any change.'

Layla blinks as she glances at the elephant again and takes a sip of her drink.

'Would he be happy to do that?'

'I'm sure he would.' Sophie hesitates. 'You know how close they are. He's devastated by what's happened.'

Layla doesn't say anything.

'I know he might not show it' – Sophie swallows the last of her coffee and lowers her voice – 'but he's not been sleeping. He woke me up last night, constantly moving around.'

Layla pulls a couple of sheets of kitchen paper off the roll and goes to wipe up the circle of pink liquid, continuing long after it has disappeared, the paper disintegrating into pieces before she finally puts it in the bin.

'Does Jude ever sleepwalk?' Her voice sounds as if it's about to crack and Sophie can see Layla's hands trembling as she clasps them together. 'I did after my parents died. Nate said he found me in the wardrobe once. I'd shut myself inside and had no memory of it whatsoever.'

Sophie frowns. 'No. Nothing like that.' She puts her empty mug in the dishwasher, wondering how she can get Layla on her own without sounding pushy. 'Will you at least consider taking a break?' she asks. 'Come out with us for a proper breakfast before you go to the hospital.'

'I don't think—'

'We can be back in less than an hour. You need to eat something.'

Layla scratches her neck, then nods.

'OK,' she says finally. 'We'll get something from one of the beach cafés, as long as we're not gone long.'

'I'll get Jude up,' Sophie says, ignoring the crease that appears on Layla's forehead. 'We'll be ready in five minutes.'

Sophie hadn't had time to put suncream on her shoulders and can already feel them starting to burn. A stinging sensation, as if someone has slapped her. They walk slowly along the road, in single file to keep away from the traffic. The cicadas chirrup constantly in the background, for which she is grateful – it helps compensate for Layla's silence. She's barely said a word since they left the villa.

Sophie feels a prick of conscience as she watches the bottom of Layla's maxi dress float just above the tarmac, her dark hair tied up casually in a messy bun. She'll wait until Layla leaves for the hospital and then return the rest of her belongings that are still in her drawer. Almost all of them, anyway. Tell Jude she's put everything back.

They find a table in the café at the end of the road and sit down beneath one of the parasols that hasn't got holes in the canopy. She can feel the sand crunch beneath her flip-flops as she orders a cappuccino, along with the breakfast special of smashed avocado with cherry tomatoes on a sourdough bagel.

'Thanks for encouraging me to come.' Layla looks at Sophie and then at the ocean, where several surfers are already catching waves. 'Nate would be out there today,' she says. 'Perfect conditions for it.'

'He'll be on his board again before you know it,' Jude says as the waiter brings over their drinks.

'You'd be happy to sit with Nate if I took Layla out for a few hours, wouldn't you?' Sophie asks. 'She needs a break.'

'Sure,' Jude says, a little milk froth stuck to his beard.

She turns to Layla, who seems to be studying Jude through her sunglasses. Sophie needs to get her away from here, away from Jude, talk to her. She hasn't come all this way to Bali for nothing.

There's a shout from further down the beach and they watch as a couple of sunbathers run over to a man gesturing from the shoreline.

'What's he doing?' Sophie asks.

'I'm not sure.' Jude walks a couple of feet away from the table to get a better look, then turns back towards them. 'I think there's someone lying on the sand.'

A few more people join the sunbathers, then a man

breaks away from the crowd and sprints towards them across the beach. He stops when he reaches Jude, bends over and puts his hands on his thighs as he tries to catch his breath.

'I need a phone,' the man says. 'Someone's drowned.'

50. Jude

Jude glances over at the crowd of people huddled together where the waves are breaking on the shore. Sophie starts to get up, but he puts his hand on her arm.

'I'm not sure we should get involved.'

She gives him an ice-cold look. He wonders if she's said something to Layla about him leaving Bearmans', as neither of them has been very chatty this morning. God knows how she'll react if she ever finds out the whole truth.

'I just meant that we don't want to get in the way.' He can hear the man who'd run up to them in the café shouting into the phone, trying to emphasize that it's an emergency. 'There are quite a few people down there already.'

'But we might be able to help,' Layla says.

Jude raises his eyebrows. 'Can you do CPR?'

'What the fuck is that supposed to mean?' Layla retorts.

'Sorry,' Jude says quickly. 'I didn't mean to sound snarky, but the guy in there' – he nods at the café – 'just said he thinks the bloke is dead. So we should probably wait for the police.'

Layla stares at him intently, her face flushed. Sophie *has* said something to her, he knows it.

'You're such a typical tourist, Jude. You forget Nate and I actually live here. We're part of a community. It could be someone we know.'

She gets up and starts to walk across the beach, and Sophie follows close behind her. Jude stays sitting for a few seconds and then, when neither of them turns around, reluctantly gets up and goes after them. Does he sound like a tourist? He's got enough on his plate at the moment and is just trying to be practical. There's no point in gawping when they can't do anything to help.

Images appear in his head that light up like flashes from a camera. Crumpled shapes lying on the ground. He pushes them away as he walks across the sand. If he's honest with himself, his hesitancy has nothing to do with getting in the way or being a nuisance.

It's the thought of seeing another dead body.

His heart starts to race the closer he gets to the shoreline. The horror he'd felt fifteen years ago rises up in his throat like a hard ball, threatening to choke him. He can feel the dampness in his armpits; the back of his neck is slick with sweat. Her face swims in front of his eyes and for a moment he's back in their university house again, standing behind Nate, staring into their bathroom, his nostrils full of that unmistakable sour, rancid smell as his brain reeled in anguish.

It had been such a shock.

Lily Harris had been the last person he'd expected to see slumped on the floor beside a pile of vomit, her green eyes staring sightlessly at the ceiling.

He'd brought her home with him the night before. Had seen her in their psychology lectures most weeks, always chewing gum, plaiting thin sections of her long blonde hair, tying the ends with different-coloured rubber bands. He'd felt himself get aroused every time he spotted her but hadn't had any signs that his feelings were recipro-cated, despite constantly searching for them. She'd acted like she wasn't aware of his existence, even though he'd asked her on more than one occasion if she wanted to grab a drink or compare notes.

In their final term, they'd ended up at the same house party – she'd sat next to him on the stairs and cried while telling him she'd just split up with her boyfriend. He hadn't listened to much of what she'd said, had been distracted by how smooth her skin was, how her hair smelled of strawberries, how stunning her eyes were despite the tears that had slid silently down her cheeks, smudging her make-up. She'd downed several bottles of WKD, swig-ging the blue liquid until her pupils had been so huge the green of her irises had disappeared into the thinnest of circles, drowned out by the blackness. He'd suggested they go back to his house, where it was a bit quieter, had put her arm over his shoulder and helped carry her when she'd stumbled getting up.

She'd given him a blow-job while Kings of Leon blasted out from his iPod Touch and then said she needed to leave, had told him her friends would be wondering where she was. She'd had to sit down on the bed a couple of times before she finally managed to pull her bra back on, but by then they'd finished a bottle of vodka between them and he hadn't been feeling too great himself. He'd felt his eyes closing as she'd stumbled around the room collecting her clothes, had thought he'd heard the front door slam as he'd drifted off to sleep.

It had only been afterwards that he'd realized the noise must have been the sound of her head hitting the floor.

If it hadn't been for Nate, he doesn't know what he'd have done. He'd been the one who'd had the foresight to get rid of the bottle of vodka, who'd made him strip off his clothes and his bedding and put it all in a black bin bag, which they'd stuffed into the loft before calling the police.

They'd both told the same story – Lily had been hammered and had decided to crash at theirs after the house party and had slept on the sofa. Jude had pulled out a few of her blonde hairs together with one of the green rubber bands she'd had in her plaits and placed them on the pillow they'd put out on the settee. Nate had laid out a blanket and left her shoes on the floor.

At the time, Jude had thought his best friend had been helping him for altruistic reasons – it had only been after the police left that Nate told him Lily had bought a bottle of GHB off him at the party. He was terrified someone would find out he had a lucrative hobby acting as supplier to several of their friends, and then he'd be asked to leave university.

But the findings of the post-mortem hadn't even mentioned GHB; they hadn't thought to test for it. After all, everyone at the party had seen Lily drinking and the report had concluded that Lily had slipped on the tiled floor, hit her head and died as a result of aspiration of gastric contents.

Jude had allowed Nate to think they'd both discovered Lily's body at the same time. He hadn't told Nate he'd actually found her a few hours earlier. Had gone for a piss in the early hours of the morning, seen her lying on the floor and panicked, gone straight back to bed, too terrified to raise the alarm. The post-mortem had suggested she might still have been alive at that point, but the time of her death was difficult to pinpoint with a hundred per cent accuracy and it's something he never lets himself think about.

He and Nate had both been called in to see the chancellor but had given the same story as they'd given the police – Lily had been fine when they'd gone to bed.

It had just been a terrible, terrible accident. And one that they'd both learned a lot of lessons from.

The huddle of people split apart as Jude reaches them. He can see Layla staring at something, her hands cupped over her nose and mouth, his wife's arm around her shoulders. The man on the ground is lying on his front, a pair of soaking-wet trousers and a black T-shirt stuck to his skin. Jude shivers. It doesn't even look like he's been in the water that long – Jude half expects him to get up and walk away.

He braces himself as he bends down and puts his hands on the man's shoulders to turn him over and check for a pulse, but a Balinese waiter who is part of the huddle grabs his arm and tells him to stop.

'We need to start CPR,' Jude says, wishing he'd stayed in the café. 'Someone's called for an ambulance.'

The waiter shakes his head.

'There is no point.' He lifts up the bottom of the man's trousers and Jude peers at where he's pointing. He can see that the man's calf is swollen and there are two large red dots above his ankle.

'Snake,' the waiter says.

51. 2007

The rapids swallow us up as soon as we leave the shelter of the pool. We're sucked in and spat out again, embraced by a force that seems intent on destroying us. No one notices as I drop my phone into the water and watch it disappear into the frothing liquid, along with all the messages Kadek and I have sent each other. If the police are waiting at the finish point, at least they won't see those.

Everyone paddles without me needing to say a word, but our efforts are pointless — we're trying to control something that has a mind of its own. The inflatable is pulled wherever the Ayung River wants to take it.

'We need to get to the bank!' Buddy can't disguise the panic in his voice and, from the look on his face, he knows he's made a terrible mistake.

We can all see what's coming, and it's too late to do anything about it. The inflatable spins in the current, plunges over a steep incline and hits a large rock side on.

I hear Kristin shriek, catch a glimpse of Mia's face, frozen in shock. The boat tips forward on its nose, hovers for a moment as if contemplating what the river will accept as a tribute, then slumps back down, plunges through a set of rapids and emerges on the other side with three of its passengers, including myself, no longer on board.

Sky. Rocks. Water. I glimpse each one for a fraction of a second before they cease to be recognizable. My lungs scream for air, my body held up only by my lifejacket. I can see the boat, but there's no way I can reach it. It's as if a huge fist has hold of me and is squeezing me in an ever-tighter grip.

'Mia!' Ashley screams. 'Mia, where are you?'

I look further downstream but can't see anything other than a frothing mass of water. The river is a roar of sound, which briefly falls silent as I disappear below the surface, pulled under by the current. I kick but can't work out which way is up. The pressure in my head builds until I can no longer bear it and I feel myself begin to pass out, panic giving way to a dizzy blur. Then, suddenly, I break through the surface again and my body's survival instinct kicks in as I gasp mouthfuls of air.

'Buddy?!' James leans over the side of the inflatable, his hands cupped around his mouth, screaming for his son. A red helmet appears at the back of the boat.

'Mia! Grab the rope!' Ashley shouts.

'Buddy!' Kristin keeps trying to stand up, but Dan pushes her back down on to her seat as the boat rocks.

Mia is pulled over the side, one arm dangling at an unnatural angle, a dark streak of red across her thigh. She slithers into the bottom of the boat in a mangled heap.

Ashley moans. 'Oh my God, look at her leg.'

There is a brief lull in the rapids, a stretch of calmer water. I start to swim.

'Buddy!'

They are all shouting for him now. In the distance, I can see the dark shapes of rocks sticking up out of the water like giant shark fins. Beyond that, the river splits: one way goes towards the meeting point, the other in a direction that we never go. Straight over a steep drop.

My arm connects with his shoulder before I see him, hitting him as I flail around.

'Buddy?'

He doesn't answer. At first I think he's unconscious, but then realize he's just in shock, his eyes staring blankly ahead.

'You need to swim,' I say. 'Come on, let's go.'

The current has started to pick up again, but he doesn't move. I pull him through the water with me, holding on to the straps of his life vest. The others on the boat are yelling his name, but he's so heavy it takes every ounce of my energy to move him at all.

A sound leaves my mouth that is somewhere between a yell and a scream. At first I don't think they've heard me, but then I can see Dan pointing in my direction, the others trying to paddle backwards to slow the boat's progress, give us a chance to catch up.

'Buddy,' I splutter. 'Please. You have to help me.'

Something in him seems to respond, and he starts to kick his legs. The rocks are closer now, their smooth, wet surfaces glinting in the sun. I'm only too well aware of the damage that will happen if my body hits them at its current speed.

We are almost at the boat, the safety rope within reach. I push Buddy towards it and he grabs it just as the inflatable spins around. I'm flung away from the boat, but Buddy holds on – one hand on the rope, his other on mine. James throws himself down on to the red fabric, Kristin gripping his life vest as he starts to pull his son inside.

For a few, long seconds, Buddy stares at me. I can feel him weighing up his options and see the brief look of remorse that flashes across his face. Then he turns towards his father and opens his hand. Slowly but surely, despite all my efforts to hold on, my fingers slip away from his.

Jen reaches her paddle over the side of the boat towards me, but it's too late. There is no escaping at this point. I surrender to the rapids, too tired to fight. When my head finally makes impact with the rocks, the pain reverberates around my skull and an explosion of stars expands across my vision. The roar of the river turns to silence, and then there is nothing.

52. Layla

Layla can't stop her teeth chattering as the taxi makes its way along the road out of Canggu. She had left the beach when the Balinese police turned up carrying a stretcher and a body bag, telling Sophie and Jude that she needed to get back to see Nate. Her hands had been shaking too much to even contemplate taking the scooter.

She hadn't needed to see the man's face to know it was him. She'd recognized the distinctive tattoo on his upper arm straight away. How can Alex be dead when only two nights earlier he'd been standing outside the villa calling her every name under the sun? She knows there are venomous sea snakes out here, but it's rare to hear of anyone being bitten. Had he gone for an early-morning swim and disturbed one by mistake? Why hadn't he shouted for help? The beach is rarely empty.

The taxi goes past Kayana, and she remembers him and Nate laughing together the last time they were there, the way that men do when they're drunk – as if they've just heard the funniest joke ever. Her mind goes back further, to Alex in HiveHub, just before he'd leaned over to kiss her and she'd felt butterflies rise up in her stomach; had stupidly thought there was something between them, hadn't realized she was being taken for a mug.

This has sorted out her problem. Permanently. She doesn't need to ask Jude for money, and she doesn't have to worry about what's happened to a wrap of fucking coke.

She tries to block out those thoughts, but they keep coming back. Beneath the shock, she feels a huge sense of relief, and this makes her teeth chatter harder than ever. She doesn't want to be the kind of person who rejoices in someone else's death.

Had Alex told anyone he was coming to visit her the other night? Had they been heard arguing? A knot of panic starts to form in her stomach. Sophie had asked if it was Alex when he was outside in their driveway; Layla can only hope that her explanation about him being someone called Chris had been convincing enough. When Alex's body is identified and the police start asking questions, Jude and Sophie are going to wonder why she hadn't said anything on the beach. She's going to have to claim she didn't recognize him. She'd only seen his back. If it weren't for his tattoo, that would be perfectly plausible.

Fuck.

She can't believe he's dead. She's so lost in her own thoughts that the taxi driver has to tell her that they've arrived at the hospital and she needs to get out.

'Thank you.' She gives him a tip, presses the rupiah notes into his hand to hide the fact that hers are shaking. She adjusts her batik bag over her shoulder, smooths down her dress and takes a deep breath before walking into the hospital reception.

Dr Purwanta smiles at her as she enters the ICU.

'Good news,' she says. 'We think Nate has started to wake up. He's been blinking and yawning, and his stats show he's breathing much better on his own. If his progress continues, we can start to think about extubating him and taking him off the ventilator.'

Layla walks around to the side of Nate's bed and threads her fingers between his, all thoughts of Alex pushed to the back of her mind.

'Nate? Can you squeeze my hand?' There's a faint but definite response. She lowers her head down until her forehead is resting on his fist.

Thank God. Or whoever you are up there. Thank you.

'Is he going to be OK?' she asks. 'I mean, will he get back to how he was before?'

'We don't know for certain yet,' Dr Purwanta says. 'We're going to see how things go today, then, if he's still stable, we'll do some more tests and another MRI tomorrow morning, so there's no point in you coming in until the afternoon. The outcome of a serious head injury is always difficult to predict, but it's a very positive sign that he's starting to respond to basic commands. We're going to take things slowly, but I am hopeful.'

Layla squeezes Nate's fingers again as she strokes his face.

'Did you hear that?' she says. 'The doctor says it's looking hopeful.'

Layla checks her phone as she goes downstairs to the cafeteria for lunch. She'd called Nate's mum, who had cried with relief when she'd told them what Dr Purwanta had said. They've agreed to keep in close contact about Nate's progress and wait to know more before deciding whether to fly out to Bali.

Sophie has sent her a WhatsApp.

Jude will be in to see Nate after lunch. Shout if you want him to bring anything. Am so pleased things are looking better. Seeing that man on the beach was so awful – hope you are OK. Jude says he's more than happy to sit with Nate tomorrow so you can have a break. Have a think about it. x

Layla picks up a sandwich and some freshly squeezed orange juice and takes them outside. There's a small garden beside the cafeteria with a few tables and chairs set out on the grass. She sits down and closes her eyes, relishing the warmth on her face, until a shadow crosses her eyelids; she opens them to see Wayan Santi standing in front of her.

'Layla.'

'Wayan.' Her heart sinks. 'What are you doing here?'

He pulls out a chair and sits down opposite her.

'How is Nate doing?'

'The doctor says he's making good progress.'

Wayan nods. 'I hope it continues.'

Layla picks up her prawn sandwich and takes a bite, the bread slightly dry and hard. She swallows her mouthful and puts the rest back in the packet. She suspects Wayan is going to ask her for more money – in which case, he's wasting his time. She's got nothing left to give.

Wayan brushes a few crumbs off the table. 'I heard there was an incident on the beach this morning.'

Layla hesitates, choosing her words carefully.

'Someone drowned,' she says. 'Tragic.'

Wayan leans over the table towards her.

'Let's be honest, shall we? I don't think you believe it was a tragedy. I think you are relieved. Because you know who it was.'

Layla doesn't answer.

'I could show you photos if you need a reminder,' Wayan says, pulling out his phone. 'The two of you looking very cosy.' She shakes her head. 'You were the one who told me he was an investor in Kayana,' he continues. 'You thought it would make me angry and hoped I'd do something about it.'

Layla feels as if someone is squeezing her heart.

'I may just be the Balinese owner of a small warung, but I'm not stupid, Layla. You wouldn't tell me something like that unless it somehow benefitted you.'

She takes a mouthful of orange juice, hopes the flush she can feel spread across her cheeks isn't too obvious.

'It took me a while to work it out,' he says. 'But then I remembered seeing Nate with Bryce in Tide. What Nate gave him. Everyone knows you don't do something like that in Canggu without Alex's permission. That man traded a lot more than cryptocurrency.' He tuts. 'Are you eating that?' He points at the prawn sandwich lying on the table. Layla shakes her head and he picks it up, takes a bite before adding, 'I think we can agree you owe me for making your problem disappear.'

The piece of sandwich she swallowed earlier sticks in her throat and she feels the lump moving slowly towards her stomach, an inch at a time.

'What did you do?' she whispers.

He holds up his hands.

'I don't think you want to know that. And I also don't think you want anyone seeing these photos. Not the police. Or Nate.'

She can feel drops of perspiration slide down her back.

'I don't have any more money,' she says quietly.

'We both understand how favours work,' he says, getting up. 'I've fixed something that was a problem for both of us, and at some point, you can do something for me. I'll be in touch. That bread's stale, by the way.'

He grins, and she watches him walk away, her legs trembling too much for her to get up out of the chair. She takes another sip of orange juice, adding to the acid that is already swirling around in her stomach.

What if the police find out?

She hadn't actually asked Wayan to do anything. But if she's completely honest with herself, she had intended to provoke him, and part of her had wondered just how far he'd go.

She takes a deep breath. Right now, she needs to focus on getting Nate better. She dumps the half-eaten sandwich and orange juice in the bin, walks back into the hospital and stops dead.

Jude is standing in reception with Wayan. His forehead creases as Wayan is speaking and she wishes she could hear what is being said. She's terrified of the ripples each word could cause, its implications spreading outwards in a pattern she has no control over.

As she watches Jude's smile fade, she feels a thudding in her chest. Why are they even talking? They've never even met, have they?

53. Sophie

'You ready?' Jude says. 'The taxi's here.'

Sophie emerges from their bedroom. She'd waited for Layla and Jude to get back from the hospital last night, had sat outside in the darkness looking at the turquoise pool with its underwater lights, swatting away the mosquitoes with their high-pitched whine, but had given up and gone to bed around ten o'clock and hadn't even heard her husband come in.

She adjusts her shorts and checks her appearance in the hall mirror before applying some waterproof mascara and lip gloss. A memory pops into her head – her standing beside Jess when she was about eight, watching their mother outlining her lips in the mirror before filling them in with bright red lipstick. She'd told them she was putting on her warpaint. One of the few things – and she could probably count them on one hand – that her mother had been right about. Make-up acts as a shield and as camouflage. And God knows she needs both today.

She double-checks the contents of her bag – makes sure she's got everything she needs.

'What if Nate suddenly deteriorates?' Layla bites her lip. 'Maybe we shouldn't go.'

Jude puts his arm around Layla's shoulder. Sophie can't help noticing the way Layla withdraws into herself, as if she's trying to disappear. It touches a chord in the very centre of her and for a brief moment sucks out all her emotions, leaving behind a blank space.

'Go out with Sophie,' he says. 'Spend a few hours in the sun. Go swimming. You need a break. You heard what Dr Purwanta said. She's not going to let anyone visit Nate this morning – I'll go in and see him after lunch and you'll be back later this afternoon. I'll call you if there's any news.'

Sophie smiles at him briefly, desperate to get going before Layla changes her mind.

'See you later,' Jude says, leaning in to kiss her.

Sometimes she forgets they've only been married a year. She can barely remember not being with him. She'd spent most of her twenties trying to find someone who made her feel safe, couldn't believe it when she finally had. She looks at her wedding ring and is transported to a long-buried memory of standing in her headmaster's office, the back of her hand covered in an indelible-ink drawing, of being so terrified she thought she might wet herself.

Jude's stubble brushes against her lips, stripping off some of the gloss. She wipes his face with her thumb, feels the stickiness on her skin and tries to rub it off on her shorts.

Layla dozes off in the taxi before they are even out of Canggu. It's half an hour to Sanur, and Sophie looks out of the window as they pass through different suburbs that have been built along the edge of the main road. Shops and buildings with corrugated-iron roofs and hand-painted signs, and kittens that wander drunkenly along the pavement. Towards Denpasar the landscape becomes more built up, with three- or four-storey buildings either side of more modern streets that look vaguely familiar from when they first arrived.

She taps Layla on the shoulder as the taxi pulls into the car park next to the pier.

'What? Is it Nate?'

Sophie shakes her head. 'We're here.'

The boat across to Nusa Lembongan reminds Sophie of one of the Thames Clippers in London and she has a sudden urge to be back home, away from the heat and humidity, browsing the boutique shops in Wimbledon Village or walking on the Common after it's rained, breathing in the fresh scent of petrichor.

Layla checks her phone as the ferry pulls into the harbour at Lembongan.

'You know Dr Purwanta will call if there's any news,' Sophie says. 'And Jude will go in straight after lunch. Try not to worry.'

They step down off the boat, helped by the crew. The other tourists on board carry their suitcases in their arms as if they were babies as they wade through the shallow blue water to the beach. Sophie and Layla wander over to one of the golf-buggy-style taxis parked up outside the restaurants that stretch along the long length of sand.

'Can you take us to Dream Beach, please?' Layla turns to Sophie. 'We can stop for brunch and then walk along the cliffs to the Devil's Tears. The views are stunning and it would be good to get some photos for my Insta grid. I've completely neglected it over the past few days.'

They drive down the main road across the island. There's less traffic here than in Canggu, fewer scooters, and no road markings on the strip of tarmac. Occasionally, through the courtyard of a building or a gap in the trees, Sophie spots the white sand and sea that surrounds the island, the water spreading out to meet the horizon in a spectrum of blue, the palest shades of turquoise to the darkest navy. She wonders how deep it gets, how many people have sunk beneath the surface, never to re-emerge.

As the taxi winds along the road towards the coast, mosaics of colour expand into beach towels and tiny stick figures grow into sunbathers.

'Look at that view! Can we stop here?'

The driver slows down as Sophie points towards the edge of the cliff that drops away into the ocean. Some teenagers are jumping and diving into the water below, their bodies flipping in the air as they do somersaults.

'Aren't they're incredible?'

Layla hesitates. 'Is it far to the beach?'

The taxi driver shakes his head. 'A few minutes' walk along the coast path.'

She looks at Sophie. 'Shall we get out here?'

They head over to the group of the teenagers who are laughing as they egg each other on. It must be at least a seven-metre drop to the ocean below – probably more – and Sophie's heart skips a beat every time one of them hits the water, disappearing underneath before resurfacing, shouting for the next person to go. She doesn't know how they do it. The total lack of control after they leave the clifftop and writhe in mid-air – just the thought of it makes her want to lie down on the ground and hold on to something solid.

They don't object when Layla asks if she can take some photos, and she snaps shot after shot of tanned bodies with sun-bleached hair suspended against the sky.

Sophie watches her and waits, all the things she wants to say circling her brain. Eventually, the teenagers decide they've had enough and head back towards the beach, jostling each other as they amble along the coastal path.

Sophie walks over to the edge of the cliffs, where two swings hang from a giant wooden frame with *Dream Beach* painted on a piece of driftwood fastened to the top. She sits down and pats the wooden seat next to her. Layla perches on the narrow plank and they watch the surfers catching the waves further out, skimming along as lines of white foam break behind them.

'You must be so relieved that Nate's getting better,' Sophie says.

'He's not out of the woods yet,' Layla replies.

Sophie nods. 'I know. But it sounds like he's moving in the right direction. And I bet it won't be long until he's back at work. It's going to be expensive, moving into your new villa.'

Layla's cheeks redden. 'It will, but I've still got some of my inheritance left. And the life coaching is going well. I need to get these photos up and start posting more regularly to attract some new clients. I don't want Nate feeling like he has to get straight back out there. We don't even know if he *will* be able to work.'

'True, but everyone will look out for him – and for you,' Sophie says. 'It's great that you've really settled into the community here. It's at times like this you find out who your real friends are.'

Layla looks across at her, a flicker of uncertainty passing across her face.

'Yeah,' she says. 'I guess.'

Sophie holds on to the ropes of the swing and pushes against the ground with her feet, watches the dust rise up in spirals of smoke as she starts to move backwards and forwards. Layla copies her movements, travelling through the air so their pendulum motions are synchronized as both swings start to gain height and momentum.

'Because sometimes it's difficult to tell, isn't it?' Sophie shouts.

The swings reach the top of their arc of motion, hanging over the edge of the cliff so that for a few seconds there is nothing but blue ocean below their feet. Sophie waits until hers is back over the sandy earth of the cliff before she jumps off and grabs Layla's seat, holding it over the edge.

'Some people always stab you in the back, given half a chance,' Sophie says. 'Some bugger off when things get tricky and leave you in the lurch. Or worse still, some don't care if they completely fuck you over. But that's not you, right, Layla?'

'What are you talking about?'

Sophie hears the fear in Layla's voice, sees her grip on the ropes tighten as Sophie pushes her seat, flying it higher than ever.

'I know what you did in London before our wedding,' Sophie yells at her. 'I know you slept with Jude.'

54. Jude

The nurse smiles at Jude as she checks the machines around Nate's bed.

'All our tests show he's doing really well,' she says. 'I think Dr Purwanta is going to look to extubate him today. We've reduced his ventilator support and he's still breathing at a sustainable rate.' She looks at another set of illuminated numbers on the screen. 'And his oxygen saturation is good.'

'That's brilliant,' Jude says. He squeezes Nate's hand, watches his chest rise, then pause for a second before it falls again. 'D'you hear that, bro? Looks like you're heading in the right direction. We should be able to get you out of here soon.'

'Let me know if you need anything,' the nurse says, pulling the door to.

Jude waits until her footsteps recede, before moving his chair closer to Nate's bed. He takes Layla's talisman pendant out of his pocket and puts it beside a pile of paper towels on the cabinet next to him.

'Doesn't look like you need this now,' he says. 'Just goes to show all that spiritual stuff is actually a load of bollocks. I knew it was.'

He tilts his head as he studies the plastic tube that weaves its way out of Nate's mouth like a transparent snake. The ventilator hisses, the only sound in the room apart from the occasional beep from the machines.

'Sophie's taken Layla out for a few hours,' he says. 'Which means I get to spend some time with you and have a proper chat. Uninterrupted.'

He squeezes Nate's hand. 'Can you feel that?' He waits, but there's no response. 'Sorry,' he says. 'Stupid question. It's not like you can answer when you're still attached to this.' He taps the hollow plastic tube and a flat, dead sound reverberates in the room. 'I'll rephrase. Squeeze my hand if you can hear me.'

He looks at Nate's fingers, which don't appear to move, but thinks he can feel a slight sensation of pressure.

'I'll take that as a yes, then.' He leans over so his mouth is next to Nate's ear. 'We need to talk about what you said to my wife.'

Nate doesn't move. Jude feels a sudden urge to put his hands on his shoulders and shake him until he opens his eyes.

'After what happened at university, I thought we had each other's backs. You were happy enough to get to know my friends and share a house, but after we started at Bearmans', you pulled away. Wouldn't even have lunch with me.'

He adjusts the sheet on the bed, pulling it across Nate's body to smooth out the wrinkles.

'Have you any idea how it feels to know you're being left behind and not be able to do anything about it? You had everything, Nate. Great parents, a great life with Layla. I had to sit and watch while you went to the important meetings at Bearmans', the client dinners where the big decisions were made. People avoided me, but they gravitated towards you.'

He squeezes Nate's hand again.

'Did you do it deliberately?' he asks, but Nate doesn't respond.

'It felt deliberate,' Jude continues. 'But I told myself it wasn't, because you were still happy to spend time with me outside of work. Meals at our flat. Nights out. You even agreed to be my best man. And then you left the country. Moved out here into your flash villa while having another built to your exact requirements.' He hesitates. 'I don't think you realize how hard it is to constantly be happy for someone else when your own life is going to shit.'

Jude squeezes Nate's fingers again.

'Do you get what I'm saying?'

Still nothing. Jude hears the sound of footsteps in the corridor and the nurse pokes her head around the door.

'Everything OK?' she asks.

He smiles. 'Absolutely fine.'

'Hearing familiar voices can definitely help coma patients,' she says.

'He's not responding at the moment,' Jude says, 'but I'll keep talking.'

She disappears again, and he waits for a few seconds before leaning back in towards Nate.

'You should have told me you were going to speak to Sophie.'

He glances down at his best friend, who still has his eyes shut, the bruising on his face turning black now, as well as purple and yellow, and wonders how long it will take until Nate looks like himself again.

'She can't find out I got fired. I will do whatever it takes to protect my wife, Nate, do you understand?'

A slight twitch of two of Nate's fingers. What's that supposed to mean?

The ventilator lets out another long hiss.

'The thing is,' Jude says, 'I know you haven't been completely honest with me. But I haven't been with you, either. Do you want to know why?'

A definite squeeze this time as Nate's knuckles turn white.

'I thought you might.' Jude smiles. 'I wanted something I could think about when you were awarded yet another promotion. I wanted to know that your life isn't as perfect as you think it is. I wasn't going to tell you, but I think as you've shown you were willing to ruin my life, you deserve it. An eye for an eye, a tooth for a tooth and all that. You screwed with my better half, so I thought it was only fair if I did the same with yours.'

55. Layla

Layla feels the wooden seat beneath her slip backwards and forwards. She looks down at the vast expanse of water, experiences a lurch of nausea at the sight of the rocks just below the surface that her body will smash into if she falls off.

'Please stop pushing me. I didn't sleep with Jude!' she yells.

'I know you did!' Sophie shouts. 'That's why you got hammered at our wedding. It wasn't anything to do with you grieving – you just couldn't stand the sight of us getting married and wanted to tell Jude not to go through with it.'

'That's not true,' Layla says.

Sophie pushes her out over the cliffs again, and Layla shuts her eyes.

'You wrote about how guilty you felt,' Sophie says. 'You carved the words into the back of your wardrobe. *It was my fault. I am a bad person.* Remember?'

'I wrote that about my parents!' Layla cries. 'I still feel responsible for what happened to them. If they hadn't been coming to visit me, they wouldn't have had that accident. What I wrote had nothing to do with Jude.' Her hands are beginning to feel slippery on the ropes and she knows she's losing her grip.

'I saw photos of the two of you,' Sophie says. 'On Jude's laptop.'

For a moment, Layla falls silent.

Sophie pushes the swing again, but harder on one side, so that it begins to twist, first one way and then the other. The two ropes meet each other, then the wooden seat flips back with a jerk. Layla lets out a shriek as she feels herself begin to slide off.

'Please, Sophie, stop. I swear on my life, I didn't sleep with Jude.'

For a moment, Sophie doesn't move, and Layla has a terrible feeling she's going to keep pushing her until she can't hold on any longer.

'I don't know what you saw,' she says, 'but it wasn't me. Let me off.'

Sophie hesitates, then finally steps to one side and allows the swing to slow down until Layla is suspended over solid ground. She slithers off and sits in the dirt, her legs trembling as she examines the rope burns on the palms of her hands.

'Are you completely insane?' she says. 'I'm sorry about how I behaved at your wedding. How many times do you want me to say it? And I know you've had a really shitty time recently – it must be horrendous to come home and find someone has broken into your flat, but that's not—'

'No one broke into our flat,' Sophie says quietly as she sits down beside her.

Layla frowns. 'You were burgled. In Wimbledon.'

'No, we weren't,' Sophie says. 'I came home from work and found Jude's laptop in our bedroom. I saw photos of you –' she breaks off, her eyes welling up '– of the two of you together. In our bed.' She takes a deep breath. 'And I lost it. Made a mess of the flat, threw things around a bit. Broke stuff. But I didn't want to confront Jude until I knew the truth; I didn't want to throw away our entire marriage, everything we'd worked so hard for. I needed time to think, so I lied and said we'd been burgled.'

Layla wipes the dust off her hands on to her dress. Her skin is soaked with perspiration. She looks at the woman sitting beside her, the one who always has her shit together, who never loses control. Whose humanity now seems to be leaking out through the cracks in her usually perfect veneer.

'I did sleep in your bed,' Layla says slowly. 'Once.'

Sophie stares at her.

'Not with Jude,' Layla adds quickly. She reaches out and puts her hand on Sophie's arm. 'I'm sorry, I should have told you.'

Sophie pulls her arm away.

'It was just before you got married,' Layla says. 'You'd gone away for work – some PR event in Manchester, I think – and Nate was on a team-building exercise with Bearmans' overnight. I did the same thing I'd done every night since the accident. Go out to a club, get hammered, sleep, repeat. Anything not to have to think about lorries and head-on collisions. And I remember drinking rum and Cokes and being a bit drunk, but not out of it; I remember not being able to find the friends I was with and then bumping into Jude; but after that I don't remember anything. I woke up in your flat in your bed, but I promise that Jude wasn't with me. He said he'd slept on the sofa. He told me he'd taken me home with him in a taxi because he'd found me outside the club with this guy and didn't want to leave me on my own.'

Goosebumps rise up on her skin and she wraps her arms around herself.

'I was so grateful to him, Sophie. But also completely mortified. I couldn't remember any of it: not going outside with some random guy, not throwing up in the taxi, which apparently I also did. I still can't. It's all just a total blank. I begged Jude not to tell Nate, or you. Nate and I were already arguing about how much I was drinking, and I thought if he found out I'd got hammered and had done God knows what with some stranger . . .'

She scratches at her neck, which itches worse than ever. '*That's* the reason I was such a mess at your wedding – I got stupidly drunk because I felt so guilty about the whole thing. Nate was being a bit off with me and I wanted Jude to reassure me that he hadn't told him about it.'

'Did you do something Nate should know about?' Sophie asks.

Layla clasps her knees more tightly into her chest. 'I don't know. I don't think so. Jude just said the guy was getting a bit overfriendly. But when I got back to my flat the next day and had a shower, I found someone had . . .'

She trails off again, the recollection flashing through her head like she's watching a film. Acid rises up her throat, hot and tight, filling her mouth with saliva, as it had done back then, before she'd vomited all over the sink.

'Someone had what?' Sophie says.

Layla buries her head in her knees. 'Having you guys to stay has brought this back up again and I'm worried I'm starting to lose the plot. I keep forgetting where I've put things, I hear noises that aren't there, and then a couple of nights ago, I could have sworn that Jude came into my room when I was asleep.'

The creases on Sophie's forehead deepen.

'I know it sounds totally mad,' Layla says. 'I thought maybe it was a nightmare, but now you've said you've seen photos of Jude and me in bed, I don't know if it was. Because when Jude came into my room here, he took a photo of me. I heard that click sound the phone makes.'

'Jude came into your room in the middle of the night and took a photo of you,' Sophie says slowly. 'And then, what, just went away again?'

Layla nods. 'And it made me think about what happened that night in London.'

'What do you mean?' Sophie asks.

Layla swallows. 'When I went to have a shower the next day, I found someone had drawn an eye on me, just above my bikini line. In black ink. It took days to get off.'

She shivers at the memory of standing in her bathroom, scrubbing her skin with a nailbrush until it turned crimson, praying Nate wouldn't ask about it.

'I thought that the guy Jude said he found me with outside the club must have done it, and I just couldn't remember, but what if it wasn't him at all?'

She looks up, expecting Sophie to say she's lying. Tell her that she's trying to blame Jude for something she has no proof of, that she's just trying to make him look bad. And maybe Sophie's right. Maybe she's just trying to find ways to convince herself that she didn't cheat on Nate with some random guy in a club.

But Sophie doesn't say any of those things. Instead, she's staring at her, a look of undisguised horror on her face.

56. Sophie

'You think I'm making it up, don't you?' Layla says.

Sophie turns away and looks out towards the horizon, the dividing line between the sea and the sky blurring into a single mass of blue. The humming in her head is so loud she can no longer hear the sound of the waves below. The heat crawls over her face, smothering her nose and mouth so she can't breathe. She wants to pretend that she hasn't heard what Layla just said. She doesn't want to think about it. She never thinks about it. She's buried it somewhere in the recesses of her mind; a box on a shelf in a locked room, the lid covered in dust.

She shuts her eyes, but that doesn't stop the smell that permeates her nostrils, making her gag. Something musty and at the same time pungent; a hint of Calvin Klein's Obsession sprayed over stale perspiration. The memories flood to the surface despite her efforts to block them out. His tweed jacket rubbing against her face, his fingers unbuttoning her short-sleeved school shirt and reaching inside. Her feet frozen to the floor, like solid blocks of ice, despite her brain screaming at her to run, out of his office, back down the corridor into her classroom. The sound of his secretary answering the phone as she returned from lunch. The relief when he'd finally put the camera back down on his desk. Running her hand under the hot tap in her bathroom when she'd got home in an attempt to scrub off the eye he'd drawn on her. A reminder that he was always watching. As if she was ever likely to forget. He still haunts her dreams, even twenty-two years later.

'Sophie?'

She's vaguely aware of Layla speaking, but can't bring herself to reply. Her mother hadn't believed her. Had accused her of making it up as an excuse to get out of detention. Had said Mr Devlin had an amazing reputation as a headmaster and would never do anything like that. Something that had hurt Sophie far more than the things Mr Devlin had done to her in his office.

She puts the lid back on the box in her mind and opens her eyes. Thoughts fly around in her head like butterflies – so fragile, she thinks they would disintegrate if she ever got hold of them.

It's just a horrible coincidence.

She wishes more than anything that was true, but as she looks at Layla, she knows it isn't.

'No,' she says quietly. 'I don't think you're making it up.'

One of the swings behind her creaks as it moves and a shudder crawls up her spine. She thinks of Nate in his hospital bed, of the moments you can never predict that affect the rest of your life. A matter of seconds where everything pauses, then turns in a completely different direction. And she thinks about Jude, her husband, the person she trusted more than anyone, the man to whom she has told her deepest, darkest secrets and now isn't sure if she has ever really known at all.

He'd always said it had been fate that they'd met. A one in nine million chance – based on London's population seven years ago – of bumping into each other in Pret when he'd been grabbing a sandwich. An instant connection. But when she runs over that moment in her head now, the way Jude had looked at her while she stood in the queue, she's not sure it was flirtation she'd seen in his eyes at all. In hindsight, she thinks it was actually recognition.

She gets up off the ground, scrapes her blonde hair away from her face and wipes a line of perspiration from her forehead as something crumbles inside her. The cliff path that the group of teenagers had walked down earlier curves around in a semicircle, the white sand of Dream Beach tucked neatly into the shallow cove below, dotted with different-coloured parasols and sunbathers. It's like a scene on a postcard – the kind of place she'd dreamed of going to before they came out here, but now when she looks at it she feels nothing. It's as if Layla's words have wiped out all her emotions.

'I need you to call Jude,' she says to Layla. 'Tell him to come and meet us.'

'But he's with Nate,' Layla says. 'He's not going to do that.'

'He will,' Sophie says, 'if you tell him that Mr Carson from the Met Police just called me.'

57. Jude

Jude can't believe he's doing this. When Layla had called him forty minutes ago, he'd jumped straight into a taxi. He'd been ushered out of ICU by the nurse a few minutes earlier as the machines around Nate's bed had beeped frantically, Dr Purwanta issuing instructions in tense, clipped tones, a concerned look on her face.

What the fuck had the police said to Sophie? She'd refused to speak to him on the phone. And how had they managed to get her mobile number? He collects a ticket for the ferry from one of the booths at Sanur and walks along the wooden pier, follows the line of other tourists on to the boat.

He bets it was bloody Patrick. Bearmans' must have Sophie's details in his emergency contacts. Or maybe they'd contacted his mum or Oliver and got her number from them. Is that even legal?

The boat pulls away across the water. It's faster than he expected; it hits the occasional wave with a jolt, like a speed bump, and the passengers let out a collective gasp as they lift off their seats in unison. Thank God it's calm – it must be a nightmare when it's choppy. He grips the back of the seat in front of him more tightly.

The boat slows down as Jungut Batu beach comes into view. They edge forward slowly to avoid the dozens of other vessels moored in the shallow bay, and he fights the urge to tell the crew to hurry the fuck up. He can hear the anchor being lowered as he files out on to the stern with the other passengers, climbs down into the turquoise water and wades a few dozen yards to reach the sand.

He checks his phone but has no new messages and feels the knot in his stomach tighten. Patrick was always telling him to get ahead of the curve, and that's exactly what he hasn't done. He's allowed this situation to escalate to a point where it's completely out of control.

Focus on the positives.

Another of Patrick's favourite phrases. The police don't have enough evidence to prove anything; it's a case of her word against his. A disgruntled employee, that's what he'll tell Sophie. Someone who missed out on promotion and is using this as leverage for a financial settlement. He takes a deep breath and follows the other tourists towards the golf buggies. The driver smiles at him.

'Where to?'

He closes his eyes for a moment, tries to remember what Layla had said. 'The Devil's Tears, please,' he says. 'Next to Dream Beach?'

The taxi heads along the coast and the road climbs upwards, allowing him to see the island spread out below him; the orange and brown pitched tiled roofs, the white sand beach that runs around the entire circumference, the mountains of mainland Bali a short distance away, across the expanse of blue. He knows he should appreciate the beauty, but right now all he can feel is the heavy beat of his heart in his chest.

The taxi stops outside a small shack and he pays the

entrance fee before walking along a path towards the ocean, to where the seawater has carved out a giant semi-circle in the lava rock. A few tourists stand around the edge that drops down vertically, straight into the water below. Jude spots Layla and heads towards her, his trainers slipping on the wet rocks.

'Where's Sophie?' he asks.

'She's gone for a walk. Said she needed to think.' Layla's voice doesn't betray any emotion and he can't work out if she's angry with him or not. 'That call really upset her,' she adds, after a pause.

Jude fishes around in the pocket of his shorts for his sunglasses and scans the landscape around them. The cliffs stretch away along the coast; parched scrubland laced with orange dirt paths wind their way through the undergrowth towards Dream Beach, but there's no sign of his wife.

'What did the police say?' he asks.

Layla shrugs. 'I don't know.'

Jude feels the heat of the sun on his head, wishes there was somewhere they could stand that was in the shade.

He pauses for a moment, runs through the various things that Sophie might have been told, dread trickling through his stomach. 'I've been a bit worried about her since we got out here, to be honest, Layla. I think she's been finding things really difficult since the burglary.'

Layla frowns. 'Really?'

He nods. 'Yeah. She'd never say anything, you know what she's like, but I think she's struggling. Mentally, I mean.'

'I've noticed she's been a bit tense,' Layla says, 'but

that's just the usual Sophie, isn't it? She never completely relaxes.'

Jude runs his hand across his beard.

'We had a row the other morning. She asked me not to tell you, but I think you should know. The things you thought had gone missing around the villa – your keys and those ornaments, the wooden gecko and elephant – I found them in Sophie's bedside drawer.'

Layla's forehead creases. 'Why would Sophie take my things?'

He shuffles slightly on the spot, hitching up his shorts, which feel looser than usual. 'I guess it was her way of getting back at you for what you did at the wedding. You've only known Sophie for what, three years? She was a very different person when I first met her. She had some issues, but I thought she'd worked through them with a therapist. Did you know she had a sister? Jess?'

Layla shakes her head.

'Jess was a year younger than her,' he says. 'She died in a fire when Sophie was thirteen.'

Layla's eyes widen. 'God, that's terrible.'

He looks out over the water.

'I don't think Sophie ever got over it,' he says. 'Especially as she felt so guilty.'

Layla frowns. 'Why would she feel guilty?'

'Because she started the fire,' Jude says. 'It was her fault Jess died.'

58. Layla

Layla's phone buzzes and she glances at the screen.

'Is that Sophie?' Jude asks.

Layla shakes her head, watches the muscle in his jaw flicker as he peers over the steep drop into the sea below.

'Do you know why this place is called the Devil's Tears?' She points towards the semicircle of water below them. 'Watch.'

A wave breaks further out in the ocean, travels in a long ripple towards them and then disappears into a cave hidden below the rockface. A couple of seconds later, sea spray shoots tens of feet up in the air. A couple of tourists shriek with laughter as they get covered in water.

'Bloody hell.' Jude takes a step backwards.

'Impressive, isn't it?' she says. 'Makes for some great photos. People love looking at stuff like this on Insta.' She hesitates. 'But you have to be careful. People have died being swept off the rocks and out to sea by waves like that.'

He nods, but she can tell he's not really listening.

'I don't think it was a great idea to let Sophie wander off by herself,' he says, looking around. 'Especially if she was upset.'

His pale, thin arms stick out of his T-shirt, reminding Layla of a skeleton. She remembers being surprised when she first met him, wouldn't have put him and Sophie together as a couple. She'd assumed Sophie was into the geek-chic look and found Jude's dry sense of humour amusing, but Layla's never found him conventionally attractive. Whereas Sophie is properly pretty – she reminds her of Cameron Diaz when she smiles – so Layla had thought she understood exactly what Jude saw in her. But after the conversation she and Sophie had just before Jude arrived, she's not so sure. Maybe it had never been anything to do with looks at all.

She taps him on the hand, trying to focus his attention back on her, rather than the surrounding cliffs. 'You said on the phone that Nate's OK?'

'Yes, he's fine,' Jude says quickly. 'Dr Purwanta was happy with the test results.' He hesitates. 'Apparently, he had his eyes open for a few minutes before I arrived, but I don't think I'm the most entertaining visitor, as he couldn't manage it when I was there.'

He smiles briefly, but Layla isn't sure if he's joking. She often finds that with Jude. A streak of cruelty sits hidden just beneath his humour; something which, recently, he seems to be making less of an effort to hide.

Jude points to the coastal path that runs along the cliffs.

'Do you think we should head over to Dream Beach?' he asks. 'Maybe that's where Sophie's gone?'

'I'm sure she'll be back in a minute.' Layla puts her hand on his arm. 'And while she's not here, it gives us a chance to talk.'

Jude moves away and pushes his sunglasses up on his nose.

'I really am grateful that you never told Nate about that

night you had to take me back to yours,' she continues. 'To be honest, I thought you would. I know how close you two are. It can't have been easy keeping a secret from your best friend. Or from your wife.'

Jude nods but doesn't say anything as he brushes something invisible off his T-shirt.

'I still can't remember much about it,' Layla adds. 'I don't remember being outside the club with anyone, I don't remember going back to your flat – in fact, I don't remember anything before waking up in your bed the next morning.'

Jude glances at her. 'That's probably because you were completely out of it. You weren't in any kind of a state to go home on your own.'

There's an awkward silence as another wave crashes over the top of the cliff, spraying them with water. Layla welcomes the coolness on her skin and points over his shoulder.

'I told you she'd be back,' she says.

Sophie appears on the cliff path and walks around the semicircle of rocks towards them. Jude's face sags with relief.

'Hi, sweetheart,' he says.

'I'm glad you came.' Sophie ignores the hesitation in his voice, wraps her arms around his waist and slides her hands into the back pockets of his shorts, holding on to him tightly. Layla sees Jude blink rapidly and his body stiffen before he leans in to fully embrace his wife. She catches Sophie's eye and sees her nod, just once, briefly. If Layla hadn't been looking for it, the movement would have been practically unnoticeable.

Jude kisses his wife on the top of her head before she pulls away, leaving him with a stupid grin on his face.

'I thought I'd give you and Layla a chance to catch up so we're all on the same page,' she says.

Jude's grin fades. 'I don't understand.'

'Layla and I had a long chat before you arrived,' she says. 'We cleared up a few things. Did you tell her it was me who'd hidden her things in the villa?'

Spots of colour appear on Jude's cheeks.

'I thought you might,' Sophie says. 'Did you tell her about Jess, too?'

Jude swallows. Layla can see his forehead glisten with perspiration.

'You didn't need to,' Sophie continues. 'Because I already told her. We agreed: no more secrets.'

'Speaking of which,' Layla says, 'I think you need to explain to us what happened at Bearmans', Jude. Because you weren't made redundant, were you? Nate told me the night we left Tide that you'd been fired.'

59. Sophie

'I wasn't—' Jude raises his voice, then lowers it again as a couple of tourists walk past with their phones out on selfie-sticks, filming the view. 'I wasn't fired.'

'Really?' Sophie says. 'So why did Nate say you were?'

'He must have been confused. His drink had just been spiked with methanol, for fuck's sake.'

'What did the Met want to speak to you about?' Sophie studies his face. She's always thought she can tell when her husband is lying, but now she's not so sure.

'I told you. About the burglary.'

She narrows her eyes. 'Are you sure it wasn't something to do with you being fired?'

The spots of colour intensify into a flush that spreads across Jude's face.

'I lied about being burgled,' Sophie says. 'I didn't come home and find anyone in our flat. What I did come home and find was your laptop, with photos of you and Layla together in our bed.'

Jude doesn't say anything, and she watches him clench and then unclench his fists as if he's trying to hold on to his thoughts, find a way out of this mess.

'Shall I tell you how that felt, Jude? Like someone was tearing out my insides. All that pain had to go somewhere. I smashed our things and broke your laptop. Me, not a burglar.'

She remembers the burning rage – a fire in her chest that she hadn't managed to extinguish even after throwing object after object on the floor and watching them shatter. Jude steps towards her, but she moves away, the noise of the waves breaking on the rocks like something being ripped apart.

'I didn't sleep with Layla,' Jude says flatly.

'Why do you have photos of the two of you in our bed, then?' Sophie asks.

Jude ignores her question.

'I can't believe you told her about Jess,' he says.

'Why not?' Sophie asks.

Jude shakes his head. 'Because if she tells someone, you could be arrested for manslaughter.'

'I was thirteen, and it was an accident,' Sophie says. 'I never meant to hurt Jess; Layla knows that. I thought Jess was already in the garden, that she'd got out. I had no idea she was still in the house until it was too late. If my mother had believed me when I told her what my headmaster had done, I never would have started the fire in the first place.'

She doesn't tell him that she regrets that decision every single day. That she'll never forgive herself for it, but she was desperate, and desperate teenagers do stupid things without thinking about the consequences. All she'd wanted to do was change schools, and destroying her house so they'd have to move had been the only way she could think of to do it.

Another wave hits the cave underneath and salt spray shoots into the air. Sophie and Layla step backwards, leaving Jude to get soaked. He staggers blindly for a few seconds, his feet slipping on the rocks.

If she reaches out now, Sophie thinks, she could catch him off balance and all it would take is one shove to send him off the edge of the cliff. The other tourists aren't close enough to notice. Layla would back her up, say it was an accident.

But she needs to understand, first. To know for certain.

'Fucking hell.' Jude takes off his sunglasses and wipes them on his T-shirt. 'I'm not staying here.' He storms off around the semicircle of lava rock before Sophie can stop him, and jogs along the cliff path that leads down to the beach.

She follows him, Layla beside her, the heat making their feet heavy, the reddish earth sending up spirals of dust that encircle their legs each time they take a step. Dream Beach appears below them, its powder-white sand glinting in the sun, and they watch Jude flop down on to it.

'You can't run away from this,' Sophie says as they catch up with him. 'You're going to have to explain why there are photos of you and Layla on your laptop.'

'And it's not just the photos,' Layla adds. 'When I got home that night after staying at your flat, I found someone had drawn a picture of an eye on my hip.'

Sophie sees the creases at the corners of Jude's hazel-brown eyes deepen as he knits his eyebrows together.

'I don't know anything about that,' he says.

'Don't you?' Sophie asks. 'The strange thing is, I had the same thing drawn on me by that pervert headmaster who took photos of me. I never told anyone about it, not even Jess, but something like that – well, I find it hard to believe it's a coincidence. Don't you?'

Jude doesn't answer. Sophie sees him fix his gaze on a surfer doing a barrel ride further out in the ocean.

'I've been thinking about the first time we met,' Sophie says. 'Do you remember? In Pret? At the time I thought you were staring at me because you fancied me but, looking back, it wasn't that instant connection you like to insist we had. It was because you recognized me, didn't you?'

60. Jude

The sand burns Jude's legs and forces him to bend his knees, lift his calves away from the heat. He's beginning to think he should have stayed at the hospital. But then he remembers the sound of the machines bleeping and the expression on Dr Purwanta's face when she'd looked at Nate, and decides he's better off here.

'I did fancy you,' he says to Sophie. 'It's just . . .'

He trails off and wipes a line of perspiration from his forehead. His tongue feels like rubber in his mouth, and he swallows in an effort to generate some saliva.

'I wanted to keep you safe,' he continues. 'I wanted to keep them all safe. Women don't realize how vulnerable they are. I help save them by making them see the risks they're taking. Change their behaviour. Stop them from doing it again.'

He looks at Layla.

'With you it was different, I admit. You can't watch someone else's life take off when yours is going nowhere without feeling a certain amount of envy. Nate and I were so close at university, I thought it would always be like that.'

He blinks as his sunglasses slide down his nose and pushes them back up again, the grains of sand on his fingers rough against his skin.

'I tried to be happy for him, I really did. I even asked

him to be my best man, for fuck's sake. But he got everything he wanted without even trying – a great family, promotions, the chance to come out to Bali, a contract to work remotely; people just kept shoving more stuff at him. And he couldn't see it. Couldn't see how hard I was trying: to win clients, to get up the next rung of the ladder, to save for a deposit. When I bumped into you in that club in London, I saw an opportunity and took it. I needed something to think about when Nate announced his next piece of great news, something to stop the jealousy that was eating me away, piece by piece.'

He watches as Layla wraps her arms around herself.

'I took photos of you when you were unconscious. Something I knew about that Nate didn't and I could look at whenever I wanted. And I drew that symbol of an eye on your hip. A reminder to be more careful, because it could so easily have been someone else who'd found you, someone who wouldn't have looked after you like I did.'

Layla puts her hand over her mouth, her body trembling.

'Did you put something in my drink?' Layla asks. 'Is that why I can't remember anything?'

Jude hesitates. 'Just a few drops.'

'Of what?' Sophie asks.

'GHB,' Jude says. 'Women need to understand the risks. They go out and get hammered, but they don't know who's out there watching them, just waiting for an opportunity when they're vulnerable. I make them realize they've experienced a narrow escape.'

Sophie shoots him a stone-cold glare. 'This is why the police want to talk to you, isn't it?'

Jude doesn't answer. He thinks of Camilla, the over-enthusiastic new intern at work, of the team drinks they'd had a few weeks ago; she'd downed several glasses of wine, the last of which he'd spiked. He'd waited until he'd seen her stumble as she'd picked up her coat to leave before following her out into the corridor. He'd been hoping to usher her into one of the empty meeting rooms, had his phone ready to take photos of her to add to his collection, but another colleague had spotted them together and had insisted on taking Camilla home in a taxi.

A few days later, Camilla had filed a complaint. Said someone had seen Jude tipping something into her glass. And following an internal investigation, Bearmans' had fired him. He'd been stupid. He should have kept his hobby separate from work. He'd never had a problem with any of the others. The dozens he'd met in bars and clubs over the years. He'd let himself get carried away.

'The police don't have any evidence to back up her allegations,' Jude says. 'It's her word against mine, and she's just an intern with a grudge.'

He fixes his gaze on his wife, the woman he vowed to love and protect, the person he wants to spend the rest of his life with.

'We don't have to go back to London,' he says, hurriedly. 'I've thought it all through. We can stay out here with Nate and Layla, and I'll work remotely. Loads of companies are letting people do it now. I'm sure Nate would give me a reference. We'll fit right in with the digital nomad community. I love you, Soph. I just want us to be together.'

He reaches for her hand, but she recoils.

'You didn't answer my question, Jude. Where did you recognize me from?'

He picks up a handful of sand and lets it run through his fingers. He's going to have to tell her. He wants the chance to clear his conscience. Start over again.

'I saw a photo of you,' he says. 'In my father's study.'

Sophie frowns. 'Oliver's?'

Jude shakes his head. 'My real father. Kenneth Devlin was the headmaster at Parkside Mount School. He was also a monster.'

He remembers standing in front of his father's closed study door when he was growing up, of hearing raised voices inside and, worse still, the other noises which filtered out when the voices went quiet.

'I saw how scared my mother was of him,' he says, 'but it took her until I was thirteen to leave. The week before she walked out, I got into his study. He always kept it locked, but that morning I came downstairs and found the door wide open. I still don't know if he'd left it like that deliberately. Whether he wanted me to discover who he really was. I saw a photo of you on his desk. In your school uniform with your shirt undone. That symbol he'd drawn on your hand staring at me. I didn't tell anyone. And then, a few days later, I came home from school to find Mum waiting for me with all our things packed and I never saw him again.'

He stares at Sophie. 'I recognized you straight away when I saw you in Pret. Your eyes were still the same. All I've ever wanted to do is look after you, protect you from people like him. I hated him for what he did to you. He

324

stole that symbol he drew on your hand from a painting I'd done – something I'd pinned up on my bedroom wall because I was proud of it, even though he said I was useless at most things, including art. So, I took it back and drew it on other women to teach them a lesson.'

He thinks he sees Sophie shiver, but she doesn't say anything. She glances at Layla, and then out to sea. He feels lighter now he's told her. Stronger. As she said, it's better if they don't have secrets. Now they can put all this behind them. Start again.

Another surfer rides a barrel wave, disappears beneath the curve of water, then reappears out the other side. He wonders whether someone in Canggu can teach him how to do that. Perhaps he should think about having lessons.

'I need a drink,' he says. 'Do either of you want anything?'

Sophie and Layla both shake their heads as he gets up and heads towards one of the bars at the back of the beach. He glances around at the other sunbathers, ignores the two policemen dressed in identical beige shirts and black trousers as they walk towards him across the sand before realizing, with a sharp jolt, that they are looking directly at him. One of them holds up his hand, stopping him as he goes to walk past. He glances back at his wife as they ask him to turn out his pockets, but she's gazing out to sea, has reached for Layla's hand and is clasping it tightly.

He smiles, to start with. Insists they are making a huge mistake. It isn't until he pulls something unfamiliar out of the back pocket of his shorts, sees the grains of white powder still clearly visible inside the squashed clingfilm wrap, that he really starts to panic.

61. 2007

I don't remember much about reaching the meeting point. My dad and Dan were shouting a lot, and Ashley wouldn't stop crying. Mum sat beside me, tried to warm me up by rubbing my arms and kept telling me I'd be OK, but I couldn't really feel her, I was shivering so much. Mia passed out with the pain from her arm and we couldn't stop her leg bleeding; a red stream that trickled into the water that covered the bottom of the boat.

When we finally got out, my dad was the one who spoke to the police who'd arrived after being called out to investigate someone acting suspiciously around the van. They'd wanted a statement, but Dad said Mum and I were too traumatized.

I can't stop going over what happened. Remembering our guide's face as he was swept away. How desperately he'd tried to cling on to my hand. The police and a rescue team are still looking for him, but I can tell by their lack of urgency they don't think there's much hope of finding him alive.

The police said we shouldn't have gone rafting at all. My father agreed and declared it was reckless and that our guide should have known better. None of us mentioned we had been the ones who pressured him into going.

If I could go back, I would. But everyone says that afterwards, don't they? When it's too late.

I take a last look at the huge stones, their wet surfaces glinting in the sun, and try to block out the memory of smashed limbs and shredded skin, of bodies travelling too fast.

Dad puts his arm around my shoulders, bends down and puts his face next to my ear, keeping his voice low so no one else can hear.

'You need to put this behind you, and move on,' he says quietly. 'Forget you were ever here.' He hesitates. 'You didn't have a choice whether to let him go, Buddy. It was you or him – I saw that. And he would have done exactly the same if the situation had been reversed. If anyone asks, you tried your best to hold on to him, but the current was too strong. The police have no reason to question your version of events, and I'm pretty sure no one else in the boat saw what really happened.'

I nod, tears pricking at my eyes.

'When we get home,' he says, 'you'll take up your place at Exeter like we planned and we won't talk about this again. We are not going to let one mistake define the rest of your life.'

He ruffles my hair and I wipe my face on my towel.

'Sometimes,' he says, 'you just have to do whatever it takes to save yourself.'

62. Layla

Layla takes a last look around the villa. She needs to be out by eleven to give the cleaners time before the next tenants arrive, and her taxi will be here any minute.

She's picking up Nate on her way to the airport before their flight to London. He's doing better, has been taken off the ventilator and is responding well to the physiotherapy sessions he's been having, but Dr Purwanta has said he still needs a lot more time to recuperate.

Nate's parents suggested they stay with them in Sussex until he's fully better, and she knows the rest will do him the world of good. Kristin had asked whether Layla was planning to work while she was with them, and Layla had reassured her that she would continue with her life-coaching sessions online from their house, but she doesn't have any intention of doing that. The thought of being stuck in the middle of the Sussex countryside with the nearest shop a two-mile car drive away is not her idea of fun.

She'd asked Nate if he could kick out their tenants in Streatham so they could move back in there; at least then she'd be able to go out for a coffee or get the train into town, but he'd said they couldn't end someone's tenancy halfway through, plus he'd find the stairs tricky with his crutches.

Dr Purwanta had said a few months of intensive physio

should fix most of Nate's issues, so Layla has persuaded Kristin to organize someone to come to the house, said they'd repay her when Nate's earning again. She knows Nate's parents are hoping they'll stay for longer, that they won't go back to Bali at all, but she's not about to give up something she loves. It's the kind of lifestyle she's always dreamed of, a million times better than anything she'd have in London. She'd be mad not to come back.

She'd met up with Wayan Santi last week. Had agreed to pay him if he took on responsibility for managing the build of their new villa. He'd assured her he could handle Nyoman, and she's promised him a bonus if the place is fully finished by the time she returns. It's a way to keep him happy, of returning the favour he's convinced she owes him. And she definitely doesn't want Wayan to be unhappy – she's already seen what can happen in that situation. But if she manages things properly, there's no reason they can't both have what they want. It seems his conversation with Jude that day in the hospital had been a completely innocent discussion about what was on the TV in reception. Or at least that's what Wayan had told her, and with Jude currently in Kerobokan prison, there's no way for her to check.

At the moment, it looks like Jude will avoid the death penalty. His mother and Oliver have paid for a decent lawyer and there wasn't enough coke in the clingfilm wrap for the police to charge him with supply. She and Sophie had made sure of that before Sophie had slid it into the back pocket of Jude's shorts. Neither of them wanted Jude's blood on their hands, although Layla isn't sure if any punishment will be enough, considering what he's done. Even if he's only sentenced for possession, he'll still be facing at least four years, which will feel more like forty in Kerobokan.

She'd heard from one of Alex's crowd that Bryce had returned to Australia, walking through customs carrying a surfboard packed with more than just foam inside it, and was now catching waves in South Stradbroke Island on the Gold Coast. She doubts he'll ever come back, but part of her wonders if at some point, when his money runs out, whether he'll be tempted. So many people are.

Sophie had stayed on for a while after Jude was arrested, but left Canggu last week. She'd told Layla she'd found the coke in Nate's rucksack, but Layla had managed to convince her that it hadn't been in there when they'd left Tide – that Layla had found it in the lining of Nate's swimming trunks when they'd given her his belongings in hospital and she'd shoved it into his rucksack.

Sophie had decided to travel around Bali for a few months. She'd said she needed to heal – and as she had nothing to go back to in London, she wanted to spend some time by herself. At the moment she's in Ubud – taking the opportunity to visit the rainforest and explore some of the shrines and temples. Layla's passed on details of some ritual purification ceremonies and hopes Sophie will take advantage of them. Further north, there's a greater sense of the spirituality of old Bali, and Layla knows Sophie would benefit from that right now. Canggu is too busy, too full of distractions. Travelling will give her a chance to sort her head out, to decide what she wants from life, going forward. Jude's revelations will take time to fully sink in – for both of them.

Layla misses having her around. Or, if she's completely honest with herself, she misses having *someone* around. The lack of another physical presence in the villa has been more noticeable than she thought it would be. At the moment she's still sleeping with the bedroom light on; has nightmares about waking up and finding Jude standing over her bed, staring at her. She wonders whether it's karma, payback for what she'd done on Mount Batur. She can still hear the crunch of gravel as Sophie's body slid down the slope. She'd tried to convince herself afterwards that she hadn't meant to push her, that she'd just been trying to steady herself, but deep down she knows that isn't true. At the time, she'd wanted to hurt her, just like she'd wanted to hurt Alex, but that was then, and now she needs to forget the past and focus on moving forward.

Nate doesn't know it yet, but she won't be hanging around in Sussex with him for long. Just a couple of weeks, until Wayan has the villa ready, and then she'll be coming straight back out to Bali. Without Nate. She might have managed to persuade Sophie that Nate would never give her a rucksack containing coke, but Layla's not stupid. If Nate was prepared to do that to Sophie, she can't be sure he wouldn't do the same to her, if it came down to it. She's realized that Nate will always save himself, and she's no longer willing to be second best.

She takes one last look around before shutting the door and putting the keys in the lockbox. In a couple of weeks, she will be back, in her new villa, and Sophie will be living with her; Layla has offered to let her rent for a few months when she comes back from travelling. They can look properly at the plans for the business they've agreed to start – with Sophie's PR contacts and marketing experience, combined with her own life-coaching skills, Layla is confident they can make enough money to continue the lifestyle she has become so accustomed to and has no intention of giving up.

Meeting friends for long lunches, having spa treatments and going out to one of the beach clubs for drinks at sunset. She can't wait.

63. 2007

THE BALI TIMES

22 OCTOBER 2007

TOURISTS INJURED AND GUIDE MISSING IN WHITE WATER RAFTING ACCIDENT

A British man has issued a warning to other travellers, after he and his family almost died during a recent 'nightmare' experience in Bali.

There were scenes of chaos on the River Ayung yesterday when a boat capsized following heavy rains, throwing several of its occupants into the water.

James Osborne and his wife, Kristin, are still recovering from the horror after their 18-year-old son was thrown into the raging rapids and almost drowned. Nathaniel Osborne narrowly escaped with his life after being rescued from the water by the others in the boat. An Australian tourist, Mia Robinson, 19, has also been seriously injured and is currently being treated in hospital.

The guide on the trip, Nyoman Suardika, is still missing, and the authorities have confirmed the search for him is ongoing. However, one of the rescuers we spoke to said it was looking 'increasingly unlikely' that he would be found alive.

'We should never have been advised that it was safe to

make the trip,' James Osborne said. 'The river was clearly flowing too fast following such heavy rains and we shouldn't have set off in the first place. We weren't given proper safety briefings and had no idea what to do when we capsized. We had to navigate our way back to the meeting point by ourselves, not knowing where we were going. Our family was lucky, but other tourists need to be aware just how dangerous this activity can be.'

64. Nyoman

He forces the lid down on the can of paint, making sure the seal is airtight, and washes out his rollers and brushes. The villa is finally beginning to look habitable – it's always the last touches of decoration that pull everything together.

He wonders what will happen to it, whether Layla and Nate will ever end up living here or whether they'll rent it out, no doubt to some other digital nomads.

They remind him of locusts – they descend in swarms, consume everything available, and when there's nothing left, simply move on to the next place. And there's no shortage of developing countries with glorious beaches and tropical climates that are desperate to take their money. All the talk about abandoning capitalism and finding a more ethical path is just smoke and mirrors, a way of justifying it to themselves. No one wants to talk about the problems it causes for the countries they go to – the environmental damage, the rising house prices, the loss of local businesses. The migration only goes one way – he's pretty sure there are very few Balinese, if any, living as digital nomads in the UK or Australia, or any of the other countries they have relocated from.

His commute home isn't far by scooter – he lives a short distance outside Canggu, in the same area as many of his friends. He wouldn't want to be in the centre of the ever-expanding town even if he could afford it – not any more. He drives past the huge villas with their heated pools set behind tall gates, past the construction sites, and wonders how many more will appear over the next year to satisfy the constantly growing demand.

He parks his scooter, walks through the small garden in front of his house, checks on the koi carp swimming among the water lilies in his pond and glances at the remains of offerings of brightly coloured flowers and incense sticks laid out in his temple.

There is an unfamiliar silence when he goes inside; he realizes his wife, three children and parents-in-law must be out. He relishes these times – a rare opportunity for quiet before chaos descends again.

He pours himself a glass of arak, mixes it with orange juice and carries it into his living room. On the dark wooden sideboard is a number of framed photographs; he lifts one up, studies it carefully.

Their faces are blurred, barely recognizable on the paper but still crystal clear in his head. The seven of them standing next to one another in a line, holding up their paddles before they set off down the steps to the boat. James has his arm around his son. Nyoman understands the desire to protect your child – can't bear to think of anything happening to his – but at the end of the day, everyone has to take responsibility for their own actions, and Nate was hardly a child, at eighteen.

When Nyoman found himself washed up on the riverbank much further downstream, he'd made a decision to vanish. He'd assumed the police would be looking for him, that his and Kadek's illegal activities had been discovered. He had left Ubud, moved away and started all over again. He'd managed to secure a job as a builder's apprentice and worked long hours and weekends for several years before finally meeting his wife, setting up his own business and having his two precious sons. He'd tried to push the horrors of the Ayung River to the back of his mind and had mostly succeeded during the day. Night-time was a different matter, however; when he finally fell asleep, he'd often wake up choking, convinced he couldn't breathe.

He had been shocked nine months ago when he'd been introduced

336

to the couple from London who were looking for someone to manage the build of their new villa. He'd never forgotten the boy who let go of his hand in the River Ayung, but Nate hadn't showed the slightest sign he recognized him.

So Nyoman had double-checked his suspicions. He'd taken a look through Nate's phone when he was at the building site one morning, then paid a visit to their villa late one night after copying a set of keys. He'd let himself in and wandered around the living room and kitchen while Nate and Layla were asleep; had run his fingers over the photos of Nate with his parents on display in the living room, James and Kristin looking just how he remembered. He had flicked through folders of paperwork before slipping out silently through the patio doors when he heard Nate or Layla get up.

He goes to put the photo back down on the sideboard but changes his mind, takes it into the kitchen and throws it in the rubbish bin instead. Time to let go. Move on.

After he'd spoken to Layla at Pura Tanah Lot and discovered that Nate prayed for someone he'd seen drown when he was younger, Nyoman had felt a knot in his stomach unravel. The anger he'd carried around with him every day since he'd climbed out of the River Ayung had instantly faded. Nate has been punished enough.

Nyoman opens one of the cupboards in his kitchen and pushes the bottle of methanol to the very back of the shelf, where his wife won't see it. She'd be horrified to hear he'd done something like that. He bows his head as he thinks about how much she trusts him, and presses his palm against his chest. If only he'd known how much Nate had regretted what he'd done earlier, it would have saved him going to so much trouble.

Acknowledgements

A big thank you to the incredible team at Viking, Penguin, for all their help in getting this book into its current shape. I feel very lucky to work with so many wonderful people – Lydia Fried, Ellie Hudson, Ellie Smith, Gray Eveleigh, Laura Dermody, Georgia Taylor, Rosie Safaty, Harriet Bourton and the entire sales team, who do such an amazing job. I owe particular thanks to Vikki Moynes for coming up with such a fantastic title and to Rosa Schierenberg for her brilliant and insightful edits. When I started writing this story, I would never have predicted that I'd be having several late-night conversations with my editor about the costs and practical difficulties involved in cocaine dealing – but Rosa, I feel we could now consider ourselves experts, just in case either of us decide on a change of career . . .

Thank you to Charlotte Daniels, who worked her usual magic on the stunning cover, and to Sarah Day, who did another fantastic job on copy-edits – I'm sure she was almost as relieved as I was that we weren't dealing with multiple timelines in this book, and I'm so pleased she enjoyed reading it as much as she did!

I'd also like to thank my brilliant agent, Sophie Lambert, for her honesty and unwavering support – and Alice Hoskyns for all her help too. I feel very fortunate to have these ladies in my corner.

Thank you also to Luke Speed of Speed Literary and Talent Management Agency for his enthusiasm about this story – it's lovely to be working together again.

The publishing industry can be tough, and having good friends who lift you up and understand what really goes on behind the gloss of social media is invaluable. There are too many people to mention here, but I would just like to say a big thank you to Lauren, Laura and Zoe for our lovely WhatsApp chats, to the Ladykillers for their wisdom and laughter, to my In Suspense podcast co-host extraordinaire, Lesley Kara, and to my fellow CoTs.

Thanks also to my lovely (non!) author oldest friends – Anna, Ceril, Els, Gill, Lynn and Nanna – over thirty years since we met, and you mean the world to me. Thank you also to Ceril for reading a very early draft of this book – I'm not sure you'll recognize it now!!

Last year, a few of my acknowledgements went astray for the paperback copy of *The Guests*, so I hope you will indulge me for including some of them here. A huge thank you to my family – my husband, Martin, to whom this book is dedicated, and to both my daughters – I'm beyond proud of you for being two of the kindest and most resilient women I know. I also want to do a shoutout to my gorgeous nephews, Ben and Ollie, and to my mum and dad, who continually champion my books – I am so fortunate to have you both still here to celebrate with.

I'd also like to thank each and every bookseller, librarian, reviewer, blogger, influencer, book-group member and fellow author who has helped get this book into your hands. My biggest thank you must go to you, the reader. Without you, I couldn't do this, and I am so grateful for your support. If you've enjoyed the book, please do leave a review, shout about it to a friend or on social media – it really helps to spread the word.

If you want to get in touch, I'm on social media in the following places and always love hearing from readers: nikkismithauthor.com (website), @mrssmithmunday (X/Twitter), @nikkismith_author (Instagram).

THE
BEACH
PARTY

**Six friends.
The holiday of their dreams.
One night that changed it all . . .**

1989: The tunes are loud and the clothes are louder when a group of friends arrives in Mallorca for a post-graduation holiday of decadence and debauchery at a luxury villa.

A beach party marks the pinnacle of their fun, until it isn't fun any longer. Because amidst the wild partying – sand flying from dancing feet and revellers leaping from yachts – an accident happens. Suddenly, the night of a lifetime becomes a living nightmare.

Now: the truth about that summer has been collectively buried. But someone knows what happened that night.

And they want the friends to pay for what they did . . .

'Bound to be the hit thriller of the summer!'
T. M. Logan, *The Holiday*

'Thrilling, twisting and gloriously '80s'
Chris Whitaker, *We Begin at the End*

'Sun-soaked and fast-paced, the perfect holiday page turner'
Ellery Lloyd, *The Club*

THE GUESTS

**The resort of their dreams.
A destination to die for.**

WELCOME TO PARADISE!

Or so the staff say as they greet the Hamiltons on the pristine shores of the idyllic Maldives resort.

And it starts off that way: snorkelling in the serene blue sea, champagne picnics on powder-white sand, and moonlit walks under the stars.

But lies lurk beneath the luxury, because each of the guests has a secret… *and they're not the only ones.*

Months later, a grisly discovery is made.

Whatever happened to the Hamiltons? And how did their once-in-a-lifetime trip turn into the holiday from hell?

'The perfect beach read'
Harriet Tyce, *Blood Orange*

'Wonderfully escapist and nail-bitingly suspenseful'
Laura Marshall, *Friend Request*

'A **sumptuous** blend of **glossy luxury and dark underbelly**'
Andrea Mara, *No One Saw A Thing*